ODD JOBS

A PETE MADDOX THRILLER

ALAN PETERSEN

STREET
BOOKS

ODD JOBS

Published by Alan Petersen. PO Box 191002, San Francisco, CA 94114. Online: www.AlanPetersen.com.

PROLOGUE

Near Llwyngwril, Gwynedd, Wales, UK

THE COTTAGE WAS LOCATED OFF A WINDING TWO-LANE blacktop almost halfway between Llangelynnin and Llwyngwril in northwest Wales.

It was an area where the locals still spoke Welsh more than English.

It stood a half-mile off the main road on a windswept hillside at the end of a gravel driveway, on land that a century ago, had been part of the Kingdom of Gwynedd.

The trespasser was greeted by a soothing cloudscape, the sounds of the howling wind, and the bay below.

One hundred feet behind the cottage was a cliffside that dropped into Cardigan Bay.

There were no neighbors to be seen or heard. Its isolated remoteness was one of the property's strong selling points for Malcolm Fitzsimmons, who had bought the then decrepit farmhouse more than ten years ago.

It had been in a sorry state back then, but Fitzsimmons had fallen in love with the property's sweeping views along the beaches of the north Wales coast down below and the Snowdonia Mountains off in the distance.

Over the years, Fitzsimmons had transformed the cottage into a home that kept its historic charm on the outside, but had upgraded the inside with a modern, fully equipped kitchen, including a commercial-grade stove, since he liked to cook.

An updated spacious living room with magnificent views of the bay and all the accoutrements for a single man's modern country living: high-speed Internet, Wi-Fi, a fifty-inch LCD smart television, a Bose home theater system, and a remote-controlled fireplace.

After twenty-two years in the SAS and eleven years offering his expertise as a freelancer in war-torn and strife-filled shit holes all over the world, he finally had his cottage as he wanted it.

He had enough money put away to hang up his guns within the next year so he could enjoy the fruits of his labor in the quiet remoteness of the Welsh coast.

Fitzsimmons stood in his kitchen. He poured himself a cup of tea and looked out to the Bay.

For the first time in this paradise, he felt *the feeling*.

He could never explain the feeling to civilians, but for a professional like Fitzsimmons, it was a well-honed skill that had served him well during his almost three decades in the trade.

He lived alone—this was by design. An ex-wife he hadn't seen in over a decade lived in Manchester, England. At least that's where she'd lived ten years ago, but they didn't keep in touch. He had a grown daughter of twenty-five living a hurly-burly life in London. She made it out to visit once or twice a year when she needed to escape the city for the rejuvenating stillness of the countryside, but he wasn't expecting her or anyone else. He never did.

But the feeling was persistent, like a kink in the neck. It nudged him.

Someone is out there.

Fitzsimmons's two English Springer dogs slept by the window where the sun shone in and kept the floor warm for them.

It's a beautiful day, stop being paranoid and enjoy it, Fitzsimmons told himself as he took in the breathtaking view of the Irish Sea from his front window. He then turned and looked down the long gravel road. It was the only way in and out of his property. He went from window to window, but he couldn't see anything out of place.

The feeling wouldn't go away.

It had kept him alive during his career, so he couldn't just ignore it. *Could I?* He instinctively reached for his pistol before realizing he had no weapons on him. *Why would I here?*

Fitzsimmons went into his bedroom and from a closet, he pulled out a small gun safe, which he opened and removed a SIG Sauer pistol. He loaded a magazine while one of the dogs looked at him curiously, its head tilted as the magazine slid into place. Fitzsimmons chambered a round.

"I'm just being paranoid, girl," Fitzsimmons said.

He walked out to his living room, putting on a light jacket. He hesitated for a moment before opening the front door and stepping outside.

"Stay," he told the dogs, who obeyed as he closed the door.

He had the pistol in his right hand, held tight against his right leg. He walked outside. It was one of a handful of clear, dry days in May with big puffy clouds that danced in the blue skies above. He walked out toward the cliff and looked around, there wasn't anything but the stillness and quietness that he loved.

He shook his head. "Paranoid, old coot," Fitzsimmons said out loud toward the sea.

He turned to head back to the cottage when the bullet tore into his chest, shoving him backward onto the ground. The pistol landed at his feet. He could hear the dogs barking inside the house and the wind howling. He tried to get up, but the life was draining out of him in a pool of blood. He lay on the ground smiling knowing he was dying.

The irony of being shot and bleeding out on the ground in his Welsh cottage—after surviving countless missions to Iraq, Afghanistan, Northern Ireland, Bosnia, West Africa—wasn't lost on him. He didn't feel sorrow but anger. Anger that the shooter had gotten the drop on him.

He yelled out weakly, "Who the fuck are you?"

The shooter replied with a second bullet. It was a headshot, and Fitzsimmons didn't have to dwell on those thoughts anymore.

ONE

PASSCODE

Key Biscayne, Florida, USA

PETE MADDOX'S PHONE VIBRATED, ANNOUNCING THE arrival of a new text message. He glanced down at the seven-digit number on the screen. It was a possible odd job from the network. Maddox was relieved that Sonia was out of the house so he wouldn't have to sneak around to check it out.

Maddox took the mobile phone, walked into his home office, and closed the door behind him.

He sat at his desk in the corner away from the window, which looked out over his backyard where the pool beckoned him. After a moment of daydreaming about the pool, Maddox stood up and walked towards a black steel lateral file cabinet that was perpendicular to his desk. He opened the top drawer and removed a blue plastic tote box. He pulled off its lid. Inside were around ten mobile phones, all unlocked and untraceable. In the same container was a stack of around fifty SIM cards bound together with a rubber band.

Maddox grabbed a phone, wiggled out one of the SIM cards from the banded stack and tossed both items on his desk. He then put the lid back on the container and placed it back into the drawer of the cabinet and slid it closed.

In a few minutes, Maddox cracked the phone open, inserted the SIM card, and activated online—it was a process he had done so often he could do it blindfolded.

While Maddox waited for the mobile phone to power up, he retrieved a hardware token card that generated randomized log-in codes every sixty seconds. After about a minute, the phone's screen flickered to life and a brief robotic chime trilled its announcement that it was now ready to be used.

Maddox installed a custom-made application on the phone that allowed him to access the deep web, instant messaging, and email without being monitored or blocked. He fired up the web browser, which was secure, hidden, and only available to members of the network. Its anonymity made the Tor browser seem like the data-hungry Google Chrome.

Maddox navigated the browser to his final destination; a white page with a single data entry field and a submit button.

He looked at the seven-digit number that he'd received via text and entered those digits into the data field. Then he looked at the secure one-time passcode provided by the token card generator and entered those digits as well.

He double-checked the numbers since he didn't have the lightest fingers when it came to entering digits on a phone, and he had to be certain the passcode was correct before hitting submit. The Network had draconian rules: you only get one attempt; Maddox's butterfingers could lock access to the lucrative network job database for a year. Do that twice and Maddox would be banned from the network for life.

Confident that he'd entered the passcode correctly, Maddox tapped on the button, and in a few seconds, he was inside the network.

The network was known as TEN, which stood for Threat

Elimination Network. It was a private network that seemed to exist only in the ether. TEN matched freelancers like Maddox with high-value targets deemed a threat to the greater good. That *greater good* could be up to debate, but in the world of nongovernment sanctioned direct action and target termination work, TEN wore the gray hat in those murky waters.

For Maddox, he had little choice. His former employer, the CIA, had blacklisted him from government contracts.

Maddox read the details about the job, which had been posted by a consortium called *The Association of the Concerned.*

The target was Jamal Ali Farah, an American-Somali from Minneapolis that been radicalized into joining Al-Shabaab. Ali Farah had become part of Al-Shabaab's upper echelon. His expertise was recruiting other young Somali men to leave their comfortable lives in the West for war in West Africa.

It was obvious that the consortium was more than likely made up of angry, grief-stricken parents who couldn't count on justice, so they would settle for vengeance.

Prosperous Somali families from Ohio, Minnesota, the U.K., and Canada who had fled their war-torn country and built a successful life in peace in their new homelands, only to lose their Western-raised sons to radicals who sentenced them to die in battle on the dusty streets of Mogadishu. These kids' demise began online where they became brainwashed into Jihadism by a recruiter, thousands of miles away. The first steps that would lead to them traveling and ultimately dying for a homeland none of them had seen since they were infants. The younger ones born in the West had never even set foot on their parents' homeland until they arrived there to fight.

Maddox next went to the Department of Justice's "Rewards for Justice" website.

He entered the name: Jamal Ali Farah.

The kid that had grown up wearing T-shirts, blue jeans, and

Minnesota Twins baseball hats, while getting high on schwag weed and hanging around the Mall of America had been replaced by a self-appointed Imam wearing a traditional white long sleeve thobe.

The photo had been taken while he was pontificating about something—probably the evils of America. He had a full black curly beard, his mouth open—no doubt spewing his twisted version of Islam—and his index finger in the air in mid wag. It was a screen grab from one of his many online sermons.

The Recruiter was the starting spark that turned into a deadly wildfire.

For Maddox, the job looked promising. Ali Farah was on the DOJ wanted list, thus meeting his own personal criteria to take on that type of contract. Odd jobs, as Maddox referred to them to his wife in failed attempts to downplay what was really involved.

Between the TEN contract money—minus their referral fee, of course—and the "Rewards for Justice" bounty, it was a very lucrative contract. But *Christ*, Maddox thought, *the out-of-pocket in pulling this off on the other side of the world would be huge without any guarantee of finding the prick.*

It was the type of operation that would take a lot of time to plan, but Maddox knew he didn't have the luxury of time. He had to make a decision on whether to bid on the job a lot faster than he was comfortable with. But there always seemed to be a young gun—Maddox assumed they were young; why else would someone bid on a job so quickly? Without thinking it through? Without doing a cost analysis and an ROI study? But the bids came in fast and low.

Maddox was trying to work out the numbers when his regular phone rang.

Maddox glanced at the incoming call's phone number; it

was his friend, Tom Rose. He took the call. "Hey, Tom, how are you?"

"Doing fine, mate, can you talk?" That was his way of asking if Sonia was within earshot.

"Yes, I was just looking into an odd job that looks interesting. I was actually going to call you about it."

Tom Rose and Maddox went back twenty years. They'd first met when Maddox was in the CIA and Rose with MI6. They shared a similar military and intelligence background—Maddox serving with the Army Rangers before joining the CIA and Rose with the British SAS before joining MI6.

It had been Rose who helped Maddox find jobs through his own contacts when the CIA blacklisted Maddox. Rose had done this not caring if it would be detrimental to his post-MI6 freelancing business.

Rose always had Maddox's back. Like the time he'd flown to Venezuela, back when Maddox had been the CIA Station Chief during the failed coup against Hugo Chavez, which had put his future wife, Sonia in mortal danger.

It had been Tom Rose who protected her while Maddox had been in the Amazonian jungle blowing up a terrorist training camp.

"We might have to back-burn that, mate. Malcolm Fitzsimmons was killed yesterday," Rose said.

"What? How? Where?" Maddox blurted.

"Sniper. At his home in Wales," Rose said.

In their line of work, death was always center stage, bringing it to their target and preventing it from happening to themselves. But at home? Maddox shivered at the thought.

"Jesus, I thought you were going to say he was killed on the job. Out in the field somewhere," Maddox said.

"That, I could understand. I could let that go. We know the dangers when we take on this work," Rose said.

"Do the cops know anything?" Maddox asked.

"No. I checked with my sources in the North Wales Police and the NCA. No suspects, no leads. It was a clean hit, two shots. They believe from a professional," Rose said.

"It sounds that way."

"One of his old jobs, perhaps?"

"Perhaps," Maddox agreed.

Maddox hadn't known Malcolm Fitzsimmons well. He had met him a few times through Rose—who called him *Fitzy*.

Fitzy and Rose were close, having met during SAS selection. Maddox knew Rose well enough to know that he wasn't going to wait around for the police to figure out who had been on the other side of the rifle's scope.

TWO
THE MORAL DILEMMA

Key Biscayne, Florida

SONIA MADDOX WALKED INTO THE HOUSE. THE MOMENT she laid eyes on Maddox, she said, "What happened?"

"Nothing, why do you ask?" was Maddox's coy response.

"Don't lie to me. I can tell something's up."

Maddox smiled. *She was always so perceptive.*

She had long brown hair and green eyes. He saw the goose bumps appearing on her olive skin as they did when she worried.

Maddox was agnostic, but that old Catholic guilt he had been spoon-fed growing up kicked into overdrive.

Everything they had been through together and all she asked, begged of him, was not to take any more of the odd job contracts in faraway lands consumed with conflict.

Maddox justified that the money was too good to pass up, but there was more to it. They had a comfortable life; they weren't rich, but they had carved out a nice homelife in South Florida.

Maddox and Sonia lived in Key Biscayne, a well-to-do

island village that had anointed itself with the tagline of "Island Paradise", even though it was located about twenty minutes from congested, and crime-ridden Miami and the International Airport.

Sonia worked as a real estate broker in the Miami-Dade area. She had been in real estate for most of her adult life, having started out in her native Venezuela.

After the failed coup d'état attempt in 2002 against Hugo Chavez, Maddox had been exposed as the CIA Station Chief— thusly Chavez's made-up boogeyman behind the coup. Maddox had been expelled from the country, persona non grata. Because of her relationship with Maddox, Sonia had to flee her home country and she hadn't been back home to Venezuela since.

She missed her country, but her mother and sister were also living in Southern Florida, and she was happy with how her new life had turned out. She'd even survived the burst of the Florida real estate bubble in 2008 and its aftereffect, which had hit South Florida like a hurricane.

At first, she had tolerated Maddox's odd jobs, but she felt, at this point in their lives, it to be an unnecessary risk. She wanted him to just work the corporate-type security consulting jobs, but those were harder to land and the pay wasn't anywhere near what the odd jobs paid.

She didn't like the danger and the fact that he would be gone for months at a time. She hadn't married a military man where deployments were part of their lives. And although he didn't talk about it, she knew that death and violence were attached to every dollar he made in that business.

She also felt hypocritical. On one hand, condemning that line of work. Yet when the granddaughter of her beloved former nanny had been forced into prostitution and trafficked by a ruthless Mexican cartel, Maddox had rescued her using those same lethal skills.

But more than the moral dilemma she felt about that work, she was mostly worried that the odd jobs would catch up with him, and he might not make it back to her alive. There was only so much luck or talent to go around to keep pushing the envelope. Eventually you're going to come up with the short straw and Sonia would be left alone, picking up the pieces.

"Cut the crap, Pete, and tell me," Sonia said, anger creeping into her voice.

Maddox sighed and told her everything.

THREE
COCKY AMERICANS

Birmingham and London, England, UK

THE STATION WAS PACKED WITH PEOPLE AS THE MAN WITH the large rucksack made his way to the London-bound train.

He had a boyish look to him, even though the right side of his face had several scratch-like scars, courtesy of shrapnel from an IED planted on the side of a crumbling road in Tikrit, Iraq.

He was lugging a large rucksack through the station. Despite the scars, the man had a knack for going unnoticed. He was just another American kid backpacking through Europe.

He had floppy brown hair and looked younger than his twenty-eight years. His face was tanned from spending most of his time on the road and he had emotionless eyes.

He donned raffish clothing of dirty blue jeans, and an olive-green Army field jacket from the Vietnam War era.

He switched trains at Birmingham International station, to continue his five-hour journey from Llwyngwril to the Euston railway station in London.

It was a long trip, but he didn't mind it. He liked watching the countryside go by. He found it relaxing.

His mind raced when he saw a person, just for an instant, walking down a sidewalk or mulling around in their backyard. He couldn't help but look at them as targets. His nose touching the window, he would close his left eye and look at them from his imaginary riflescope, and wonder if he could make the shot. *It would be an amazing hit from a moving train.*

The man felt eyes on him so he turned. Two attractive blonde girls across from him were giving him a flirty smile. He had heard them incessantly talking since the moment he'd sat down. They were Russian or Ukrainian—he was still learning how to pinpoint accents; they all sounded like Russian to him. He smiled back politely, then dismissively stuck white earbuds into his ears and turned his attention to an iPad—the twenty-first century way of telling someone to fuck off, without saying a word. After about a minute, he glanced up and the girls seemed confused. It didn't seem they were used to being ignored.

An overweight businessman sitting kitty-corner from him, in a suit one size too small, shook his head, wishing it was himself those pretty girls had flirted with.

It was the part of public transportation the man hated, dealing with the *public.* He went back to his iPad, reading *One Shot - One Kill* on the Kindle app and Metallica's "Ride the Lightning" blasting in his ears.

The Euston Station concourse was jammed with commuters. The man made his way outside, which was as crowded as the inside of the station.

The plan was to walk to the nearby London Underground Station, but the man decided he'd had his fill of crowds and trains, so he hailed a cab.

He soon regretted that decision. *Should have walked,* he thought, as the cab inched along the busy London streets where the traffic was thick and slow and it kept the cabbie busy maneu-vering around cars, trucks—or lorries as they called them in the

UK—iconic red double-decker buses, and people. Lots of people. Until, finally, the driver turned onto Cumberland Gate, paralleling Hyde Park.

"Pull over here, driver," the man said, staring out the window.

The cabbie did as instructed. The man paid the driver and jumped out of the cab. He shouldered the rucksack and walked into the park.

He was meeting his contact at the Hard Rock Cafe in London, which was about a mile away from where he'd exited the cab, he never took a cab right to his destination.

It was actually a nice day for London, so the man made his way through the park to that crowded, tourist mecca that was the Hard Rock Cafe. The type of garish location where people just blended into oblivion, so the man knew why his contact had chosen to meet there.

He went inside and looked around. There was rock-and-roll memorabilia hanging on the walls and in every nook and cranny of the restaurant which was crowded with hungry tourists craving American style burgers — seemingly ignoring the clutter on the walls.

The man stood there, lost in thought when the hostess, a pretty blonde with short hair and skin white as milk smiled and welcomed him to the restaurant with a cheery English accent.

She caused a stirring down in the man's groin—a feeling he had fought off for over two years. He shook her off and walked past her without saying anything.

He glanced around the restaurant and nodded at the man he was meeting.

Mr. White was sitting in one of the side booths toward the back, facing the front door.

The man walked through the restaurant toward Mr. White

in a saturnine silence, a direct opposite of the loud, bright, and fabricated perkiness imbued by the restaurant.

He slid into the other side of the booth.

"Hello, Axel," Mr. White said as the man dumped his backpack on the chair and nodded.

Mr. White and Axel only used codenames to address each other.

Axel had chosen his codename after Axel Kilgore, the author of *They Call Me the Mercenary* action books he'd loved to read as a kid. Hank Frost was the one-eyed mercenary that Axel had dreamed of being like when he'd joined the Army. That dream came too close to becoming a reality when IED shrapnel in Iraq nearly cost him an eye.

Axel didn't know Mr. White's real name or his identity, and he didn't want to know. But Mr. White—who had selected Axel for these jobs—seemed to know everything there was to know about Axel.

Mr. White was in his mid-forties with thinning black hair. He was a spindly, gaunt-looking man. He was wearing a blue sweater which made his skin seem a few shades paler than usual.

"I trust your trip went smoothly," Mr. White said with a trace of an Eastern European accent that Axel hadn't been able to place. If he were a gambling man–he was not—he would bet on Russian, or one of its former Soviet Bloc nations.

"Like taking candy from a baby. In and out," Axel said.

"You cocky Americans," Mr. White scoffed.

"Fucking-A," Axel said with a smirk just as the cheery waitress arrived.

Axel ordered a double cheeseburger. "Meat, cheddar cheese, meat. Bun. No special sauce or anything else on it. An order of fries. Do you have Mountain Dew?"

The waitress looked like he had kicked her dog when she

apologetically informed him that they did not have Dew. So, he ordered a Coke.

Mr. White ordered a club sandwich and a bottle of Perrier water. Both men watched as the waitress scurried away to put in their order. Mr. White leaned in toward Axel.

"Here's the next target," he whispered as he slid a small jump drive across the table. "I've made the arrangements. You're on the red eye, tonight. Word is already getting out there about your the last target, so we must strike quickly before every freelancer on the network finds out about your work in Wales."

Axel pocketed it and said, "No problem."

Mr. White sat back and smiled. *Cocky Americans.*

FOUR
HIRED HELP

AXEL LOOKED AROUND THE DARKENED CABIN OF HIS VIRGIN Atlantic flight from London to New York City.

It was the red-eye flight and most of his fellow passengers were fast asleep. He envied them. He always struggled to sleep on an airplane.

It didn't help that he kept thinking about how he would be trapped in a tin can hurtling, thirty-thousand feet in the air, over the Atlantic Ocean for about eight hours.

As passengers slept, he bided his time, watching movies he had downloaded onto his iPad and listening to heavy metal music. The hard rock thundered through his headphones as he learned the details of his next target.

He had a two-hour layover at John F. Kennedy International then another five-hour flight to Luis Muñoz Marín International Airport in San Juan, Puerto Rico. From there, he would drive ninety-minutes south to Ponce.

Axel had plenty of time to think about the disrespectful way

Mr. White treated him. He could feel his disdain deep in his bones with every glance and conversation.

It was the way Mr. White looked at him and talked down to him, like he was nothing more than hired help like the waitress who fetched their food with a fake smile and pleasantries in the hope to be rewarded with silver.

"Don't be impatient," Mr. White would lecture.

You have no idea how patient I can be. Had Mr. White ever lain in the prone shooting position, hidden in the bush for hours, even days with a sniper rifle, waiting for the right time to take that kill shot?

The flight landed on time and Axel deplaned. His lack of sleep was catching up to him. The last thing he wanted to do was to go through customs. But he lined up with the rest of the herd.

At least the line for "US Citizens" seemed to be moving a bit more swiftly than the line for foreign visitors.

The customs officer in the small tollbooth-like cubicle was overweight and aloof. He flipped through Axel's passport. It was real and less than a year old, so it didn't elicit as much scrutiny as his previous passport, with its pages stamped from countries like Afghanistan, Pakistan, Egypt, Libya, Russia.

The customs man eyeballed him for a few seconds before he stamped the passport, muttered, "Welcome," and waved him into the United States.

Axel had to wait twenty minutes in line to spend about one minute with the customs official.

After waiting around the baggage carousel for ten minutes, he picked up his rucksack and went through another line.

They didn't check his rucksack, but he didn't care either way—it wasn't like he would check his work gear through customs.

After a few minutes, he was walking down the busy JFK

terminal. He hated both New York airports with a passion but, since it had been a while since he'd been back to the States, he actually stopped and took it in.

Someone bumped into him from behind and muttered something—sounded like *move, asshole*—but Axel didn't care.

He inhaled American air and smiled. He was surprised how good it felt standing on U.S. soil again for the first time in ten months. Even though he wouldn't be setting foot outside of the terminal.

He had a connecting flight to San Juan, Puerto Rico. He looked at his watch. Eighty minutes. *Plenty of time,* he thought as he went looking for a cheeseburger and a Mountain Dew.

FIVE

SWAGGER

"MI VIDA, I'M GOING TO THE GYM. I'LL BE BACK IN A COUPLE hours," Hermes Ramos said to his wife, his gym bag in hand.

"Okay, have a good workout. I'm going to yoga in an hour. We can meet up afterward," his wife said.

"Sounds good. Text where you're at and I'll meet you there," Ramos said, heading out the front door.

A minute later, Ramos pulled out of his driveway.

Ten minutes later, he was on Baramaya Avenue and pulling into the Planet Fitness parking lot.

Ruben Blades was blasting inside his black Lexus. Ramos loved the salsa classics, and for him there was none better than 1970s Ruben Blades singing the story about Pedro Navaja.

There were plenty of parking spots, one of the reasons why Ramos liked to workout during nonpeak gym hours—the benefits of being a retired Army soldier and freelancer. He could now pick his hours.

Ramos parked the car and looked around. Special Forces

habits never went away. Especially since a Lexus was a popular target for carjackers in Puerto Rico.

Ramos got out of his car and headed toward the gym with his usual swagger, even if no one was paying attention.

He was whistling as he strutted up to the front door, Pedro Navaja style, he saw a beautiful raven-black haired woman exiting the gym. They reached the glass door at the same time. Ramos was more than happy to turn on the charm for the beauty. He quickly grabbed the door handle, flung it open, stood to the side like an eager New York City doorman.

"Please, after you," the ever-flirtatious Ramos said in Spanish with a huge smile.

The woman ignored him as she walked past him.

Ramos was leering at her when the shots rang out. Two shots hit their target as he stumbled into the front lobby, and collapsed onto the floor.

The staff and gym members had hit the floor at the sound of gunfire. After about a minute of eerie silence, they began to reemerge.

The smell of gunpowder hung thick in the air as the witnesses gathered around and looked down at Ramos's body.

Someone in full gym workout attire identified herself as a doctor and knelt next to Ramos, but there was nothing she could do.

"He's dead," she said, as the crowd gasped and sobbed. Sirens could be heard from a distance.

Axel saw the first responders speeding towards the gym as he was getting on the Luis A. Ferré highway toward San Juan.

SIX

PUSHING FIFTY

Key Biscayne, Florida, USA

MADDOX AND SONIA ALWAYS ARGUED WHENEVER HE TOLD her he was considering another odd job.

The only change to the argument was the location.

"Somalia? Are you nuts!" Sonia said as tears welled in her eyes. She was angry, disappointed, and scared—all at once.

Maddox knew that taking on an odd job would only exacerbate the problems that work had brought their ten-year marriage.

"You said no more odd jobs," Sonia reminded him.

For Maddox, it was like they were on a prerecorded loop when it came to the subject of his work. Sonia upset that he would be willing to yet again, go off to some strife-filled far away land to kill someone for money.

Maddox downplayed it.

You don't waltz into a country like Afghanistan, Iraq, or Somalia and walk out with a captured target when a kill shot and a photograph paid the same. It was like being a bounty hunter during the Wild West.

She didn't care to hear his litany of excuses. To her, they were just Maddox's rationalization to take on these dangerous jobs and she had heard them all before.

"It's the type of work I would be doing if I were still in the CIA or with Special Forces."

"The CIA has blacklisted me from the plum, fluff jobs."

"I only go after targets that are being sought by the US government. I'm being patriotic. I'm ridding the world of very bad men."

Sometimes he would shout-out the overlying truth to it all. *"I'm damned good at it. It pays ridiculously well, and I'm doing the world a favor by putting down that vermin trash."*

Sonia knew that, and she actually understood it. She just thought he had done enough. They weren't in the poorhouse by any stretch of the imagination. It was time to stop.

Although they never talked about it, she knew he'd killed more than one of those bastards who had kidnapped her friend's granddaughter. He himself had been shot, saved only by his bulletproof vest.

And that was the cusp of her angrily pleading for her husband to stop taking on these dangerous jobs—forget killing people, she was terrified that *he* would be killed.

The house always wins, and with every job like the one in Somalia his odds of returning home to her alive dwindled.

You can't keep betting against the house and expect to walk away a winner every time.

It couldn't help in that line of work that he was pushing fifty. What is he thinking?

To Maddox's relief, their fight was interrupted by a phone call.

Maddox picked up the call from Tom Rose and the two friends exchanged greetings.

"Did I catch you at a bad time?" Rose asked, sensing tension in Maddox's voice.

"No, it's fine, what's up?" Maddox said, looking over at Sonia, who rolled her eyes and walked out of Maddox's home office.

To be continued, Maddox thought.

"I'm afraid I have bad news," Rose said.

"What is it?"

"It's Hermes Ramos. He was just murdered near his home in Puerto Rico," Rose said.

Maddox felt light-headed, like a simple push would knock him down, so he sat in his chair.

"When?"

"A few hours ago," Rose said. "Sorry, Pete, I know you two went way back."

"As far back as you and Fitzy. And now they're both dead within days of each other. What the hell is going on, Tom?"

"I don't have an answer, but there is no way this is random."

"Agreed. Even if it's a past job catching up to them." Maddox stopped, thinking about the worst fear he had about the odd jobs—that somehow, someday, someone would come seeking revenge at his front door, putting Sonia in danger. Or that they would hurt her, knowing it would cause him more pain than anything they could do him.

"You there, mate?" Rose asked.

"Yeah, sorry. Just thinking what this could be about." Maddox looked out his door. He didn't see or hear Sonia, so he continued, "And about Sonia's safety."

"That's why I'm calling, mate. We need to hold off on that Somalia job and figure this out," Rose said.

Maddox agreed.

"I'll make the travel arrangements," Rose said.

Maddox hung up. On the one hand, Sonia would be happy he wasn't going to Somalia. But the reason for backing out of the job wouldn't send her running into his arms with joy.

SEVEN
ASK ALICE

Amsterdam, Netherlands

Maddox and Rose met at Schiphol Airport, Amsterdam. It was one of the busiest airports in Europe, ushering travelers from across the pond and all over the world.

It was also the location where network business was discussed in person.

Maddox had taken the nonstop red-eye from Miami. Rose had flown in from his villa that overlooked the Atlantic Ocean in Tenerife, the largest of Spain's Canary Islands.

Rose had arrived in Amsterdam first and had waited for Maddox to emerge from the passenger arrival area.

The two friends embraced and smiled at seeing each other for the first time in over a year. As always, they picked up right where they had left off previously and were getting on as if they had just seen each other days ago, the seriousness of the occasion be damned.

Maddox and Rose took the NS train sprinter from the airport to Centraal station in Amsterdam.

Then, mostly so they could talk freely, they slowly made their way on foot to *'t Loosje,* a café on Nieuwmarkt.

"I take it Sonia wasn't too happy about this trip," Rose said as they walked.

"No, she pretty much doesn't want me involved with this type of work anymore."

"Mate, why do you tell her the truth?" Rose asked. He was half-serious, half-joking.

Maddox shrugged. "I can't tell her I'm working another risk analysis corporate job. She knows those jobs don't last that long, and they don't take such a toll on my ass like the odd jobs. I prefer to keep her in the loop. This work is hard enough on her anyway. Lying about it just makes it worse."

"Well, what the hell do I know, that's why I'm thrice-divorced, and single now," Rose said with a laugh.

"I don't know, Tom, I'm going to have to retire from this shit in order to save my marriage," Maddox said.

It was something that he had been thinking about for a long time, but it was the first time he'd said it out loud to anyone. To his surprise, he felt okay with it.

"Well, mate, you should have enough money squirreled from all the other jobs we've pulled off over the years," Rose said.

"Yes. But what the hell am I supposed to do with myself for the next twenty years or so?" Maddox said, grinning.

"You'll figure it out, mate, you always do," Rose said.

The 't Loosje Café on Nieuwmarkt Square was better known for its pot and hash than its coffee. They sat at one of the small sidewalk tables away from the haze of weed and hash.

Rose ordered a Heineken. Maddox ordered an Old Speckled Hen beer.

Rose raised an eyebrow at his beer choice. "You're in Holland and you order an English beer."

"I can drink Heineken anywhere. Old Speckled Hen, not so much," Maddox said.

"I like your logic."

Maddox and Rose killed time at the cafe for over an hour. After two beers, a sandwich, and a slice of clean chocolate cake —ordered clean to ensure it wasn't infused with THC—they headed out to the rendezvous location.

EIGHT

DOCKLANDS

Amsterdam, Netherlands

MADDOX AND ROSE MADE THEIR WAY FROM THE CENTER OF Amsterdam toward the eastern docklands on foot.

They made it to the Jan Schaeferbrug Bridge and walked over, into the Java-eiland neighborhood—which was located on a peninsula.

It had once been an area that bustled with business on behalf of the Dutch East Indies Company, but that had been a long time ago.

The area was now transformed into a desirable residential neighborhood with postmodern-looking row houses dotting the canal and small dinghy like boats tied up to the pier and swaying in the water.

It was quiet and a bit off the beaten path for the typical tourist. It was a good place to meet.

A man sat on a low wall with his back toward the canal.

As agreed upon, the man wore a black Chicago White Sox baseball hat. It was that black hat with the distinctive White Sox logo that Maddox saw first.

Maddox nudged Rose and nodded toward the man on the wall.

They walked up to him and shook hands. His handshake was limp and sweaty. Maddox fought the urge to wipe his hands on his jeans as they greeted each other with their TEN codenames.

"Hello, Larkspur. Foxglove," the man said.

"Homer," Maddox said. Homer was Ben Gold, Maddox, and Rose's liaison with the network.

The three men exchanged brief pleasantries. Even in this business it's the polite thing to do.

There was an uncertain cadence to Gold's voice that Maddox hadn't heard before. He remained sitting. He was a tall man, so his lanky legs and stooped shoulders awkwardly took more space than needed.

"I trust your flights went well?" Gold asked as he stood.

Maddox was six feet, three inches tall and Rose was six feet tall, both above average height, but Gold towered over them at six feet, six inches and he was thin like a rail.

"Let's walk," Gold said.

The three men strolled by the river.

Riverboat homes gently swayed on the calm waters of the canal.

Rose had been part of the network for a year before Maddox, and he had been the one that had referred Maddox to the board.

Once Maddox had been admitted into TEN, Rose's liaison, Ben Gold had become his connection to the network as well.

Gold was organized and efficient. He seemed to have connections everywhere—Russia, Turkey, Jordan, Uganda, Albania.

He served as a broker and logistics expert, the operational

middleman that was required to get men like Maddox and Rose the things they needed in order to do their jobs.

You don't hop onto Expedia when traveling to Baghdad.

Gold's wheeling and dealing and relationship building, which had him palm-greasing everyone from local warlords, chieftains, mayors, governors, senators, and even presidents, allowed Maddox access into tightly secured areas in foreign lands where he could track down and execute the contract at hand.

And it was Gold who could procure the necessary arms and equipment to carry out those jobs with the expertise of an Adnan Khashoggi.

Maddox figured the network paid him very well on top of ten percent of the contract that was paid out to the liaison — for Maddox, Gold was worth every penny of that ten percent.

TEN operated in murky waters, but unlike the black-market networks, TEN was more exclusive with the contracts they took and the freelancers they allowed to bid.

The board refused to list the type of contracts that were deemed nefarious, in an already shady business world of war and death. No jobs for drug and war criminals or known terrorists were allowed.

That mantra of exclusivity and vetting the jobs that were posted had become part of the network's mystique.

TEN's business model was rather simple—it brought freelancers and job contractors together.

It was the brainchild of a man known as the chairman, who had founded the network and served as its leader, and head of its Board of Directors.

Their identity was a mystery. Rumors and tidbits of information culled from here and there pegged the chairman as the former head of Mossad. Or perhaps he was just a high-ranking

Mossad agent or a general. Or maybe a former prime minister of Israel. The rumors were rampant.

Ben Gold and two other liaisons were the only people free-lancers met with in person on contract-to-contract bases.

The chairman's idea for TEN had come from the explosive growth in private military contracts after 9/11.

By the time TEN had been formed in 2003, private military contracts had more than tripled to over $300 billion from around $100 billion in 2001.

The Department of Defense's online bidding system, known as FedBizOpps, was the biggest source for these contracts.

By law, every Pentagon contract was required to be open to public bidding so companies—from behemoths like General Dynamics and Northrop Grumman to small mom-and-pop operators to shady brokers and war dogs—could bid for a piece of the pie.

Everything from requisitioning Kevlar helmets, bullets, and bulletproof vests to screws, paperclips, and fuel was outsourced and open to be bid on.

Then, there were the type of contracts that would never be posted on the FedBizOpps website or the privately funded work, which is where the chairman's TEN website filled the void.

For the liquidation jobs, the chairman wanted to keep the contracts in the gray market, so the network would only accept jobs against targets deemed to be a threat to a legitimate govern-ment. The type of contracts that might be found on the DOJ's Rewards for Justice website.

The chairman would not cross the line and open the network to drug cartels, Russian mobsters, or to a billionaire looking for someone to kill his wife.

Only former top intelligence agents or Special Forces operatives would be considered for membership, since these individuals understood and appreciated the need for secrecy in that line of work. And only those individuals invited by the Board could apply to join.

You didn't ask to join the Threat Elimination Network. You were invited.

After a few minutes by the river, Maddox asked Gold, "Is there a security breach in the network?"

Gold stopped and looked at Maddox, "Only the administrator could tell you that. He runs the system, the database, the nuts and bolts of the network. I'm not privy to that type of information."

"Can we meet with the administrator then?" Maddox asked.

"I'm afraid that is not possible. Liaisons are the only representatives of the network that meet, or talk with the members of the network," Gold said.

"Okay, let me try a different question. You are aware that Hermes Ramos and Malcolm Fitzsimmons have been killed. Within days of each other," Maddox said.

"I'm aware of that," Gold said. He turned, and looked out to the canal. It seemed so peaceful.

"Is the board aware of it?" Maddox asked.

Ben mulled it over trying to decide whether to answer the question.

"They are aware."

"Jesus, didn't the network think that's information that should be shared with the membership?" Rose asked.

"You knew the rules of the network, gentlemen, and you agreed to abide by those rules when you joined. A network, no matter how secret, no matter how well protected, is still vulnerable, and we all knew that when we joined it. The rules will not be changed over these deaths. Therefore, the only communication coming from the network will be about the jobs," Gold said.

"So why did you agree to meet with us then, mate? It seems like there is nothing to discuss according to the rules," Rose said.

"That is an accurate assessment, Foxglove. I read out of the same playbook as you do. But you see, I was the liaison for the two contractors that were terminated making me feel a bit uneasy about my safety. But unlike you gentlemen, I'm strictly logistics. I don't have your set of skills. And there appears to be someone, or a group out there picking off the best in this business like they were buck privates. So, I worry if those under my charge are being killed, perhaps they'll go for a clean sweep and take me out as well. A scenario I would much rather avoid," Gold explained calmly.

"So you're scared you'll make the hit parade," Maddox asked.

"I'd figure it's in all of our best interests to have that threat eliminated before they get a crack at taking us out."

"Don't you risk the same outcome by meeting with us?" Maddox asked.

"I would suspect the board would put out a termination contract on me if they knew about this unauthorized meeting, but you're the only two members that have reached out to the network about this situation, at least officially. As you're both highly rated members of the network, I thought it would be in my best interest to agree to meet with you," Gold said.

"For self-preservation," Rose said.

"Indeed. Isn't that why you're here as well?" Gold asked. It was a genuine inquisitive reaction from Gold, not meant to be a put-down.

Maddox grinned, "Indeed it is. No shame in self-preservation."

"I believe this might be about all of *our* self-preservation," Gold said.

"Have you brought this up with the board?" Rose asked.

"Even if I knew how to get in contact with the board, I don't think this is something I would want to discuss with them. I work for the network administrator. He reports directly to the board. I did bring up my concerns to him, and he told me to stop being paranoid and get back to work. So I did try to follow protocol," Gold replied.

"Can you get us in touch with the administrator?" Maddox asked.

Gold sighed. "I wouldn't know how. I've never met him face-to-face. I don't even know from which part of the world he operates."

"So what exactly can you do to help us out here, mate?"

Gold pursed his lips for a moment and said, "I made a copy of my hard drive. I don't have administrator type access to the network, but it could perhaps shed some light as to what is going on here. If you're interested, I can provide that to you."

"Do you have it here?" Maddox said.

"No. That was too risky. I have it in a safe location in my apartment," Gold said.

"Please tell me you live in Amsterdam," Maddox said.

Gold shook his head. "Brussels."

"Fuck," Maddox muttered.

NINE
7212

Axel felt emboldened with his recent successes including terminating two targets on two continents in the same week.

He had spent a couple days laying low in New York City. All five boroughs were trash as far as he was concerned but it was a good spot to blend in and go unnoticed.

The latest instructions from Mr. White was for him to pack his bag and head out to Kennedy Airport.

Axel took the train from Penn Station to JFK. He had barely made it into the terminal when his phone vibrated in his pocket. He dug it out and saw he had a new text message.

He clicked on the obfuscated number and read the text: 7212. That was the code Mr. White was using for the day.

Axel looked around the terminal at the throng of hurrying people.

The phone he had on him wasn't secured and he didn't have a disposable one on him, so he'd need a public pay phone.

He had learned that lesson the hard way when he'd first

started... TSA gets mighty suspicious when traveling with multiple mobile phones.

He was certain that airports were one of the few remaining bastions of public pay phones.

Axel was right. It didn't take long to find one.

He was amused by the fact that he had probably walked by those phones before but had never noticed them. He couldn't recall the last time he had used one, if ever—not uncommon for members, like him, of the millennial generation.

Axel dug out a prepaid calling card and slid it into the payphone's card-reading slot. After a few seconds, he began punching numbers on the keypad.

It took about a minute for the phone to ring through. The dial tone sounded odd to him, like it was ringing in a tunnel.

Mr. White had a security system in place where each ring-back meant something, so Axel had to count the number of rings.

Mr. White picked up on the third ring, meaning it was clear for him to talk.

But even then, he demanded the use of codenames and passcodes every time they communicated.

"Pennington Travel." It was Mr. White's voice.

"Arthur Franklin returning your call," Axel said.

"Do you have the travel confirmation number, Mr. Franklin?"

Axel read back the numbers he had received via text: 7212.

Satisfied the lines were secure, Mr. White blurted, "What took you so long in calling me back?"

Axel looked at his watch. It had been about ten minutes since he received the text message.

"You know I'm at the airport, right? I don't have a burner handy, so I had to track down a pay phone. Not an easy task nowadays. So give me a break," Axel said.

"We have a problem."

Axel didn't say anything.

After a few seconds, Mr. White said, "We need to meet right away, in Amsterdam."

Right away. Amsterdam. Does he think I'm around the block?

"You do know I'm in New York?" Axel said.

"Of course. I always know where you are," Mr. White said.

Axel gripped the black receiver tighter.

"There is a red-eye, tonight on Delta. I've made all the travel arrangements, and the boarding e-ticket is waiting for you."

"What's going on?"

"Like I said, we have a problem. It's just come up, and we need to take care of it right away, so be on that flight," Mr. White said.

"But ... hello?" Mr. White had hung up.

Axel slammed the phone down loud enough that two Tommy Bahama-clad old coots glanced over in his direction.

Axel looked away, shouldered his rucksack, and split.

He stewed as he headed toward the Delta terminal, muttering under his breath, "We. *I'm* the one doing the actual heavy lifting. It's me, asshole. Not *we*."

He wanted to show Mr. White up and not be on that flight. So he did the breathing exercise he'd learned from that counselor he had been forced to see after his last tour in Iraq.

To his chagrin, the shrink's bullshit breathing trick actually helped him calm down.

Axel reminded himself that this was the line of work he had sought out so desperately and now that he was doing that work, he couldn't just pick and choose.

Soon enough, he told himself. *Be patient.*

TEN
AGAINST THE RULES

Amsterdam, Netherlands

THE PLANE TOUCHED DOWN AT 7:00 A.M. LOCAL TIME. AN
hour later, Axel met up with Mr. White at a safe house near
Schiphol Airport in Amsterdam.

Axel got there tired and bedraggled.

They went to the kitchen where Mr. White had a teakettle
heating.

"You look tired, Axel," Mr. White said, eyeing him
carefully.

"Wales, London, New York, Puerto Rico, New York again,
and now Amsterdam. I wonder why I look tired?" Axel said, his
voice snarky.

"I know. You've done well. But something has come up and
it's truly an emergency. So after this assignment, you can take
more time for yourself. You've earned it," Mr. White said.

Axel tilted his head like a dog. It was the first time Mr.
White had given him a compliment and shown an inkling of
appreciation for his work.

"So, what is the emergency?" Axel asked.

"Someone inside the Network has been a very naughty boy. Made an unauthorized back up of his hard drive. The fool didn't think I would know," Mr. White said.

The teakettle screamed, so Mr. White removed it from the burner and poured the hot water into a cup letting the tea bag steep. He didn't offer Axel anything.

"So what did he do, give it to someone?"

"That's not important right now, and frankly, it doesn't matter what he plans to do with it. It's against the rules. He knows that damned well, so now he needs to go," Mr. White explained.

He filled in Axel about his next target in Brussels between sips of mint tea.

"I stashed my gear in London, I can swing over there—" Axel began to say before Mr. White interrupted him.

"No time for that. I want you on the next train to Brussels. I'll provide you with everything you need there. Besides, you won't always have the luxury to stalk and set up a sniper's nest for your targets. There will be times you'll need to be quick, up close and personal. This will be an excellent training assignment for you," Mr. White said.

ELEVEN

TRAINING ASSIGNMENT

Brussels, Belgium

BEN GOLD LIVED IN NORTHWEST BRUSSELS IN A COZY apartment with a beautiful view of the Basilica of the Sacred Heart. He looked out the window to the street below, which was quiet that early in the morning.

That doesn't mean it's safe out there, he thought. Then he stopped himself.

Don't get yourself worked up.

Gold's apartment building was stylish and sought-after by the working young, but it was an old building that creaked and popped during the stillness of the night. It always had, but since he had met with Maddox and Rose, that noise sounded more ominous. He tensed up at the creaking wooden floor, certain an assassin was creeping up to him.

"You need to keep it together," Gold said to himself.

He knew how the network internal security forces operated better than anyone else, and if they suspected him of wrong-doing—like making a copy of the network hard drive—they would watch him first in order to assess if he still had the hard drive, and what his plans were.

He felt that he was being watched, but that didn't mean he would be terminated. How could they possibly know about the hard drive?

Maddox and Rose would arrive on a later flight. They would observe the place to ensure he wasn't being watched, and then he would pass them the hard drive.

"Okay," Ben said as he went into his bedroom, determined to get on with his regular day so that if they were watching, he wouldn't raise red flags with TEN.

He was going to go on his regular morning run in Parc Elisabeth, which was across the street from his apartment. He changed into his running gear, grabbed his phone and earbuds, and left his apartment and down a flight of stairs. He walked by the mailboxes, opened the front door, and stepped onto the sidewalk.

The crisp morning air felt good. He stretched for a minute on the sidewalk.

He knew he should do more stretching, but he was eager to run. He popped in the white earbuds and hit *play* on his iPhone as he walked down half a block to a crosswalk. Traffic was light this early in the morning so he jogged across the street and into the park, picking up the pace.

He was running down the path that was surrounded by trees with groves and flowerbeds. He glanced up at the cloudy sky and he could feel the morning dew and fog on him as he ran.

He had made it less than a mile when he reached the part of his run that paralleled the tracks of the tram railway.

One of the streetcars passed him by and even though he had techno music blasting in his ears, he could feel the rattling of the streetcar roaring past.

The music thumped in his ears so he did not hear as Axel

ran up behind him. Axel had been waiting for the streetcar to come up and took off in a sprint alongside the train. He used it to hide the sound of his approach.

Axel was jogging a few steps behind Ben. The streetcar clanked past him, then Ben, Axel took that opportunity to close the gap to get within striking reach.

Axel had been glancing around that whole time. There wasn't anyone around near enough to cause him to abort the mission. He got so close that Ben finally sensed the presence that someone was running up behind him. He began to turn his head in midstride to see what was going on, but it was too late.

Because of Gold's height, Axel had to leap like a lion taking down a zebra. He wrapped his left arm around Ben's neck and then he sank the blade of his dagger into the base of Gold's neck.

He pushed the blade deep enough to sever Ben's external jugular vein.

Axel had trained for this type of kill many times before, but it was his first attempt tat it, so he had been nervous. And even as he sank in the blade, he kept thinking, *What if I miss the jugular? What if the knife ends up getting stuck? If that happens, just leave the knife—you're wearing running gloves, no prints.*

The thoughts bombarded his head as he removed the blade and Ben fell to the ground like a sack of stones.

Axel knew it was a clean hit. There was no coming back from that.

As he kept on running, he unzipped the blood-splattered hoodie he was wearing and tossed it into the bushes without breaking his stride. He looked back once at Ben Gold's lifeless body on the trail behind him.

Mr. White will be pleased, Axel thought as he cut through the pathway, resisting the urge to get into full run-out panic mode.

Just keep jogging, he reminded himself. He ran onto Avenue des Gloires Nationales where he could easily disappear into its residential neighborhood.

Axel made it back to the safe house. He looked at his watch. He had plenty of time to wash up, pick up his stuff and be on the red-eye train to Prague.

TWELVE

GAULOISES

Brussels, Belgium

Philippe Bouhouche was a natty dresser with Louis Jourdan movie-star looks.

He was an inspector with the DJSOC, the department that fought against serious and organized crime at national, and international level.

But more importantly to Maddox and Rose, he was part of TEN's extensive collection of well-placed paid sources throughout the world.

He had agreed to meet with Maddox and Rose in a café not far from where Ben Gold had been murdered the day before.

Bouhouche was dressed in a twill-woven cloth suit, with a skinny silver tie, and a crisp white cotton poplin dress shirt that twinkled with a silk-like gleam.

It was not clothing that Maddox and Rose were used to seeing a detective wear.

The three men sat around a small table toward the back of the café where all three could keep an eye on the front entrance.

Bouhouche chain-smoked Gauloises cigarettes and drank

black coffee like it was water and he had just been rescued from the Sahara.

Bouhouche struggled to speak since he always was either puffing on a cigarette or drinking.

"We don't have any leads about the killing," the detective said without bothering to remove the cigarette from his lips. "Mr. Gold went for a run and was killed. That is all that is known by the inspectors handling his homicide."

He had a heavy French accent, but he spoke English well.

"Was anything amiss in his apartment?" Rose asked.

"What do you mean, please?" Bouhouche asked, not familiar with the word.

"Anything stolen from his home? You know, when burglars toss a place looking for items to steal, jewelry, televisions, computers, that type of stuff," Maddox asked.

"Ah, I understand now. The apartment was not broken into. Nothing seemed out of place. The police did take his laptop, an iPad, and a phone for evidence."

"What about an external hard drive, did the police recover one of those?" Maddox asked.

"Not that I recall. One moment," Bouhouche said, grabbing his mobile phone and began scrolling and tapping on it.

After about a minute, he looked back up and said, "There wasn't an external hard drive recovered. It's not on the evidence list so I doubt they found one."

Maddox and Rose looked at each other.

"Tell me about this external hard drive," Bouhouche said.

"Mr. Gold was going to give it to us last night. It's the reason we came to Brussels. There was very important data on that hard drive that we need. He stood us up and when we couldn't reach him, we reached out to you and found he'd been murdered that morning," Maddox said.

"We can't help but think his murder might have to do with

the hard drive. Perhaps the killer wanted to make sure he wouldn't pass that along to us," Rose said.

"Possible," Bouhouche said. "Do you know what type of information was on the hard drive?"

"He didn't tell us." Maddox and Rose had decided not to let Bouhouche know it was a copy of TEN's network since Bouhouche was on the network's payroll.

"What about video? Did you get anything from that?" Maddox asked, changing the subject.

"We obtained the CCTV from near his home and from various points along his running route. He was spotted on several occasions, just running. Once he entered the park, there was no CCTV available and therefore his murder wasn't captured on video. There were no suspicious individuals seen on any of the footage," Bouhouche said. He reached into his pant's pocket and removed a jump drive, which he handed to Maddox. "That's a copy of the preliminary police report on the Ben Gold investigation. Make sure you destroy it when you're done with it."

"We'd like to take a look in his apartment. For the hard drive," Maddox said pocketing the jump drive.

"It's still secured as a crime scene so you will need to be careful. There is no guard detail. But I'm certain the forensic investigators would have taken a hard drive for evidence had they found one, so not sure it's worth the risk, but here you go," Bouhouche said, sliding a key toward Maddox.

"Mr. Gold's apartment key."

Maddox took the key and pocketed it as well.

"Thank you," Maddox and Rose said at the same time.

"Please, don't get caught in his apartment with that key or the jump drive with the report I gave you. It would make my life very difficult."

THIRTEEN

CHARLES BRIDGE

Prague, Czech Republic

THAT EVENING, MR. WHITE WAS STANDING IN THE MIDDLE of the Charles Bridge in Prague.

It was a beautiful bridge made of sandstone that had stood over the Vltava River for more than six hundred years.

Axel was walking toward Mr. White from the Malá Strana side of the bridge.

Mr. White looked at him a couple times as he got closer. Axel could read it in his face. Mr. White wanted him to pick up the pace, so Axel began to walk slower.

Axel could hear Mr. White sigh as he walked up next to him. Mr. White was leaning against the bridge with his front side overlooking the river. Axel followed suit and didn't say anything.

Mr. White finally broke the silence. "Your work in Brussels. Did it have to be so messy?"

"You're the one who said that sometimes we need to get up close and personal in this line of work. I did the job the only way I could do it quickly. I don't have the luxury to overthink these things. And it didn't seem messy to me. It was in and out," Axel said.

"According to my sources he bled out like a stuck pig. It was undignified," Mr. White said.

Axel shook his head in disbelief. "What business are you in?" he asked.

Mr. White said nothing, knowing Axel was right.

It was a bloody, messy business, that's why Mr. White needed soldier ants like Axel to do the grunt labor.

"I just wish it didn't have to come to that. He was highly capable at his job," Mr. White said.

"What is that regret you have? You're the one who said he had been a naughty boy and all that shit, so that was his own doing, now wasn't it?"

Axel seemed to enjoy the kill. That worried Mr. White, but he had proven to be far more efficient and reliable than he could have ever imagined.

"You're correct. But unfortunately, the disloyalty of the man in Brussels has become even more of a distraction," Mr. White said.

"What now?" Axel said, sticking a piece of gum into his mouth and tossing the wrapper to the wind.

"Are you just trying to annoy me?" Mr. White said as he watched the wrapper dance over the bridge and gently land in the river.

Axel chewed his gum and grinned.

"As I was saying, because of the man in Brussels, we now have to deal with that damned hard drive. Its contents must not get out. I have been unable to recover it, but I will. It's just a matter of time. In the meantime anyone that knows of its existence, must be liquidated."

"How many people are we talking here?" Axel asked.

"He met with two network freelancers violating network

protocol in Amsterdam. One of the men was already a target for other reasons. The other man with him, well he has to go now too. So start with them. I'll send you their details," Mr. White said.

"So why was the other guy's head on the chopping block?"

"Those details do not concern you. Your concern should be that these two men are highly trained professionals."

"No problem," Axel said, blowing a bubble with his gum.

Damn his cockiness, Mr. White thought.

"They are the best in this business, so don't get too cocky," Mr. White said.

"Fuck that, so am I," Axel replied, sounding offended.

"They were handpicked to be in TEN for a reason," Mr. White said.

It was a cheap shot since Axel had been turned down by the network.

It was Mr. White's way of knocking the cocky young man down a peg or two.

He could see the anger in Axel's brown eyes and couldn't help thinking that the kid had a chip on his shoulder the size of Ayers Rock and although beneficial for his current needs it might be a problem he would have to deal with later.

"You can't take this lightly, or with overconfidence."

"I never take killing lightly. It's an art form," Axel replied, smirking.

That didn't reassure Mr. White.

FOURTEEN
THE SAFE

Twenty minutes after leaving Bouhouche in the cafe, Maddox and Rose pulled up in front of Ben Gold's apartment building in a rented cherry-red Fiat 500X.

Rose stayed in the vehicle while Maddox went inside.

Once at the door, Maddox was relieved that were wasn't yellow crime scene tape to deal with. He looked around the hallway as he put on a pair of black lightweight running gloves. He tried the key. It worked.

H quickly went inside. He wasn't sure what he was looking for. The police had already gone through the apartment, so he started looking in the one spot where he would hide something like a hard drive with stolen data on it—the walls.

Maddox fired up a stud finder app on his iPhone and began to scan the walls, looking for hidden compartments.

The best spot for a hidden safe was a special compartment between the studs of the interior wall.

The app wasn't a CIA type gadget—it was a civilian-developed app, available from the app store for less than ten dollars. He was amazed how well it worked.

After about fifteen minutes of scanning the walls, and moving furniture out of his way, Maddox found a loose section of the lower wall that had been conveniently blocked behind a couch.

It was a good spot, Maddox thought, as he got on his knees and began jiggling the section until he was able to remove a square section of the drywall.

He was looking at a hole in the wall, but it was too dark to see inside so Maddox reached for his pocket Maglite and pointed the light into the cutout hole that Gold must have been using as a hidden compartment.

Maddox got excited at seeing what looked like an ammo box tucked inside the hole.

He put the flashlight in his mouth and, with both hands, reached inside and slowly removed the object.

Once he had it out of the hole, he shined the flashlight on the box. It wasn't an ammo box, but a small safe with a digital keypad. He tried to open it, but it was locked, so Maddox took off his jacket and wrapped the safe within it.

He replaced the cutout wall and moved the couch back into place. He looked around to ensure he was leaving the apartment as he'd found it. Satisfied, he grabbed the jacket-draped safe and tucked it under his arm, like a wide receiver holding onto a football as he's heading for the end zone.

The moment Rose saw Maddox walk out, he started the car and flung open the passenger door.

Maddox ducked into the small Fiat. As soon as he shut his door, Rose checked for traffic and pulled out onto Avenue du Panthéon.

"What did you find?" Rose asked.

"A safe, hidden behind the drywall. Not to get too excited, it could be just his valuables he was hiding from burglars. But it was locked, so I couldn't look inside, so I just took the whole damned thing," Maddox said.

"Look at you, all Ronnie Biggs like," Rose said, laughing.

FIFTEEN

MAGNETS

Brussels, Belgium

IT WASN'T THAT BEN GOLD'S SAFE WAS STATE-OF-THE-ART — he had probably bought it at the local Carrefour Hypermarket.

It was like the safes found in hotel rooms, but the digital keypad lock rendered Maddox's lock picking tools powerless against it and he didn't have any drills or power tools to crack it open.

"A crowbar might do the trick. We could ask the front desk," Rose said, looking at the safe.

"I don't know. That might make them ask questions. It's too risky," Maddox said.

They decided against calling the front desk and instead called Philippe Bouhouche.

The inspector arrived twenty minutes later with a backpack over one shoulder.

After a minute of small talk, all three men were standing in front of the safe, staring at it.

"A hidden safe, right in his apartment," Bouhouche said,

shaking his head in dismay and embarrassment that the Belgium Police had not found it.

"Ben cut a square hole through the drywall. He placed the safe in there. Covered up the hole with the cut-away piece and, for good measure, he placed a couch in front of it. It was easy to miss," Maddox said.

Bouhouche groaned. "We've made a lot of improvements to our policing services in Belgium, but looks like we have more work to do. I had three inspectors go over that apartment supposedly very, very thoroughly."

"I'm sure it would have been found eventually. Finding secret hiding spots is more our expertise than police officers'," Maddox said with a smile.

"And as you can see, we can find it, but we can't open the bloody thing without drilling it, that's why we called you," Rose said, "we don't have any tools."

"And we wanted to turn this over to you anyway," Maddox added.

Bouhouche grinned at Maddox's bullshit. "I'm sure that was on your mind."

"Did you bring a drill or a crowbar?" Rose asked.

"When you described the safe and the brand over the phone, I knew just what to bring in order to open it. I don't need a drill. I did bring a crowbar, since that always comes in handy, but I probably won't even need that," Bouhouche said, inspecting the safe closely.

Maddox and Rose exchanged curious glances.

"So how will you get it open?" Rose asked.

"It won't be difficult to open this," Bouhouche said. He reached into the backpack and took out a small hard case. He clicked it open and removed what looked like a hockey puck. He held it up so Maddox and Rose could see it.

"Is that a magnet?" Maddox asked.

"It's a lot more powerful than a regular magnet. It's a rare earth magnet," Bouhouche said, still holding it. He put it down and asked, "Do you have a sock?"

Maddox and Rose looked at each other, confused. "Like a regular sock?" Maddox asked.

"Yes, yes, like a sock you put on your foot," Bouhouche said.

They were in Maddox's room so he walked over to his suitcase, flipped it open, removed a pair of black socks and held them up to Bouhouche.

"Yes, perfect. I just need one. And don't worry, I won't damage it," Bouhouche said.

Maddox handed him the sock, "Don't worry about the sock. It's fine if it's damaged, as long as you can get that safe open."

"Won't be a problem, but these rare earth magnets are extremely powerful. If you get your fingers in between the magnet and the metal surface, it could crush them. I've seen it happen, very painful," Bouhouche said as he dropped the rare earth magnet into the sock, "The sock offers some protection without affecting the usefulness of the magnet."

"You got me curious as hell as to how you're going to open that bad boy with a magnet," Maddox said, leaning in.

"It's simple with these basic safes. The safe uses a solenoid device that is built into the interior panel of the safe. There isn't much to it—just a cheap cylinder stuffed with coils and pins that acts like a magnet when the code is entered into the digital keypad, which sends little electric shocks when the right combination is entered. That is what opens the safe. All I have to do is put the rare earth magnet on top of where the solenoid is located," Bouhouche said, getting the sock-covered magnet closer to the safe.

"Since I do not have X-ray vision, it's a bit of guessing game, but the solenoid is almost always located right around the keypad," Bouhouche said, rubbing the area of the safe with his hand where he believed the device was located.

"Magic time," he said with a smile as he carefully hovered the sock over the chosen spot until the pull of the magnet and the steel of the safe took over. The magnet seemed to jump out of his hand onto the safe with a loud thwack.

Once the magnet was tightly attached to the safe, Bouhouche grabbed the sock by the gusset and said, "Okay, now I just slide the magnet over the solenoid." Bouhouche grunted a bit as he struggled to move the magnet over it until they all heard a click. He quickly pulled on the lever and the safe's door flung open.

"Voilà," Bouhouche said proudly.

"That. Is. Awesome," Maddox said.

"Brilliant," Rose said at almost the same time.

"I have to get me one of those magnets," Maddox said, smiling, and looking at Rose.

"They're cheap, around fifty dollars US. Cheaper, probably, for you in America," Bouhouche said.

"I knew there is no such thing as an impenetrable safe, especially civilian retail brands like that one, but that was ridiculously easy," Rose said.

"I wouldn't put anything of value into a safe. I don't care if it's gold, cash, jewelry, or documents," Bouhouche said.

"At least bury it, or hide it like Ben did," Rose said.

"You still found it," Bouhouche said, smiling.

He removed the magnet from the safe by sliding it toward the edge until it detached. He then casually removed the magnet from the sock and gave the sock back to Maddox with a smile.

"Still good."

Maddox and Rose were so impressed with the ease of

Bouhouche's magnet safe-cracking skills that, for a few minutes, they fussed over the magnet before finally turning their attention to the contents of the safe.

The inspector stepped aside from the opened safe. "Mind if I smoke out on the balcony?"

"Be my guest," Maddox said.

He was leaning against the railing, smoking and watching as Maddox and Rose emptied the contents of the safe.

After a few drags, he flicked the cigarette over the balcony and walked back inside.

"What was in there?" Bouhouche asked. The smell of tobacco radiated around him.

Maddox had laid out the contents into separate piles on the carpet.

"Cash in US dollars, Euros, and Pounds. Looks like around a thousand in each denomination. We have different IDs with his photograph. Different names. From Bulgaria, Togo, and Norway. And one external hard drive," Maddox said, smiling.

"That's what we're interested in," Rose said as he fired up his laptop.

"Indeed," Maddox said, handing Rose the hard drive. Rose connected it to his laptop's USB port and began sliding his index finger on the trackpad to navigate the hard drive's contents.

He didn't get far.

"Shit, password protected," Rose said.

"He couldn't make this a little easier for us?" Maddox said.

"Philippe, I don't want to jam you up, but I need to take the hard drive. If there is anything on it that can help with your investigation, you have my word that I'll pass it along to you as soon as I can," Maddox said.

Bouhouche had little choice in the matter since he had

already poisoned the investigation by taking money to help Maddox and Rose, but he appreciated that Maddox, unlike many American and British operatives, showed him respect by asking before taking it.

SIXTEEN

BEATRIX

Reston, Virginia

Troy Sennight and Pete Maddox had started their working relationship back in Maddox's CIA days.

He had been Maddox's Field IT Technician when he had been the Station Chief in Caracas, Venezuela.

After Maddox had been branded rogue by Langley and fired, there were few colleagues in the agency that dared to carry on a relationship with him.

Sennight was one of those few.

The tech whiz had risen through the CIA technical ranks, serving in senior roles as an IT tech, system administrator, and later as a tech supervisor at CIA stations in Mexico City, Beirut, Moscow, and London, before spending the last decade of his agency career as a Senior Data Engineer with the Directorate of Digital Innovation at CIA Headquarters in Langley, Virginia or, as he liked to describe himself, a real-life Q.

He had been tasked with the design, implementation, and the operation of data management systems for the CIA.

He was a grown-up hacker who had worked for the CIA

and unbeknownst to them, had continued providing his expertise to Maddox on the side for almost the entire last decade of
his CIA career.

Sennight had officially put out his own shingle after he had
retired from the CIA, two years ago, and business was booming.
But no matter how busy he got, Maddox always got to the top of
Sennight's queue.

Part of it was loyalty to his former boss, and because he had
been disgusted by the way Maddox had been hung out to dry,
after Venezuela. Fired, publicly exposed, and charged with a
litany of felonies by the Department of Justice which were all
dropped.

Maddox had been humiliated, and that had stayed with
Sennight.

The other part of it was the adventure. Maddox's work fed
his inner hacker child and Maddox provided a lot of fun for that
inner child. Hacking into the databases of the federal government, police departments in the United States and around the
world, creating black software and algorithms customized for
Maddox.

Tools that would make CIA contractors drool so Sennight
liked helping the blacklisted Maddox get an edge. It was like
rooting for the underdog.

Maddox and Rose were five hours ahead of Sennight, who
lived in Reston, Virginia. They called him from a secure cloned
phone.

Maddox and Rose were on speakerphone. Maddox gave
Sennight the background on how they had come upon that hard
drive and he was immediately intrigued.

"Is there a way to upload a password protected external
hard drive to Beatrix?" Maddox asked.

"It would be better if you overnight the hard drive and I'll
get to it right away. Once I crack it, I can upload the data to

Beatrix," Sennight said.

Beatrix was the dedicated secure server that had been set up exclusively for Maddox. The server was located in Sennight's home-based data center, tucked away in a hidden room he'd built as an addition to his home's basement.

A fake wall hid a steel fire-resistant door that could only be opened by sliding a slab of wood in the baseboard then pressing the locking mechanism in the right sequence, which was only known by him.

He had built the door and wall in his woodworking shop himself to avoid nosey construction contractors from knowing about it.

Inside the temperature-controlled room there were two 800mm depth rack-mount server cabinets on wheels.

The entire setup was up to CIA and NSA standards.

But, being the paranoid, tech-loving geek that he was, he didn't stop there. He had also rigged the server cabinets so that, in the unlikely event that someone was able to break into it and tried to remove any of the servers, an alarm would alert him.

If he didn't enter a passcode only he knew within forty-five seconds of the breach, the entire server would be wiped clean to agency standards.

"Okay, I'm going to send that to you overnight. I'll send you the tracking ID. Please get to that bad boy as soon as it's in your hands," Maddox said.

SEVENTEEN
THE COWBOY FACTOR

Brussels, Belgium

Maddox was back in his hotel room twenty minutes later. Rose was drinking a gin and tonic and reviewing the police report from the jump drive provided by Bouhouche.

"Did you get that drive out to Sennight in time?"

"I did. The hotel's business office guaranteed it would be delivered to him first thing in the morning, Virginia time," Maddox said.

"Excellent," Rose said.

"Not bad service for two hundred bucks," Maddox said. Rose whistled at the amount.

"You get anything new out of that stuff," Maddox said, pointing at Rose's laptop screen.

"No. Poor bastard. Bled out paralyzed on the ground," Rose said.

"Yeah, I understand sometimes that type of hit is necessary, but why not just pop him in the head? Faster, cleaner," Maddox said.

"I was thinking the same. Maybe this bloke is into the killing," Rose said.

"Great, a cowboy," Maddox said.

"I hope not. Makes these things so much harder to handle," Rose said, finishing his drink.

The cowboy factor had always been a scourge on the business. But in the last decade, with the seemingly never-ending global wars, it appeared that a new generation of freelancers was being spawned from video game players to the military, and these cowboys became addicted to the action.

Once out of it, they missed it. They craved it. They viewed odd jobs as a way of staying in the action after their service and making a lot more money than the military paid.

The cowboy's impatience and eagerness to kill put everyone at risk.

The private military companies had been started by professionals, but they had too much work around the world to be too discerning in their hiring practices. To the point that eventually they eagerly took in almost anyone with a military or law enforcement background, and paid them three times their salary.

It made matters worse that many of these contractors suffered from PTSD or were vastly undertrained for that type of work. It was a recipe for disaster.

Professionals like Maddox had to be out in the field with freelancers that didn't know what they were doing or skilled operatives that liked killing for the sake of killing.

To Maddox, they were kids playing cowboys and Indians with real-life deadly consequences, not professionals.

It was under this bloodthirsty environment that the Threat Elimination Network had been born.

Abner Tarkay was the octogenarian founder and the chairman of the board of TEN.

Tarkay had been a young soldier during the Israeli-Arab War of 1948.

Moshe Dayan had been his mentor. He had been there when Dayan had famously lost an eye during battle, ensuring that he would become the legendary eye-patch leader for Israel.

The State of Israel had been founded on contested land that was surrounded by bitter enemies.

A strong military, but an even stronger secret intelligence agency was needed. And Mossad was born.

Tarkay was an early member of Mossad and he was there for just about every war, conflict, and major intelligence operation on behalf of Israel.

In retirement, Tarkay had founded TEN to be an elite network of professionals that could only join by an invitation from the board.

He kept his identity secret and he delighted in providing fodder to the rumor mill about who he was.

TEN's mission was to keep the cowboys and adventure-seekers out and thus keep TEN as a light, mobile, and highly effective network of professionals that were considered the best amongst the best.

It hadn't taken long for TEN's reputation to grow, which meant it became harder to stay hidden within the community, and eventually, joining its ranks was considered a badge of honor—its illusive invitations became heavily sought after by freelancers.

Maddox had heard through his personal network of contacts that the CIA and the FBI were making cursory inquiries about its existence.

Rose said he heard the same hubbub from MI6 and MI5. And Ben Gold had once confided to Maddox that freelancers wanting to join the network ignoring the invite-only rule were now approaching them.

In those situations, not only was its existence denied, but the board ensured those seeking admittance to TEN without a board invitation were permanently banned from joining.

EIGHTEEN

THE CENTER

RESTON, VIRGINIA WAS ABOUT TWENTY MILES FROM DC. It's where Troy Sennight lived with his wife, Carrie, and their daughter.

The Sennight family went through their regular morning routine—a breakfast of scrambled eggs, oatmeal, and toast.

He ground the coffee beans that he'd specially ordered from Ritual Coffee Roasters in San Francisco. Damned beans were expensive, but worth it.

They both tagged off in getting their eleven-year-old daughter out of bed and ready for school. It was Carrie's turn that morning.

Carrie took care of the drop-off on her way to work at the Virginia Hospital Center in Arlington, where she was a Finance Director. Troy would pick up the kid in the afternoon.

"Okay, hun, have a good day," he said as he stood by the door, waving at his wife and daughter like he was June Cleaver. All that was missing was an apron.

He was amazed how his daughter was looking more like her

mother every day—down to the dark brown hair and big bright hazel eyes.

He marveled how a tech schlub like him had landed a woman like Carrie.

They made the odd couple, like Julia Roberts marrying Lyle Lovett.

Once the car left the driveway, Sennight headed into the kitchen and filled his workingman-sized thermo with coffee and warm milk.

It was around 8:30 in the morning when the FedEx man showed up at his door with an urgent delivery from Belgium.

He signed for it and the deliveryman took off.

"Time for work," Sennight said to an empty house. He headed out to his backyard. It was a quick walk to The Center, as Sennight called his home office.

The Center was actually a large backyard shed that he had transformed into a CIA-worthy SCIF.

SCIF stood for Sensitive Compartmented Information Facility and was pronounced "skiff".

In the intelligence community, these were secure, sound-proof rooms where intelligence officers, US military and other federal government agencies go to discuss big secrets, knowing that spies couldn't listen in.

Sennight had ensured his skiff was impervious to eavesdropping from all sides, even from up above.

He also ran bug scans three times a day and had an illegal home-built cell phone jammer that he could easily activate.

Every morning, he made the quick walk to the center with a thermos full of coffee in one hand and a laptop tucked under his arm.

He always dressed comfortably for work: sweatpants, T-shirt, and a pair of well-worn Keen sandals.

The best part of being retired from the CIA and working

from home—besides the money his skills fetched in the open market—was not having to start each day crawling on the 267 highway.

Sennight had outgrown the excitement of Foreign Service after going through a coup in Venezuela, two winters in Moscow, and working from an Afghanistan substation near Tora Bora.

Sennight disarmed the alarm to The Center with his key and turned the biometric doorknob to open the thick vault-like door to his office.

The door closed behind him, automatically locking, as he walked toward a large wraparound desk where a desktop computer, a laptop docking station, and four large interconnected monitors were waiting for him.

He plopped down on his Herman Miller chair and slipped on a pair of blue Beats headphones—Sennight didn't do cheap when it came to his gadgets and the creature comforts for work.

Sennight took a sip of coffee from the thermos and he opened the FedEx box.

Inside was an antistatic bag made of strong Bubble Wrap.

He tore it open and shook out a slim gray USB External Hard Drive.

He inspected it for a few seconds. He wasn't sure why he did that since, from the outside, it looked like any of the other thousands of portable hard drives he'd handled in his career.

He connected it to his computer and moved his mouse to the external hard drive. He clicked on it and a box popped up demanding a password, just as Maddox had said.

He couldn't recall if he had ever been thwarted by a basic, password-protected drive. He knew it wasn't a matter of if he could crack it, but when.

The when part was always an issue since his clients, like

Maddox, rarely had the comfort of time on their side in these matters.

Encryption would be the killer, not a password and even spooks hated having to deal with ever-changing, hard to remember, easy to forget passwords, so they follow similar protocols for coming up with passwords across their devices as anyone else.

It was usually bits and parts of words and numbers that had some meaning to them in a way they could remember, like a combination of their dog's name and their mother's birthdate.

If they used password-generating software, even if they closed their eyes and banged on their keyboard like a chimp to come up with a password, dollars to donuts they would write that password down somewhere on their computer or in the cloud where someone like Sennight could find it.

It amused him when targets would go through a lot of hoops to come up with an obscure, difficult to guess password, only to type it into an unsecured Excel spreadsheet, Word document, or into a text file on their computer.

Like taking candy from a baby, Sennight thought.

An external hard drive would be even easier to crack for someone with Sennight's skills and tools.

He connected the hard drive to his computer then he fired up a custom coded hard drive recovery application. He ran the application then he selected Gold's hard drive from the hard drive list. He clicked on NEXT and the application began to start the unlocking process.

A window with an unlocking progress bar popped up as the application went to work.

Sennight worked on other client's projects while the application did its work. Every now and then he would glance over at the progress bar. It was going well, he thought.

He was engrossed in other work when he heard a ping. He looked over at the computer running the unlocking application and the progress bar was completely filled indicating the process was finished.

He shut down the computer and booted it up again then he navigated to Gold's Hard Drive and clicked on it, the password had been removed. Sennight smiled.

NINETEEN

WHAT'S HIDDEN, CAN BE FOUND

Belgium and Virginia

It was about eleven o'clock at night in Brussels. Five in the afternoon in Virginia.

"Okay, I've left him alone all day," Maddox said to Rose as he picked up his phone and punched in Sennight's number.

He picked up on the second ring. "I was just going to call you."

"Let me put you on speaker. Tom is here with me," Maddox said.

"Hey, Tom, how's it hanging?" Sennight said.

"To the floor, mate. It's a real drag."

"In your dreams, you John Holmes wannabe," Sennight laughed.

"I hate to break up such rippling soliloquy, did you get in?" Maddox asked.

"Oh, I got in. Let me ask you guys, when you joined TEN, you didn't fill out a form with your name and address and your social security number and all that stuff like you were applying for a regular job?" Sennight asked.

"No. I mean they have my contact information and other things that they need to do business, but you know the drill. I use that mail drop box run by Moses in Hialeah. Anything on their database is supposed to be on via codenames only," Maddox said.

"But someone knows who you really are because joining TEN is by invite only," Sennight said.

"Yes, but trust me, I never gave them my home address and the network is run by professionals they know better than to use our real names on a database. My name isn't even on my goddamned mortgage. Are you telling they have that?"

"Yes. I found it on a database that was in a hidden hard drive on the network. I doubt Ben Gold knew it was there, but when he copied the network's drive, he copied it all, even the hidden folders that, unless you know how to search for them, will never show up for most end users. The board probably didn't even know it existed either. It was well hidden. Whoever did it really knows their shit. They weren't simply creating an extra drive and stashing it like some IT flunky can do, this person really hid it so it would never be found. Unlucky for the person that created it, they didn't know I would be snooping," Sennight bragged.

He was always cocky about his work and Maddox liked that about him. He was good and he took pride on doing the work and figuring things out. No matter how complicated it might be, Maddox knew Sennight would find a way to get to that data.

"My info was on there?" Rose asked.

"Yes. It's a database with your real locations; including your home address. I checked for you, boss, and they have your address in Key Biscayne down to the zip code. And, Tom, they have your places in Isleworth and Spain, and even your office in England."

"Shit," Maddox said.

"How difficult is it to get that data?" Rose asked.

"Well, I help Pete cover his tracks and I scrub his name and info from Google every month, but anything on a database can be found. There is no magic bullet that will keep it secure one hundred percent. The goal is to make it as difficult and time-consuming as possible. Hackers usually follow breadcrumbs so they would need to know enough about Pete's background then be able hack something else, like an Army database or the CIA, and *then* you might begin to get some of this info, but that's for someone on the outside. But if you're on the inside as part of TEN, then it makes this so much easier since you already know his background with the Rangers, the CIA. So it starts getting easier to triangulate and collate the data," Sennight said.

"The board was adamant that data like that would never be collated on their system, even though they swore their system was practically unhackable," Maddox said.

Sennight snorted and said, "Nothing online is unhackable, I don't care how deep down in the dark web they have it. If it's connected somewhere online, it can be hacked. The hidden web is just that—hidden. But remember, what's hidden can be found. I warned you about joining something like TEN, boss," Sennight said.

"That ship has sailed," Maddox said.

"There's more."

"Jesus, what else?" Rose asked.

"I noticed a lot of spreadsheets with what appears to be financial data. I just looked at a few and I'm not an accountant, but it looks like the type of spreadsheet a bean counter would put together," Sennight said.

"That is interesting. We've been thinking the catalyst to these killings was revenge. Someone with money and means, getting vengeance for one of our past operations, but maybe it's just about good old-fashioned greed," Maddox said.

"Well, I'm not sure about that. I just took a glance. I can look at programming code that is as clear as the alphabet to me. *But* looking at the financial transactions—they might as well have been written in Chinese. I can't make anything out of it," Sennight said.

"Well both computer code and accounting formulas are like Chinese to me, so I'm worse off," Maddox said.

"I have a friend in the CIA. She's a forensic accountant. Looking at this type of shit and figuring out fuzzy math is her bread and butter. She reached out to me last month—about putting out her own shingle and wanted my advice on how to go about that. I could give her a call. Maybe she can take a look at these spreadsheets," Sennight said.

"You trust her?" Maddox said.

"Hell, yeah, I wouldn't even suggest bringing her into this if I didn't trust her," Sennight said.

Maddox looked at Rose he shrugged his approval.

"Okay, send her the spreadsheets. We'll take a look at them too, but might as well have an expert take a gander," Maddox said.

"Will do," Sennight said.

"You mentioned this hidden drive was something put together by someone that knows what they're doing tech-wise, so it couldn't have been Ben?" Maddox asked.

"No way. He probably didn't even know this stuff was on that hard drive. It was buried well. I checked the user logs and Ben Gold never accessed it. There is only one user ID that created the hidden drive, its folders, and spreadsheets, and that same user kept accessing those folders and the database. So we have one person. Or it could be multiple persons using the same username, but I find that doubtful. And the way they set this up is beautiful. Someone who really knows their shit and has admin level access to the entire system," Sennight said.

"Admin level. Like the system administrator?" Maddox asked.

"That's right. At the very least, that's whose door I would come knocking first to see what the hell is going on," Sennight said.

"Easier said than done. Our contacts were with the liaisons, like Ben Gold, aside from a few digital messages once in a blue moon from the system admin. We never dealt with the admin directly. I have no clue who he or she is or where they're located," Maddox said.

"He's good at covering his tracks. Every move is buried deep in proxy layers. He bounces around the globe multiple times, but I've written a nice piece of code that is stripping the layers as we speak, I should know where he's physically located soon enough," Sennight said.

"Even if you know the area where he's at, won't it be like finding a golf ball in a ball pit?" Maddox asked.

"Theoretically, but the admin is basically on 24/7. Not sure if he sleeps, but once I find the ball pit he's playing in, I can pinpoint that golf ball so you can just reach in and grab it," Sennight said.

"Nice. How long is that going to take?" Maddox said.

"The program has been running for five hours so far. Like I said he's good, but I can't imagine more than a few more hours to go," Sennight said.

TWENTY

EASTER EGG

Brussels, Belgium

The next morning at their hotel, Maddox and Rose were eating a breakfast of buttered bread with jam, sliced cheese, cereal, and a strong coffee that perked Maddox up nicely. Rose stuck to tea.

Maddox's phone buzzed. He wiped his mouth and hands with a white cloth napkin and glanced at the screen.

"Ketchum," Maddox said, referring to Troy Sennight by his codename.

Rose didn't say anything as he motioned to the waiter for the check. They finished their breakfast like they were back in an Army chow hall, fast.

Back in the room, Maddox grabbed one of the half-dozen throwaway mobile phones he had handy. He pressed the "on" button and waited for it to fire up.

Mobile phones were a boon to the businesses in the shadows. Maddox bought them by the dozen at a time from a dark website on Tor that even offered free and discreet shipping from China.

"Okay, boss, I've uploaded my detailed analysis report of the hard drive to Beatrix, but there is a more pressing matter you need to worry about. There was an Easter egg in the hard drive."

Maddox cringed knowing that Sennight was referring to a tactic that developers used to sneak files, messages, scripts, all hidden in a computer program and the average end user would be oblivious to it.

"What was its purpose?" Maddox asked.

"The quick and dirty: whenever someone runs a backup, it copies everything on that hard drive. Basically, the program creates a clone of that drive, which is what Ben Gold did. He then copied that onto the external USB Hard Drive you recovered from his apartment. He did it manually, which activated the hidden Easter egg which sent a message to someone with system administrator rights on the network. The message was sent instantly, so whoever is the TEN system administrator, they knew right away that Gold created a backup of his entire hard drive. I'm taking a wild guess here, but that can't be a good thing," Sennight said facetiously.

"Not a good thing at all," Maddox said, rubbing his forehead.

"You think this admin person knows he was planning to give you that hard drive?" Sennight asked.

"Doubtful. That's why he wanted to meet in person and why he left the hard drive hidden in Brussels. He wanted to make sure he could trust us then and only then, would he give us the drive," Maddox said.

"So they killed him to prevent that from happening," Sennight said.

"That's how they knew what he was up to," Maddox said.

"So you guys still have the upper hand without them knowing who you are, and that you recovered the hard drive," Sennight said.

"Unless he was being followed," Rose said.

"Possible. Especially since the administrator was notified right away of the copy. He could have put a tail on Ben to see what he was going to do with it. But I would think they would have killed all three of us right on the spot in Amsterdam if they had been tailing him. It would have been nice and neat," Maddox said.

"That is how I would have handled it," Rose said.

"We need to find those pricks, the admin and his shooter," Maddox said.

"I'm still running my program. I'll locate the son of a bitch in a day or two," Sennight said.

"We need to let the chairman know that they have the fox guarding the hen house," Maddox said.

TWENTY-ONE

HOUSEBOAT

Amsterdam, Netherlands

AXEL WAS SUPPOSED TO WAIT FOR MR. WHITE TO CALL with further instructions. Instead he decided to take some RNR while in Amsterdam so he shut off his phone.

One of the reasons he'd left the Army to work on his own was to be his own boss; he wasn't keen on sitting around waiting to take orders from Mr. White.

But that would soon stop, he thought, *I'm getting better with each job and I'll go solo.*

He had to admit that acquiescing to Mr. White's demands was paying off dividends for his long-term plans.

But he was tired and he needed to recharge, if Mr. White had a problem with that he could go and kill the people on his ever-growing list himself. Axel scoffed at the idea of Mr. White killing anyone himself.

Mr. White had set up a safe house in one of those Amsterdam houseboats. The bedroom and bathroom were a bit cramped, but Axel found the living area pretty spacious. He looked around and he liked what he saw; he could see himself living on a houseboat like this.

He dumped his backpack on the floor, kicked off his hiking boots, stripped down to his underwear, and crashed on the bed, lying on top of the sheets.

He woke disoriented as the houseboat gently swayed on the canal. It took him a moment to get his bearings and he smiled. He stretched and checked the time. *Damn. I slept eleven hours.* He dropped to the floor and peeled off twenty push-ups, went to the bathroom and took care of business there.

He put on sweatpants and a shirt. He was feeling much more alert. The sleep had worked wonders. He felt ready to get back to work.

For the first time since leaving the Army, he was making steady money and a lot more than his E5 army salary. So even though he didn't care much for Mr. White, he did appreciate that he had brought him into the business.

Not that money was all that important to Axel. He considered himself a modern hobo. Riding the rails looking for work. He could live cheaply. Even though he was sticker shocked at the price of Mac and Cheese in Amsterdam.

"This is considered cheap food back home," Axel said to the grocery store clerk, who had just rolled her eyes at the complaining American tourist.

The look of contempt on her face and the disrespectful way she treated him, a paying customer, had made Axel's blood boil. He'd steadied himself. Later, he took pride in his remarkable feat of self-control in walking away without slicing her throat open where she stood.

Axel made the short walk back to the houseboat with his food. Four boxes of mac and cheese, a packet of hot dogs, a bag of chips, several bars of Toblerone chocolate, six dozen eggs, ham, a gallon of drinking water, and two liter bottles of coke.

It was noon and he was starving. He walked into the kitchen

and poured water into a pan. He removed the packet of hot dogs and the Mountain Dew from the grocery bag.

He cut up three hot dogs while the water boiled, then proceeded to empty the hard, little shells of macaroni noodles into the boiling water and poured himself a glass of Dew.

He took a big drink and felt the jolt of super caffeine kick in. He liked it, so he poured himself some more.

Once the shells were tender, he drained the water and tossed in the packet of orange powdered cheese, half a stick of butter, and the chopped up hot dog bits, and stirred. His feast was ready.

He sat down to eat and finally decided to turn on his cell phone. He was chewing a mouthful of food when multiple messages from Mr. White had been sending while he slept began to popup on his phone's screen. Axel dialed Mr. White back.

"Where the hell have you been? I've been trying to reach you for hours," Mr. White said without saying hello.

"I needed to sleep," Axel replied nonchalantly.

He could feel Mr. White's frustration over the phone, but what was he going to do about it?

"Fine," he finally grunted. "Can we get back to work now? A lot has happened while you decided to go offline."

"Sure," Axel said, forking the last two pieces of hot dog and using them to mop up the last of the cheese sauce from his plate, and into his mouth. He chewed loudly because he knew it would bother Mr. White. He knew it was childish, but he liked needling Mr. White. Gave him a sense of control and it was the only power he had – short of killing him.

"Where are you now?"

"I'm still in Amsterdam in the safe house you arranged."

"Okay, good, you're still there and you're not too far," Mr. White said.

"From where?"

"The targets are no longer there. You need to go back to Brussels, right away."

"I was just there, why did you send me here?"

"It's normal in this line of business. Targets move. We need to be able to adapt and be flexible."

"Easy for you to say, you're staying put."

"I'm not going to debate you. I've made the arrangements for you to get back to Brussels. Just do it, please."

TWENTY-TWO

DIME A DOZEN

Directorate of Intelligence, CIA Headquarters, Langley, Virginia, USA

Bob Guy was twenty-eight years old and had been with the CIA for two years. He was a corn-fed college All-American who was losing his athletic body. He had freckles all over his face and arms and he kept his red hair short, combing to the side, Ivy League style.

The bulk of his nascent CIA career to that point had mostly consisted of training and more training. Until finally, ten months ago, he'd had his training wheels removed. But that didn't mean he was trusted with doing much more than observing and writing reports, while senior officers and supervisors hovered around him like helicopter parents at their kid's soccer match.

An overachiever his entire life, Bob Guy was desperate to prove his mettle, so he worked fifteen-hour days and eschewed a social life as he pored over magazine articles, journal reports, and online content from the mainstream internet, and its dark unindexed bastard cousin where you were more likely to find ISIS beheading videos than cute cat ones.

Guy was impatient and on a Neo-like obsession to find Morpheus. He wanted to find that nugget of intelligence that would lead to one of his in-depth analysis reports catching the attention of someone worth a damn in the chain of command that would kick-start his career.

It was ten o'clock at night. Bob Guy was ready to head home. He stretched, yawned loudly at the empty cubicle farm, and rubbed his reddened and hazel eyes.

He took a swig from his coffee mug, but gagged. It was luke-warm, at best. For sixteen hours he had been like a needle pulling thread—he was on to something, and it felt big. Big enough to let that natural adrenaline rush kick in like an Adderall wave of focus and determination.

Guy looked at his cell phone watch and began to do the math in his head. *Write the report; should take me about two hours. Go home for a few hours of sleep. Review the report in the morning to make sure it still makes sense. Upload it to the database, then figure out how to get it into the hands of someone that matters.*

For a junior analyst like Bob Guy, getting someone that mattered—maybe a senior analyst or even better, someone at the associate/assistant director level—was the uphill battle. Regardless of how thoroughly the report had been written, it was written by a rookie, and would probably sit unnoticed in a database for eons.

Bob Guy hated that Catch-22, but it was the reality he had to deal with. He knew he had to be aggressive and in your face to get on the executive leadership's radar.

Guy looked at his computer monitor and the report he had just finished rewriting for fifth time and thought, *this is my ticket.*

It wasn't a move to be done lightly. A shit report with shit data can attach the stink of that shit to a young analyst's career for a long time. Satisfied it was ready, he powered down his computer and headed home.

The next morning, Bob Guy nervously fidgeted in his Toyota Celica on the GW Parkway, going over the same pros and cons from the previous three nights.

By the time he arrived at CIA headquarters, he knew he would make the move and personally deliver his report to Dale Shaw. It was the only way to ensure it wouldn't take space and be ignored on the database.

It took Guy fifteen minutes from the time he pulled into the Langley employee parking lot and made his way to his cubicle.

Guy waited ninety minutes, and drank way too much coffee during that time. He had psyched himself enough. He was doing it.

At first Dale Shaw snapped at the young analyst for poking his head into his office unannounced.

Guy sweated nerves and caffeine, and felt like in-laws dropping in unannounced at dinnertime.

The "open door policy" had come from DA director himself. An edict that made it very clear that his directorate and its leaders were to welcome intelligence officers if they thought it was important.

But it was the midlevel leaders that had to deal with the annoying interruptions not the director.

So Shaw ensured he would make it as unpleasant an experience as possible in the hopes of scaring off the new wave of needy millennials slinking into his office with bullshit.

"You're sure this can't wait? I'm quite busy," Shaw said, studying Bob Guy's face with a scowl.

Bob Guy swallowed nervously and he was certain the entire floor could hear it.

Dale Shaw was in his forties and sported an H.R. Haldeman high and tight haircut. He glared at Guy from his desk in his blue suit, white shirt, and blue and gray-striped tie. Shaw reminded Guy of a high school gym teacher. One you feared when you're thirteen years old then couldn't help but laugh at after running into him fifteen years later.

When you couldn't help but wonder: *I can't believe that pipsqueak scared the shit out of me.*

But people in positions of authority tended to have that effect to those under them.

"Well, sir, I know you've been looking for a chink in the armor on those private paramilitary freelance networks, and well, I, I believe I found one," Guy stuttered nervously.

That was good, keep calm, don't fuck it up, he thought as Shaw sat back in his chair.

He was intrigued so he waved him in.

Guy walked into Shaw's office without much confidence.

"Let me see it," Shaw said, holding his hand in the air impatiently.

Guy walked toward Shaw, realizing that he had been clutching onto his report with both arms crossed over his chest like his life depended on it.

Guy panicked for a moment that he had wrinkled up the report or that his sweaty palms had soaked through the binder, but to his relief, the report looked clean, crisp, and ready to jumpstart his career.

He handed it over.

Shaw had two visitor chairs and a small round table kitty-corner from his desk, but he didn't offer Guy a seat, so he stood.

Shaw took the report, flipped it open, and read the cover sheet—it was a standard CIA template with the agency's logo and "Top Secret" stamped on it.

Shaw sat further back in his chair and read the synopsis.

Two former Special Forces soldiers and private contractors (former Delta Force and SAS) were murdered by what authorities believe was a sniper. One victim was in Europe and another in the Americas (Wales and Puerto Rico, respectively). Both kills were within one week of each other. The killings have all the markings of a professional assassination from a highly trained sniper.

Further analysis uncovered chatter about these killings in a dark web message board that the FBI has been able to infiltrate (this is covered in-depth in the report). This leads me to conclude that there is a breach in one of the privately run paramilitary free-lance networks, which offers the services of former Special Forces and Intelligence Officers in a mercenary capacity to conduct privately funded military operations in hostile territories for profit. Any security lapses or breaches could provide an opportunity for the intelligence community to access one of these networks. This is something that the Agency has been unable to do so far.

Guy stood there in Shaw's office awkwardly as Shaw read the cover page. He looked at the light switch then out the window toward the wooded area of the sprawling CIA campus in Northern Virginia.

Associate Deputy Directors were high up the CIA food chain, especially to a two-year analyst like Bob Guy, but they were basically middle management and a dime a dozen like a vice president at a bank. But there was a Machiavellian reason he'd brought this report to Dale Shaw specifically.

It was well known in the agency that Shaw was on a Captain Ahab mission to infiltrate a working private freelance network that was operating, hidden in the dark web.

To Shaw, these freelancers on private networks were nothing more than glorified bounty hunters and hitmen.

What they used to call, back in his day, mercenaries. A

private citizen can't hire a hitman in the back of one those mercenary want-to-be magazines—why should these networks be able to?

Guy's mind was drifting, but he was still standing there, bending his knees to avoid locking them. The last thing he needed was to pass out in the office of Dale Shaw.

Dale Shaw stopped, glanced at his desk, and retrieved a rubber fingertip which he put on and began to turn the page from the synopsis to the table of contents.

He hadn't looked up or acknowledged Guy. He hadn't said a word, but Guy felt his heart pounding, for he was certain that that was a good sign.

It meant that Shaw was intrigued by the synopsis enough to actually peruse the table of contents of the report and that must be why he was still standing in Shaw's office.

Had Shaw not been interested, he would have dismissed Guy flatly.

"Looks like a thorough report," Shaw finally said as he flipped through some of the forty-seven pages. Guy beamed inside.

"I try to be very thorough, sir."

"Okay, thank you, Robert," Shaw said. He had the tendency to call everyone by their proper name whether or not that was their preferred way of being addressed. So Bob was Robert, Mike was Michael, Tim was Timothy, Chris was Christina and so on.

The analysts didn't know if it was just snobbery from the Stanford and Harvard educated man or if it was some sort of odd power play.

"I'll go ahead and read through your report and I'll call you if I have any questions. Thank you."

"Thank you, sir," Guy said, taking the hint. When Dale

Shaw said *thank you* and went back to his paperwork that "thank you" meant *get out of my office*.

Guy walked back to his cubicle. He could feel the sweat under his armpits, spreading to his back, and moistening his upper lip. *Some spy you're going to make.*

"How did it go?" one of his cube mates asked as Guy walked by, but Guy ignored him and he beelined to the bathroom.

"Went that well, huh?" Guy heard him say, laughing.

STAGING GROUND

Amsterdam, Netherlands and Brussels, Belgium

AXEL LEFT THE HOUSEBOAT HOISTING HIS BACKPACK ONTO his shoulder and walked toward one of the OV-fiets bike share program stations in the nearby town center. He rented a bicycle and rode the two miles to Amsterdam Centraal Train Station, where he dropped off the bike and bought a one-way second class train ticket to Brussels.

He stowed his backpack, sat on aisle seat, and settled in with his iPad and earphones. As the train began to move, Axel read the dossier on Foxglove on his iPad.

Foxglove was Thomas Gary Rose. Thirty years of experience. Ten years in the SAS. Twenty years with MI6. But Axel wasn't intimidated by that. He found it pathetic. *That's the background that the board creams itself for. Bunch of Luddite old fucks with bullshit honor codes. Hypocrites.*

He was going to show Foxglove, just like he'd shown Fitzsimmons in Wales and Ramos in Puerto Rico. The two other old codgers that TEN had invited to join their network, while not thinking that Axel was worthy enough to belong. He put them down easily. He was showing the network now.

There wasn't much information on the other freelancer that was traveling with Rose. Not that it mattered to Axel. He smiled wide as he looked out the window while Guns 'N Roses "November Rain" played though his headphones.

Two hours later, he arrived at Brussels Midi Train Station. He exited the train and made the quick walk to Gare du Midi Zuidstation and down into the Brussels Metro.

He took the subway to Delacroix metro station and walked to the safe house that Mr. White had set up for his staging ground.

The house was a small loft located on Rue de Birmingham. It had a basic sleeping area, one bathroom, a tiny kitchen, and a common area that served as a living room and dining room with a television set and dining table.

The home was nicely renovated and in a quiet neighborhood.

Axel went up the steep stairs that looked more like a ladder that led to the open bedroom.

He moved the bed frame to the side, then removed a section of the flooring, revealing a compartment in the floor where Mr. White had hidden tools for the job. An Uzi submachine gun, a Glock 22 .40 pistol and ammunition.

Axel laid out the weapons and ammo on the bed, turning his attention to his rucksack.

He had to remove most of his clothing and items before he reached the disassembled M40 rifle. He pulled it out of the rucksack and began to assemble it methodically and reverently.

Axel was excited about the Foxglove assignment. Fitzsimmons and Ramos had been more straightforward hits because the target locations were known and fixed, so he could hunt and set up the shot with more leeway. And since the targets didn't know a contract had been placed on them, he had the element of surprise going for him.

After the two hits, he knew Foxglove would be on high alert. That suited him. The greater the challenge, the more he enjoyed it.

Pulling it off would be his final self-imposed test for the business. After Foxglove, Axel would confirm what he had always known, that he could go up against any of these TEN so-called professionals and that he would be better than the best of the best.

Mr. White could kiss his ass after Brussels. He was going to be a true freelancer—completely independent.

Axel smiled as he inspected the weapons laid out on the bed.

TWENTY-FOUR

A SERIOUS MATTER

Prague, Czech Republic

THE ADMINISTRATOR SCANNED THE SERVER AND connection to ensure it was secure. Satisfied, he added the five participants to the group call and clicked the video button.

In mere seconds, five screens appeared on the monitor with darkened images of fidgeting people on the other side.

The administrator looked at the IP addresses, which he bounced around a series of hacked computers distributed across the globe in order to hide their true locations, which were only known to him.

One from Tel Aviv, Israel, one from Galway, Ireland, one from Monte Carlo, Monaco, one from Budapest, Hungary, and one from Toronto, Canada.

It was the Threat Elimination Network's Board of Directors and the five directors were online.

"Good afternoon. I've made sure this call is secure so you may proceed when ready," the administrator said into the headset mic.

"Okay then, is everyone ready?" one of the talking heads on the video asked.

The TEN board meeting began.

"Are we sure this is safe?" a British voice asked.

The administrator sighed. He recognized the voice of Damond, whose IP Address was from Budapest.

"Yes, I guarantee it, and I'll continue to monitor the system security during the call."

"Okay, let's get started," the chairman said.

His IP address indicated he was in Tel Aviv, Israel.

The board met infrequently, by design. The five members of the board met twice a year and, if needed, they would meet more often. This was the second unscheduled meeting of the year.

The administrator only knew them by their code names: Saul, Damond, Gabriel, Gawain, and Belisarius and their IP address.

The chairman used the codename of Saul and he would connect in from Tel Aviv. Damond would sign in from Budapest. Gabriel from Galway. Belisarius from Monte Carlo. And, the only female of the board, Gawain signed in from Toronto, Canada.

"So what is it, Mr. Chairman? Why have you called us to meet, yet again?" Gawain asked.

"We've been having too many of these meetings. This is highly irregular and this is how mistakes are made," Damond interjected.

"Don't think that I don't know that, but there is a serious matter that needs to be discussed and what action to take must be voted on tonight. Belisarius, please illuminate the other board members on the importance of this meeting," the chairman said.

"One of our liaisons was murdered in Brussels."

The gasps from several members were audible.

"Has it been determined if it has anything to do with this Network?" Gawain asked.

"My contact in the Belgian State Security Service said that Mr. Gold was stabbed once through the neck, in expert fashion and he died on the scene. His expensive mobile telephone and his wallet were not taken. It appears there wasn't even an attempt at robbery," Saul said.

"We must be one hundred percent certain that this isn't a threat to the Network," Gawain said.

"Exactly. We don't want to overreact," Damond said, sounding cautious.

"One of my most trusted freelancers is already in the area so I move that we activate Foxglove to look into this matter," Saul said.

"I second that," Gabriel said.

"Okay. Let's vote then. We have two votes for yes. Gawain?" the chairman said.

"Yes."

"Damond?"

"No."

"Not that it matters since the yesses have it, but I too vote yes, so the motion passes. We activate Foxglove," the chairman said.

The administrator was supposed to be monitoring the connection to ensure it was secure, but he wasn't supposed to be listening into the call, but he was. He wiped the sweat from his brow and upper lip as the board members began to disconnect from the conference one after the other.

TWENTY-FIVE

ON ICE

Office of Terrorism Analysis, CIA Headquarters, Langley, Virginia, USA

It was supposed to be Bob Guy's big day. He wore the best suit he could afford from Brooks Brothers only to find out he couldn't attend the meeting where Dale Shaw would be presenting his report to the head of OTA.

Dale Shaw instead had chosen to bring Tanya Girard, who was a highly respected analyst.

Being excluded stung Guy's ivy league ego, but he understood. He was on the bottom rung of the career ladder at the agency while Tanya Girard was one of the best analysts in the company. She could provide concise and detailed information on the political situation in some obscure country like Nauru right from the top of her head. Plus, she had sixteen years on Bob Guy when it came to intelligence experience. So, Guy sat in his cubicle and waited.

Henry Benavidez had been in charge of the Office of Terrorism Analysis in the Directorate of Intelligence for two years.

He had been with the CIA for twenty-seven years and everyone knew this was his last rodeo. He wasn't about to do anything that would buck him off his horse on the final lap.

He was fifty-four years old and with his overseas service, he could have retired at fifty. But the promotion to be the director of OTA and a deputy DI director—reporting directly to the DI—would pad his pension nicely and was too prestigious to pass up.

But retirement to Florida loomed in his horizon, so although he took the job as seriously as he always had, he wasn't about to make waves or take unnecessary risks—not at the twilight of his career.

He was not part of the Ivy League elite, yet he had achieved a lot during his career. He was a Cuban American, born in Cuba two months after Castro's Cuban Revolution.

It hadn't taken long after Castro's guerrillas swept down from the mountains and into Havana and power for Fidel Castro to begin seizing farms and cattle ranches–even his own wealthy family's land.

As bad as that land grab was the beard also began to take control of the press, businesses, homes, and soon after those who criticized or posed a threat to Fidel's revolution began to disappear.

That was enough for Benavidez's father who fled with his family to Miami when Henry was just two years old. He grew up in the feverishly anti-Castro Miami community of Cuban exiles and joined the CIA in the 1980s during Reagan's amped up Cold War against the Soviet Union. He was eager to fight communism. That was over twenty years ago. The spitfire anti-communist had morphed into a savvy careerist nestled comfortably in the CIA bureaucracy.

The meeting was a standing weekly meeting with his deputies.

Shaw had the floor, he had given a detailed presentation based on Bob Guy's report, which Shaw and his senior analyst, Tanya Girard, had worked on, to improve and expand on the rookie analyst's original.

Benavidez cleared his throat after Shaw's presentation.

He was a stocky, balding man who looked fit, and younger than his fifty-four years.

"Well," Benavidez said slowly. He cleared his throat again, and went on, "It's an intriguing report, excellent research and analysis, but I'm not sure what you exactly want to do with this information, besides feed it to the database."

Shaw felt the wind knock out of him. He glanced around the long conference table as several of his cohorts shifted around awkwardly, avoiding eye contact, while his two top competitors in the department smirked.

"Well," Shaw hesitated, choosing his words carefully. "We've always suspected the existence of these private networks. It looks like there is a good opportunity to gather intelligence from one of them. Besides, there is a US Citizen, a highly decorated, retired Delta Force soldier murdered. I think we should look into the matter further."

Benavidez sighed.

"Your report states that these networks operate outside of the United States. It appears they're doing the type of work we'd love to do ourselves, if we didn't have a bunch of pansies in Congress. Hell, some of the suspected targets of this network in your report are on the DOJ's Rewards for Justice program, for chrissakes. The DOJ probably paid them the reward. So why would we stick our nose into this? It seems they're doing a good job of taking out the trash for us. I don't see why we should be wasting resources on this. And as for the dead Delta Force Soldier, that is a tragedy, but they know the risks when they sign up for this type of work. That goes double as an independent contractor. Had he died working for us, he would probably have a gold star on the wall."

"Yes, sir," Shaw said, knowing it was over.

But Benavidez wasn't finished.

"Besides, we're not the FBI. We don't investigate crimes. We're analysts, so good report, but as to your request to run an op from the Amsterdam station to look into this further, that's a no-go, Dale."

Benavidez shoved the report to his right, where his assistant picked it up and added it to the bottom of the report file.

"What else?" Benavidez said, looking around the conference room.

Shaw sat stoically. Inside he wanted to crawl out to lick his wounds in private.

Guy waited anxiously in his cubicle until finally, his phone rang, then came the second blow of the day when he was told his report was to be filed and put on ice. The operation was not approved.

Guy was surprised when the man the analysts called *the jackass* had kind words for him.

"The director was very impressed with your report. I was also impressed," Shaw told him. He hung up the phone before Guy could thank him.

Well that saved this shitty day, Guy thought.

TWENTY-SIX

FOXGLOVE

Brussels, Belgium

MADDOX WAS IN HIS HOTEL ROOM. HE WAS SITTING ON THE edge of the bed in front of the television, navigating to the checkout screen with the television's remote control when there was a knock on the door. It was followed by three more quick knocks—the prearranged sequence that Maddox and Rose had agreed upon.

Maddox still looked through the peephole, and there was Tom Rose, making a goofy face that looked even goofier through the fisheye view of the peephole.

Maddox chuckled and opened the door. Rose went inside and shook his head, saying, "You're not going to believe this."

Rose plopped on the bed while Maddox stood and shrugged, and asked impatiently, "What?"

"Just received a contract for a job with TEN from the board itself," Rose said.

"No shit. What are the odds that this isn't all interconnected?" Maddox said.

"Zero, my friend," Rose said.

"What's the job?"

"They know about Ben's death and they're worried. There is also concern about a possible data breach," Rose explained.

Maddox laughed.

"Exactly."

"You didn't happen to mention we have the hard drive with the breached data?"

"No. I decided we should keep that card close to the chest. But this means we can continue to look into this on their dime," Rose said, smiling.

"Ah, Jesus, Tom. I just told Sonia I was coming home soon."

"Fitzy and Hermes were killed on their home turfs. Not on a job, but on the bench. You know I'm not one to hit the panic button without cause, but dammit, I'm hitting that button. I'm not keen to go home and be having to look over my shoulder more than I have to already," Rose said.

Maddox slowly sat down on the leather club chair and sighed.

"It's obvious the board is also feeling a bit panicky for them to put out this contract. Come on, mate. A few days we check things out, see what the hell is going on. I prefer to be proactive than hanging around home worried that there is a sniper out there with my head in his scope," Rose said.

"If the goddamned sniper doesn't kill me, Sonia might," Maddox said, shaking his head. Rose grinned as Maddox shook his head some more.

"Well, you better get out of here. I'm going to call her and it's not going to be pretty."

With Maddox onboard, Rose went back to his room to give Maddox his privacy while he called Sonia. He powered up his laptop and logged onto the network under his Foxglove codename to accept the contract.

He navigated to the right web page and clicked on the

"accept" button. He sat back and waited for the board to confirm the contract so he could have access to further instructions.

While he waited, Rose flipped open the minibar and took out an overpriced bottle of Canada Dry Tonic and a more over-priced baby bottle of Beefeater gin. *It will be on their dime anyway*, the always-frugal Rose thought as he prepared his drink.

He had taken two sips of his gin and tonic when he heard his laptop ding. He pressed a key to wake it up.

The board had activated the contract and set up escrow accounts from a small bank in Estonia.

One account was for the job fee. As usual for a TEN contract, Rose would have access to twenty-five percent of the fee upfront. He would receive an additional twenty-five percent once operational and the remaining fifty percent upon successful completion of the job. The second account was for expenses. The board provided more than enough to get the ball rolling and for another gin and tonic.

Rose finished his second drink. He felt terrible knowing these types of jobs, the "odd jobs" as Maddox called them, were causing a strain in Maddox's marriage. But it was the business they chose. He knew Sonia would be afraid for Maddox and upset all at the same time. But Rose figured it would be better she is mad at an alive Maddox than risking a sunroof in his skull. *What good would that do Sonia?* Rose thought as he drained the last of his drink.

With the contract accepted and confirmed by the board, Rose began to download the documents provided from a secure dedicated server set up for just that job. Once the documents were downloaded the drive self-destructed. No second chances.

The process for posting and accepting jobs on the network worked the same way every time—a contract was posted and the employer either opened it up for bids from all TEN freelancers or they open a closed job, which meant they offered the contract to a specific contractor only.

Tom Rose had worked other jobs for the board. For being so secretive and reclusive the board members were actually creatures of habit.

Once they liked a freelancer, they stuck with that person. Right now, Tom Rose, codenamed Foxglove was the go-to freelancer to the chairman he knew as Saul.

Rose turned on the television to the news. He didn't pay attention to the talking heads pontificating, but he liked to have white noise in the background.

Rose began reviewing the documents. He looked at his watch. It had been almost thirty minutes since he'd walked out of Maddox's room and he hadn't heard back from him.

The call must not be going as well as he had hoped, Rose thought.

He wanted to walk over and knock on the door to make sure he was okay but figured it would be best to give Maddox the space he needed.

Being married to someone in this business was a tough proposition for the spouse. And unfortunately, it took a lot more than love to make it work.

It's not uncommon for these problems to end marriages and relationships for active-duty soldiers, law enforcement people, firefighters, and the like.

Jobs that demand duty come first, above all else.

Being a freelancer seemed to make it worse, because they had already put in their time in the army, CIA, MI6, or the police, so spouses didn't understand why they're still doing that work as a private contractor.

Before, there were orders—now it was their choosing the job over them.

Rose had retired with thirty years of service between the SAS and MI6. He had a pension. His former wife didn't understand why he continued to do that type of work. But Maddox was fired from the CIA. Blacklisted without a pension. He had to work and he was damned good at his job.

But there was no doubt that odd jobs were relationship killers. They took the freelancer away from home for months at a time. The risk of death or serious harm loomed heavy over every job, and he was still taking lives himself.

It was a perplexing parallax that Maddox and Rose had discussed many times. They did the same work as a soldier or for the government and they were paid poorly for it, yet they're anointed a hero, a patriotic warrior, risking their lives for their country. Do the same work as a freelancer, killing the same type of bad men, but as a private citizen being paid extremely well to do the same job and they were viewed as war dogs, an immoral mercenary making money from death and war.

None of that mattered to the spouse who has to wait back home, worried every single day on the job might be their loved one's last day on earth.

Rose cared a lot for Sonia. It was Rose who helped Maddox smuggle Sonia out of Venezuela while they were hunted down by the Secret Police.

It had been a hell of a way to start a relationship. Yet over ten years later, they had made it work.

It was difficult for Rose not to feel jealous when he visited Sonia and Maddox. They had been through a lot and had built a nice home together. And after ten years, he could see the way they looked at each other hadn't changed much from when Rose first saw them together back in Caracas.

But those odd jobs were toxic to relationships. Rose had three marriages under his belt as proof, and he wasn't eager to try again.

But he never said never because he knew that if he doubled down and swore off marriage for life, karma would have a laugh and make it happen all over again. Better to stay quiet on these matters, he would often joke.

Rose was poring over the documents for the job when he heard coded knocks on the door. It was Maddox.

Rose opened the door. Maddox walked in and he looked spent.

"How did it go?" Rose asked.

"Like I need some of that," Maddox said, pointing at the empty little bottles of liquor on the desk.

"Sorry, but I've been draining the hard stuff, you're a beer man anyway," Rose said.

"Indeed," Maddox said, opening the minibar. He examined the limited choices and settled on a Heineken beer.

"How deep in the shit house are you?" Rose asked as Maddox used his pocketknife bottle opener to get at the chilled suds.

"I'd say about waist high," Maddox said, taking a long drink of the Dutch beer.

Rose whistled, "Sorry, mate."

"No need to be. I put myself in this situation by doing this work. And you're right, we need to nip this in the bud, before *they* nip *us* in the bud," Maddox said.

"Okay, so what's going on here?" Maddox asked, changing the subject.

"Job's been approved, so we're on. They've released the first twenty-five percent of funds from escrow plus the money for expenses, so we're good to go on that front."

"Any good intel there?" Maddox asked.

Rose and Maddox went through the documents.

"You think they got hacked?" Maddox asked.

"That was their train of thought, but the admin insists they have not been hacked."

"And we trust this admin?" Maddox said.

"The board does. I don't trust anyone involved with this but you, mate," Rose said. They clinked their empty bottles of booze in the air.

"Did the admin set up the workroom for this contract?" Maddox asked.

"Yes. He sent me the login info. Looks like you're thinking what I'm thinking," Rose said.

"We don't use anything set up by the admin," Maddox said. "We'll have Troy run the tech side of this, so we can bypass the network's admin and we'll use Troy's servers, not TENs."

TWENTY-SEVEN

AMERICAN BRAVADO

Brussels, Belgium

Axel was eating breakfast at a McDonalds on Elsensesteenweg Street in Ixelles. It was a bustling Brussels neighborhood with narrow streets and sidewalks full of shops, cafes, and restaurants.

He poured syrup from a little plastic container on his pancakes while he chewed the last of the Egg McMuffin he had ordered. Hash browns and a cup of coffee completed his fast food feast.

He people-watched as he ate, something he enjoyed doing.

He would come up with a random person's backstory and the best way to kill them on the spot.

Just like in the Army, Axel had found that freelance work consisted of a lot of downtime.

There was a lot of hurrying up and waiting. With that much time on his hands, he would keep busy by picking a random person to follow.

Sometimes just for a block or two; sometimes for an hour or even the entire day.

He enjoyed the challenge. Would they find him out? Could he stay invisible?

He would follow them home or to work and he would strategize how he would enter undetected.

He would think of the best ways to kill them by scoping out the rooftops and buildings, looking for a perfect sniper's nest. Or perhaps he would break into their home or place of business for closer contact since he wouldn't always have the luxury of a sniper's nest.

If he could enter their home or office undetected, he would think about how he would kill them. Shoot them? Stab them?

Ben Gold had been his first stabbing kill and it had gone down flawlessly. His sniper skills were without reproach.

His longest confirmed kill was 1,100 meters, which had given him a bit of a celebrity status when he had been with the 2nd Ranger Battalion.

The truth was most sniper kills weren't from that impressive distance.

Next time, Axel wanted to try strangulation. He imagined that would be a handy skill set to have.

You weren't always going be able to take care of business from a comfortable distance. And you couldn't always just shoot someone with a pistol or have the opportunity with a knife like he had with Ben Gold, so it made sense to try strangulation.

With a garrote, perhaps, like Clemenza did to Carlo in the Godfather, he thought.

He contemplated testing that with a civilian, but decided against it. *Too much risk,* he thought.

Besides, Foxglove was a highly trained professional so it wouldn't be as easy to get the drop on him with a garrote in comparison to one of these civilian idiots.

Axel was looking out the McDonalds window at the throng of people walking to-and-fro on the crowded sidewalk.

The brief JFK layover and eating at McDonalds had made him homesick for the United States.

Axel liked traveling and loved being a nomad, but he missed that American way of living. The "I'm the King of the world and I don't care what you think, so fuck you" American bravado that rubbed Europeans the wrong way.

But look at them, he thought, *so docile, laid back, so dependent on the state to take care of them that they were like little children without any spunk or fight in them.*

He laughed out loud—which caused a young couple to glance at him and giggle—thinking how, by law, the police in Belgium could not raid a home or business between the hours of 9:00 p.m. and 5:00 a.m. Everyone knew this, especially the criminals. So as long they operated their meth labs or made bombs to blow up the metro between those hours, they didn't have to worry about the police busting through the door in the middle of the night.

He marveled at the dysfunction of the police in Belgium and other European countries—a disorganized conglomerate of competing interests that were spread out amongst municipalities, towns, cities, regions, and on the federal level.

And most of the cops in Belgium didn't even carry a gun. That part of Europe he liked. He could be fearless if he had to kill a cop in Europe.

It's why he wasn't worried about being back in Brussels just days after killing Ben Gold. He knew the Brussels police would be clueless.

Axel didn't think much of the police anywhere in the world. He disliked the trigger-happy authoritarian bent of cops in America but, at the same time, he found the docile nature of law enforcement in Western Europe to be pathetic.

He wouldn't think twice of killing a cop in Brussels or in Amsterdam.

Back in the United States, killing a cop unleashes the fury of Armageddon.

Axel would never dare do what he had planned for that afternoon against a Belgium Federal police officer in the States.

TWENTY-EIGHT
BAD FOR BUSINESS

As usual, Philippe Bouhouche had a Gauloises cigarette dangling from his lips as he exited his lime-green Renault Scénic.

He wasn't happy that TEN had reached out again asking for his help with another of their contractors.

In his mind, he had already risked far more than what he'd been paid to help Maddox and Rose, and now he was supposed to do the same with another contractor?

That was another area of concern for him. Three TEN contractors running around his city—that could be bad for business. His police business and the other work he did on the side.

TEN set up the meeting at the Bois de la Cambre, a park on the edge of the Sonian Forest.

The park was best known for the cricket match played by members of British troops before they had gone up against Napoleon at the Battle of Waterloo.

He lit up a new cigarette with his old one as he walked toward the lake flicking the old cigarette into a thicket of shrubs.

He didn't like meeting outdoors in the open, or at night like a spy or like he was cruising. He might be on the take and on TEN's payroll, but meeting this way felt undignified to him. But the board insisted so there he was.

He arrived at the agreed location by the lake and he saw the young man waiting for him.

He approached Axel and they exchanged the prearranged codes. Once their bonafides were established Axel said, "Let's sit on that bench over there," he pointed at a wooden park bench nearby that overlooked the lake.

It was late in the evening the park was empty.

Right off the bat, Bouhouche didn't like Axel, and his instincts were always correct.

For one, he was young. He had never met a TEN freelancer that young. He dressed rather shabbily in dirty blue jeans and an unbuttoned flannel shirt over a black T-shirt and an olive-green jacket. It was thick. Like the ones GIs used to wear before they began to camouflage their field jackets.

Axel sat first. He studied the well-dressed Belgium cop.

A real pretty boy that one, Axel thought.

He took the final drag of a cigarette, which he had smoked down so thoroughly that he struggled to hold it between his fingers. He took the last puff holding it like a roach of weed.

"Is that pot?" Axel asked.

"What, this?" Bouhouche asked, holding the stub of cigarette out for Axel's inspection.

"Yeah."

"Of course not. It's tobacco." He sounded offended at the suggestion.

"You hold it like a joint and it smells like ragweed," Axel said.

The cop shrugged, dropped the small stub to the ground, put it out with his foot, then joined Axel on the bench.

"Do you have the information we requested?" Axel asked.

"Yes. But I must ask, being such an unusual request, why do you need it?"

"It's not your concern, Inspector," Axel said tersely.

"Excuse me?"

"Look, Inspector, it doesn't matter what you or I think on the matter. I'm just a courier so hand over the information that they have requested and I'll be on my way," Axel said. He looked directly into the inspector's dark eyes and said nothing until Bouhouche broke the silence.

"They're staying at the Hotel Sofitel. Here is the address," Bouhouche said, handing Axel a piece of paper torn from his pocket notepad.

Axel took it without saying a word. He glanced at it.

The address meant nothing to him. It was just his third time in Brussels, so he would have to locate it on Google Maps.

"What else?" Axel said.

"It's not just Foxglove, but he has a friend. American. His name is Pete. Told me his last name was Wall, but I have a feeling that's an alias."

Bouhouche reached for his weatherworn pack of Gauloises.

"Just wait until I'm gone before you light up again. I don't want to inhale your toxic fumes," Axel said.

Bouhouche lit up anyway and said, "They found a safe in a hidden compartment inside the wall of Mr. Gold's apartment. I opened the safe for them and there was some amazingly well done fake identification cards, cash in euros, dollars, and pound sterling, and a hard drive, which they took. They're going to report back to me as soon as they figure out how to get through the password." Bouhouche blew smoke toward Axel on purpose.

"Okay, that's it?" Axel asked.

"Yes."

"Any leads on who killed our man, Ben Gold?" Axel asked with a thin grin.

"Not yet," he said.

"Okay, then. I'm heading back to the safe house," Axel said as he began to walk away.

TWENTY-NINE

INTO THE LAKE

Brussels, Belgium

As agreed upon beforehand, Bouhouche would remain on the bench for five minutes after Axel left before getting up to leave.

After a couple minutes, he looked down at his watch to check the time and felt something wrap around his neck.

He dropped the cigarette and tilted his back, trying to figure out was happening.

Axel stood behind him on the other side of the park bench with a garrote that he was tightening around the inspector's neck.

Axel felt the power of a boa constrictor as he choked the life from his prey.

Bouhouche began to swing his arms wildly behind him like a windmill, trying to break free from his assassin's grip.

He landed a couple feeble blows, but the garrote just got tighter.

In a panic, he found the whereto to reach into his coat and, without even removing the pistol from the coat pocket, managed to get to the trigger and began pulling it.

Several shots rang out.

One of them grazed his leg before embedding itself into the ground as chunks of dirt and grass kicked up into the air.

Two more shots hit the ground.

The shots were loud. Axel's ears rang and he loosened the wire enough so that Bouhouche was able to get his left hand in between the wire and his throat, preventing Axel from finishing the job.

Bouhouche's leg was bleeding from the self-inflicted shot, and his hand and neck were bleeding from the garrote's wire, but with a boost of air and surge of adrenaline, he was able to wriggle himself off the bench.

"Motherfucker," Axel grunted as Bouhouche began to stand. Axel shoved him back down as he tightened the garrote again. It was now cutting deeper into Bouhouche's hand, but that wasn't going to kill him.

The wire sawed at his flesh and Bouhouche had enough air in his lungs to scream.

It was a primal shout of anger and pain and Axel knew that meant he was getting air in his lungs.

Axel realize he had botched the hit and had to do something quick since the shouts and shots fired would soon bring a swarm of police to the area.

Axel reached for his pistol at the same time that Bouhouche managed to remove his black .38 from his coat. He pulled the trigger two more times.

The gun shots exploded near Axel's ear. It felt like a boxer had used his eardrum as a punching bag.

Axel dropped the garrote. He struggled to get a grip on his pistol with one hand as he grabbed Bouhouche by the wrist and he twisted it with his free hand.

Bouhouche fired one shot toward the lake, then Axel heard *click, click.*

Bouhouche was out of bullets.

Axel tried to reposition himself to shoot him in the head, but Bouhouche wrapped both his arms around Axel's neck from behind and leaned forward with all his might, causing Axel to topple over the park bench and onto the ground.

Bouhouche attempted to drop a knee onto Axel's groin, but missed as the two men scuffled on the ground.

Axel dug into Bouhouche's leg wound, causing him scream in pain and to let go, and Axel began punching Bouhouche's face with balled fists. He kept slamming his fists until the inspector rolled off him and lay on the ground dazed from the haymaker punches.

Freed from his grip, Axel jumped up and took three steps back as he glanced around to ensure no one was coming, but this gave the inspector a chance to get up.

He tried to run away, but the self-inflicted leg wound caused him to fall again as Axel pulled the trigger five times.

Axel was exhausted. He tried to breathe but felt like he was sucking air through a straw.

He was covered in dirt, grass stains, and blood.

He stood there for a moment, hunched over, until he got a second wind. Or was it a third or fourth wind? He couldn't keep track.

He knelt next to the body to make sure Bouhouche was dead. He was. Then he riffled through his pockets until he found the dead man's key chain.

He pocketed it then grabbed the body by the ankles and dragged him to the edge of the lake, where he was able to roll it in using his foot. He watched for a moment until the body began to float away, face down in the water.

He tossed the .38 into the lake.

He went back to the park bench. He picked up the garrote and took off, running.

It felt like he was running with cinder blocks for shoes and his entire body was sore. He was parched. The inside of his mouth felt like he was chewing on a kerosene rag. He tried to spit blood from a busted lip, but the little saliva he had was thick and stringy.

He was drained of energy when he approached the only parked car on the road. He pressed on the fob, which, to his delight, caused the car to chirp and flash its lights. He climbed in and sped away in Bouhouche's car.

Axel ditched the car about three miles from the park. He wiped it down clean. And he walked to the Metro Station, tossed Bouhouche's key chain and the garrote into a sewer drain.

He zipped his jacket tight to hide the Glock and the blood and grime as best he could.

During the metro ride Axel felt that every single person in the subway car was staring at him, aghast at the bloody clothing on the sweat-drenched foreigner that was breathing heavily. But when he looked up at the smattering of passengers, he was relieved no one was paying attention to him. They were too engrossed with their mobile devices or sleeping. No one cared. No one noticed him. He sighed in relief.

Thirty minutes later he was back in the safe house. He removed his cell phone, wallet, holstered Glock, and his knife, and placed them on the kitchen table.

He stripped off his clothes and socks so he was standing in the kitchen naked. He drank two bottles of water. Then he put the clothing, including his gloves and shoes, into a plastic trash bag, which he would toss in a dumpster a few blocks away.

His body burned and ached. The physicality of strangling someone to death was more complicated than he'd imagined.

He would have practiced on a civilian first if he'd known it wasn't as easy as it was in the movies.

I should have just shot him in the head instead of trying that stupid garrote. Mr. White would shit if he knew what had happened and the thought of that made him snigger.

He drank another bottle of water then he went to the bathroom and took a scalding hot shower. It felt good to have the hot water send the blood, sweat, and shame of his screw up down the shower drain.

He stood in the bedroom naked. His skin was prickly and reddened from the hot shower, but he was starting to recover.

THIRTY

THE NEXT TARGET

Brussels, Belgium

AXEL GOT DRESSED. HE CAUGHT A GLANCE OF HIMSELF IN the mirror. The deathlike pallor of the face staring back at him amused him.

He wanted nothing more than to be back on that houseboat in Amsterdam so he could sleep for ten or twelve hours, but there was too much to do so he settled for a twenty-minute catnap.

He got five minutes of sleep before the phone vibrated. It was Mr. White. He didn't want to deal with Mr. White or talk about killing Inspector Bouhouche. He needed to focus on the next target. He sent the call to voicemail.

The most important detail, he had: Foxglove was staying at the Sofitel Hotel.

The hotel was a thirty-minute metro ride away from the safe house. It was tricky working in the hotel since just about every square inch of the building was covered with security cameras.

There would also be cameras at the metro station and on the buildings and the private residences, so he would be leaving breadcrumbs the size of boulders for the cops and spooks to find. Avoiding security cameras was a luxury a modern-day assassin like Axel could not enjoy.

Axel brainstormed a work-around. Perhaps he could wear one of the black head to toe burqas. Back in Iraq, they were issued warnings about male insurgents who had passed themselves as burqa-wearing women so they could get past security point checks with an explosive belt strapped on under the robe.

A burqa could work. It would hide his face and weapons. And as a bonus, maybe he could pin the attack on ISIS. But it seemed impractical to him since he had to go find a burqa and a white American going to the Muslim neighborhoods of Brussels would stick out like a lion in a kitty condo.

It didn't help that the recent terrorist attacks in Toulouse and Montauban in France and the Burgas Bus Bombing in Bulgaria had police and citizens on edge to the point that a burqa-clad woman might be looked at a bit too closely for his purposes.

I need to find another way, Axel decided.

Axel fired up his laptop and browsed to Google Earth and Street View to study the hotel and the buildings near it.

There weren't many buildings directly across from the hotel, and of those, there weren't many that were appropriate height wise. There was also the common problem in Western European cities that many of those old baroque buildings didn't have the flat roofs needed to set up a sniper's nest.

The building kitty-corner from the hotel was a residential apartment building, so he had the option of picking an apartment with the best vantage point into the hotel, but he would have to kill whoever was living there. With the limited time he had that could lead to more risk than he was comfortable with. What if that person had a lot of friends and family coming and going? Or if they happened to have a plumber coming that day? Or a UPS delivery?

The logistics and the time constraints meant he needed to come up with another way. A sniper kill would be out.

The only choice was to kill Foxglove up close and personal, but unlike Bouhouche, he wouldn't be that careless and sloppy.

Axel was thinking about his choices when the cell phone vibrated again. This time he took Mr. White's call.

"Don't ask me why I haven't picked up. I've been busy figuring things out," that was how Axel, not wanting to deal with Mr. White's condescension, answered the call.

"Okay, Axel. It's good to know that you're alive and that you haven't been arrested by the police or rendered by the CIA, MI6, or both."

"I took care of the policeman in Brussels," Axel said.

"We didn't agree on that. Not only was he an excellent source of information and logistical help for many years, but also I took a big risk in telling him you were a TEN contractor."

"More reason to kill him. He could have talked to someone else in the network and found out you sent a ringer," Axel said. "Besides, he was too close to Foxglove. He would have told him about my being there and asking about his location. I couldn't risk that. And he knew about the hard drive. You said anyone that knew about it had to go," Axel said.

Mr. White hated to admit it, but Axel was right. It would have been too risky for Bouhouche to live but that's not why Axel had killed him. He did it because he liked to kill and that worried Mr. White just as much. But he would deal with that concern later.

"I trust you, Axel. I'm sure you did what needed to be done for the mission and to protect us both. I won't second-guess you on those types of on-the-field decisions," Mr. White said.

Axel was taken aback by Mr. White's confidence since it was the first time he had shown him any.

"So, what did he tell you, specifically?"

"Foxglove is not working alone. He has a partner, goes by the name of Pete Wall. An American. They found a hidden safe in Ben Gold's apartment that the police had missed. They recovered a hard drive, which they took. It was password protected so they haven't been able to access the drive. But they told Bouhouche that they would be able to get around the password and that they would share its content with the inspector."

"Ben Gold met up with them in Amsterdam and they probably came to Brussels to get that hard drive," Mr. White said.

"Any idea of what might have been on that hard drive?" Axel asked.

"Yes, and it's not good for us. That imbecile Gold is going to screw up everything from his damned grave," Mr. White said, now sounding agitated. "Making matters worse, the board has contracted Foxglove into looking into Gold's death, so I can't stress this enough, you must ensure Foxglove and his American friend don't leave Brussels, alive."

"That's what I'm working on."

EUROTRASH GHILLIE SUIT

Brussels, Belgium

AXEL SHAVED HIS HEAD FOR A LOOK THAT HE HADN'T sported since Army Basic Training. He ran his hand through the stubble on his head and smiled. He liked it. *And now for the face,* he thought as he grabbed a small bottle of amber-colored liquid. It was a resin liquid adhesive that is used to apply crepe hair, mustaches, beards, wigs, and fake noses.

It was the stuff used by actors, private investigators, snoops, and freelancers like Axel to disguise themselves in a world where there was a security camera to cover just about every step a person takes.

Axel had a nice selection of mustaches and beards. He went with a thick black goatee that would also cover up his scars. He glued it on. Next, he slipped on a short-haired blond wig. The shaved head made it easier to adjust and wear the wigs. He adjusted it for a while until he was satisfied with the look. He stepped back to check himself out in the mirror and was startled at the transformation.

Next up: the clothing.

Axel was still learning the tradecraft but, as Mr. White had advised him, when on a job, try not to dress like you normally dress. And avoid any clothing apparel that might provide clues of his whereabouts—like your home team's baseball hat.

Axel had gone shopping in Prague, buying clothing he would never wear in his real-life. Clothing he would happily burn afterward. Axel called it his Eurotrash look: gray skinny jeans and to match, tight-fitting shiny red shirt.

He slipped on a short, double-breasted black overcoat of coarse woolen cloth, formerly worn by sailors, appropriated by hipster douchebags.

The jackets had deep inside pockets where Axel could carry the Uzi and the Glock undetected.

Axel looked in the mirror and turned around to make sure the weapons weren't creating any bulges that would be hard to hide from untrained eyes.

He topped off the look by donning a New York Yankee's baseball hat. Like most Americans not from New York, Axel hated the Yankees, so it was the one hat he would never wear. He wore the hat down low to offer a glimmer of protection from the prying eyes in the skies that would be watching and recording him.

He checked back on the television news station. Although his French was spotty and his Dutch was nonexistent, he didn't see any news stories about a body being fished out of the Bois de la Cambre Park or about a dead or even a missing Belgium policeman. That was a relief.

He took one last look in the mirror with pride at the Eurotrash Ghillie suit he had put together.

Satisfied, he inhaled and walked outside, making his way toward the hotel where Maddox and Rose were staying.

Forty minutes later, Axel sat in the lobby of the hotel on his laptop. He blended in well.

Mr. White had sent him additional information on Pete Wall. His real name was Pete Maddox. Like Axel, he was a former Ranger.

And he wasn't just any Ranger.

Maddox had been in the CIA and fired, exposed as a spy, and humiliated for being a rogue agent in Venezuela. *A badass*, Axel thought to himself. And there was Foxglove, who Mr. White had finally revealed to Axel as being Tom Rose, was SAS and MI6. He and Maddox went way back and had worked several jobs for TEN. It hadn't been a surprise to Mr. White that Foxglove had asked Maddox to back him up in this new job from the board.

This would be Axel's toughest assignment yet. Axel figured Maddox and Rose knew they were targets. It wasn't going to be easy to kill them on any given day, but now they would be on the lookout for it. Axel smiled. He liked challenges and was becoming more confident in his skills.

Mr. White had hacked into the hotel's registration software system. It was a skill that Axel wished he had. Axel hadn't seen a computer or database that Mr. White couldn't get into. He didn't know how those geeks did it, but it was impressive.

Axel's burner phone trilled. He looked at the incoming text. It was from Mr. White, passing along Maddox and Rose's hotel room number.

Axel thought about the information he had just received. It gave him an advantage, no doubt about that, but with these types of professionals, he had to carefully consider every angle. He couldn't just knock on their door and shoot them in the head like some untrained asshole civilian.

Breaking in and ambushing them was out of the question. They were too good for that, so he figured he would wait until they left the hotel.

The odds of striking in a crowded lobby were low. He knew

that was what they would calculate. He would too if the shoe were on the other foot. So that was what he would do.

Axel exited on Rose's floor. He didn't want to wander down the hallway or get anywhere close to Rose's room, fearing they had it surveilled. Axel looked both ways down the long corridor. It was empty. He placed a pinhole-sized video camera on the frame of a large mirror that hung on the wall opposite three elevator doors. He carried cameras in four colors: wood brown, black, white, and metallic silver. Those would cover most frames typically used for paintings and mirrors. The silver one matched the frame so Axel removed a strip of adhesive tape and used that to stick the tiny camera on the frame. The camera was motion activated. The tiny button-sized battery packed enough juice for three to six months. Axel figured he would need just a few hours before his targets made their way down to the lobby.

In less than two minutes, Axel was back in the elevator, going down to the lobby.

The lobby area was peppered with small tables and comfortable leather chairs for guests and visitors to order sandwiches, chips, and drinks.

It was also the one spot in the hotel that offered free Wi-Fi so it was a popular spot for guests to lounge. Axel found a spot between the bank of elevators in the lobby and the front door. All guests and visitors had to walk by him.

Axel fired up his laptop. He opened an app, and with just a few clicks he was looking at a live feed from his pinhole camera. He watched the brass-colored elevator doors in all their high-definition glory.

Next, Axel reversed the camera of his laptop so he could monitor the elevator banks behind him. If they were on the lookout for possible hitmen, they might not suspect someone sitting with their back to the elevators, so that's how Axel sat. But with the pinhole camera on their floor and the reversed view of his laptop's camera, there was no way Maddox and Rose could leave the hotel without him seeing them.

Axel thought about gunning them down right in the lobby. Two birds. One stone. Even if he followed them outside, he was going to be on video, so it didn't matter where he shot them. The hotel was brimming with surveillance cameras. There was no way to avoid that. Thus his transformation—let everyone look for a slickly dressed goatee-wearing douche bag in a Yankee's baseball hat with dirty-blond hair from the wig jutting out.

Axel had made his decision. He would kill them in the lobby. Following Maddox and Rose would be too dangerous. As much as he hated to admit it, they had a lot more experience than he had at this work, so they would probably pick him up pretty quickly.

It would be a bold move, Axel thought.

Bold or stupid? His inner voice asked. He ignored it.

He was working himself into a sweat. Not good. *Focus. Focus. Think about the plan.*

Axel mulled over his plan for what must have been the hundredth time: after gunning down Maddox and Rose, he would not run out the front door since that was heavily trafficked and what security might expect. After casing the place, he had decided he would run into the hotel, toward the back, into the restaurant then into the kitchen.

The whole time he would be yelling, "Allahu Akbar" as loud as possible, since he figured that would cause everyone to run and hide in terror, even more than the sound of gunfire and the two dead bodies.

At the back of the kitchen, there was a push bar door which led to a relatively quiet narrow alley behind the buildings.

He would toss the baseball hat and the hideous red shirt in a preselected dumpster a block from the hotel. From there, he'd spill out of the alley where he could cut through toward

Chaussée d'Etterbeek street and hop a small black aluminum fence into Leopold Park, where he would ditch the wig and fake goatee in the trash can by the pathway.

He would then calmly make his way back to the safe house, where he had a stolen 2002 Toyota Noah with a German license plate. Mr. White had stashed a clean license plate for each of the EU countries in the safe house.

Axel would drive the two hours to Bonn, Germany, where he would abandon the car at the Heiderhof Shopping Center's parking lot and make his way to another safe house located a few miles from there.

The authorities would know it was a professional job. They more than likely would find the pinhole camera on the victim's floor. They would also find the Yankees headgear, the wig, fake beard, and shirt. Axel figured they would be impressed at his skill. It made him smile as he pretended to look at a complex color-coded spreadsheet on his laptop.

Until Maddox and Rose appeared, he could do little else but wait in that lobby.

The fact that he was American helped. It was quite common for Americans to be hanging out in hotel lobbies, but he had set a time limit of ninety minutes. You can't hang out in a fancy hotel lobby all day without drawing attention to yourself, even if you seemed to fit in.

THIRTY-TWO

EMPTY PROMISES

Brussels, Belgium

It was 10:30 in the morning. Maddox was preparing to check out of the hotel.

Maddox and Rose knew that they were targets, so they decided that Maddox would take the stairs down to the lobby and sneak into the gift shop.

From there he could keep an eye out for anything suspicious and provide cover for Rose as he made his way through the lobby like bait.

If the shooter were to bite, Maddox would get the drop on him.

Maddox glanced at the phone. He wanted to call Sonia so he could hear her voice, but it was too early in Florida.

He didn't make the call.

There was a lot he wanted to tell her, like how he would no longer do the odd jobs, but he figured it would be better off to save that conversation in person.

It would be a hard sell to get her to believe him with his track record of empty promises in such matters.

But now he felt a resolve that he hadn't felt before. Perhaps it was because he felt that Sonia was slipping away from him.

The long absences, the dangerous work. Maddox prided himself in his skill at compartmentalizing. How else could he do the work he did, then go home and be a functioning husband? You don't say much. The thought being that he was protecting her; instead he was driving her away more each day.

But he couldn't just leave.

He wasn't away for just another odd job, far from it. This time it was self-preservation. He had to put a stop to the threat.

There wouldn't be any happy reunions back home without knowing who was after them, and why.

Back in his room, Rose had his bag ready by the door. He checked the time and sat down at the desk. He had to make a call before meeting Maddox in the lobby.

Rose swapped out SIM cards from the burner phone and dialed the chairman. After the correct exchange of passcodes, Rose filled him in with what had happened in Brussels.

"This tech person, Mr. Sennight. Do you trust him with the hard drive?"

"One hundred and ten percent," Rose said.

"Good," the chairman said, his voice low and barely audible.

Rose cleared his throat and asked, "Speaking of trust. How well do you trust TEN's administrator?"

His question went unanswered for a few moments. Rose waited, despite the awkward silence until the chairman finally spoke up.

"We trusted him well enough to make him the network's administrator."

"With all due respect, sir, you're sounding like a politician with that response. I need you to be frank with me if I'm going to be out here trying to contain whatever this is," Rose said.

More silence. A cough. "There have been signs that maybe

we've trusted him too much. Perhaps, we gave him too much autonomy in matters of technology," the chairman said sheepishly.

"What makes you think that?" Rose asked.

"Is there a reason for your questions? Do you suspect him?"

"It's just that the person behind this appears to have administrator rights to TEN. It doesn't mean it's the administrator. Perhaps he has an assistant or a staff for tech support. Or perhaps TEN has been hacked," Rose said.

The chairman sighed heavily. "The technology changes. It's hard to keep up. When I started TEN, the Internet was just a small guppy swimming around enthusiastically unafraid. Now you have one big fish getting swallowed up by an even bigger fish, until another even bigger one comes along to swallow that fish up. It's maddening. My thirteen-year-old grandson's mobile phone has more firepower than the first computer I used on the job. In those days, it took true expertise, usually found in academia, military, and government to hack into complex, hidden systems like TEN. Now I fear even my grandson could figure it out. Finding an expert in China, Ukraine, or Slovakia to do that kind of work is rather simple. I'm afraid that the idea of a network like TEN might be going the way of the Dodo bird."

"That might be the case. Our tech expert found a hidden database. It included the names and addresses of the contractors and financial records. They have all our personal data including Fitzsimmons and Ramos. That database was created and hidden by someone with administrator rights. Now you understand my concern with your administrator," Rose said.

"Yes, I understand. You continue your work. I will see what I can find on my end," the chairman said.

"Mr. Chairman, it wouldn't be prudent of you to alert the administrator to any of this until you hear from me," Rose warned.

"Of course."

"You can save us a lot of time by telling me who he is and where he is located," Rose said.

"I cannot do that for you. I'm sorry. But it goes against the very principles that have guided the network. Even with proof, I would need to put it to a vote with the board to terminate his services, permanently."

"I understand, but I fear you're the only one playing by the old rules," Rose said.

"I can live, and die with that, Foxglove."

Not me, you old coot, Rose thought as he ripped out the SIM card and burned it.

THIRTY-THREE
I'LL WALK

Brussels, Belgium

AXEL COULD FEEL HIS HEART THUMPING FASTER AND faster upon seeing Tom Rose appear on the video feed.

Then panic. Foxglove was alone.

Axel's mind began processing what that could mean. Maybe they had made him and they were laying a trap, or maybe they were leaving separately.

Either way, he couldn't make a move without knowing the whereabouts of Foxglove's partner.

Axel calmed himself down.

Perhaps the second target would join Foxglove down in the lobby. Axel watched the video feed carefully then switched to the laptop camera covering the lobby.

About a minute later, Axel watched as Rose got out of the elevator. He began to make his way through the lobby, there was still no sign of his partner.

Axel double-checked the facial recognition app that Mr. White had provided him and it was a one hundred percent match with Tom Rose. Thinning, dirty-blond hair, cleft chin, six foot tall, with an athletic build that was impressive for a man in his early fifties.

Axel switched from the app to his reverse laptop camera as he followed his target through the lobby.

He could shoot him at any moment. *Where the hell is the other target,* Axel thought as he scanned the video feed. Axel appeared calm as he sat there staring at his laptop, but he was panicking inside. His stomach burned, and it felt like he had a tight band around his throat that kept getting tighter.

He couldn't make a move without knowing where the other target was. He could be providing cover from somewhere else in the lobby. It would be a perfect way of drawing Axel out so they could ID him. Even if Axel was just being paranoid, it made no sense to kill Foxglove and leave his partner out there. They would be in the same vise grip they were already in.

And Mr. White had been adamant: kill them both at the same time or abort the mission.

Rose walked past him. Dammit. He could shoot him in the head so easily, right now.

Axel had been so focused on Rose, and in trying to find his second target, that he hadn't noticed that Foxglove was rolling his suitcase behind him.

Shit. He's checking out. He's leaving Brussels.

His phone vibrated. He looked at the incoming text from Mr. White, who was monitoring the hotel's guest system.

Targets have checked out.

Axel's heart and mind raced a mile a second. Where was Maddox? His plan was falling apart in front of him.

Rose looked around the lobby, but he walked with confidence, like he didn't have a care in the world. It pissed Axel off.

Axel watched impotently as Rose walked outside into the front foyer where one of the many bellhops approached him.

In one single motion, the bellhop grabbed Rose's suitcase and gestured for a cab.

In less than a minute, a black car with a yellow-checkered stripe running across its side drove up.

The bellhop sprang into action, placing the suitcase in the cab, and holding the door open for Rose, who smiled and tipped the young man in the funny getup. Rose climbed into the cab, which then took off. The bellhop glanced at his tip. He smiled widely, seemingly very pleased.

Axel remained seated in the lobby. He didn't want to blow his position.

A few minutes later he finally saw Maddox emerge from the gift shop, which was to the left of where Axel was sitting.

The passage between the gift shop and the front door flanked the pathway Rose had taken from the elevator to the outside area in front of the hotel. Maddox was also rolling his suitcase behind him.

Son of a bitch, Axel thought.

He must have snuck into the gift shop providing cover for Rose and had been there the whole time.

But how had he gotten past him?

Axel got angrier as he watched Maddox exit the hotel. They had one-upped him, but it didn't appear they had discovered who he was.

Axel watched the same bellhop fetch Maddox a cab.

He waved off the offer of taking his suitcase. He tipped the bellhop enough cash to make him smile widely again.

Axel wanted to shoot that fucking bellhop in the head.

The cab sped off.

Axel packed up his laptop. He looked around the lobby and spotted signage for the stairs, then he saw the door for the staircase behind him.

You didn't cover the damned staircase. That's how Maddox made it to the gift shop without you seeing.

He was impressed, jealous, and relieved at what he witnessed.

Had he acted on his impulse to gun down Foxglove, Maddox would have pounced from the gift shop and would have shot him dead before he could even unholster his pistol.

Axel took respite in the fact that he was only one man. He couldn't possibly cover every nook and cranny like a team of two. He still had a lot to learn in this business, he thought.

Axel went outside and glared at the bellboy. He was just a civilian doing his pathetic job in that stupid polyester costume. But that tip-seeking stupid grin and fake laugh grated on him. Axel wanted to pull out his Glock and kill that asshole of a bellhop.

Axel walked up to him. He was older than he'd looked from the lobby. The bellhop smiled wide at Axel, his eyes eager to greet him. He was dark-skinned. Perhaps Moroccan.

"New York Yankees, my favorite baseball team," the bellhop said in English.

"What?" Axel said before remembering he was wearing that stupid baseball hat. "Go Yanks."

Axel still wanted to shoot the fucker, but instead paid him fifty euros for the location of the last two cabs he had hailed.

"Brussels Airport, sir," he said, stuffing the cash into his pocket. "Can I fetch you a taxi, sir?"

"I'll walk," Axel said, turning away from the bellhop, and merging into the crowded sidewalk.

THIRTY-FOUR

THE BANNED

Brussels Airport

MADDOX AND ROSE WERE WAITING TO BOARD THEIR FLIGHT
by having a drink in the British Airways Galleries Lounge in the
main terminal of Brussels Airport.

Their nonstop flight to London departed in forty minutes.

It was too early for beer, so Maddox was drinking a Bloody
Mary garnished with carrot, celery, with extra pitted manzanilla
olives, served with ice cubes and liberally splashed with
Tabasco sauce and lemon.

"You've got a regular Carmen Miranda hat in that drink,"
Rose teased, as he drank a Screwdriver.

Maddox grinned, lathering cream cheese on a sesame bagel
while Rose took a bite of his wheat toast spread thick with
butter and apricot marmalade.

They went about their debriefing.

"Any red flags back at the lobby?" Rose asked.

"Just one. There was a young guy wearing a New York
Yankees cap. He was sitting on one of the lounge chairs in the
lobby. He's the only one that got my attention. Male. White.

Age. All fit the typical profile. And I don't know. He seemed to be trying to blend in a bit too much the way he was staring at his laptop. But then again, today's youth, they live with their noses in their electronic gadgets. And he didn't make a move. Hardly moved, actually. So maybe it was nothing."

"Sometimes staying still can be a tell," Rose said.

"I took his pic," Maddox said, handing his phone to Rose.

Rose took it and looked at the photograph on the screen. It was a peripheral snapshot of Axel. Looking down at his laptop.

"Never seen him before," Rose said, handing the phone back to Maddox.

"Me neither. Probably nothing. But I'll send it to Troy so he can run it through his facial recognition software," Maddox said.

Rose then filled in Maddox about his conversation with the chairman. Maddox had been against letting anyone on the board know what they were doing and who they suspected since he no longer trusted anyone at TEN.

But Rose trusted the chairman. When TEN had been founded, Rose was one of the first contractors invited to join.

And it was because of Rose, that Maddox had been invited. Usually a man with Maddox's background—fired from the CIA, charged with Federal crimes, and blacklisted by the CIA— would bar him from joining TEN for life.

It didn't matter that within the industry, people knew that the CIA had scapegoated Maddox and the charges, which were bogus, were eventually dropped.

But he still had a stain in the freelance community that wouldn't wash off.

But Rose had made his case to the chairman.

The board deadlocked on a two-two tie in letting Maddox join TEN, so it was the chairman that cast the tie breaking "yes" vote in Maddox's favor. And he did so out of respect and admiration for Tom Rose.

After several years and several successful jobs, Maddox had proved himself to embody the valued TEN code of operating a clean dirty business.

"He didn't flat out say it, but there is concern about putting too much trust in the administrator," Rose said.

"What are they waiting for?" Maddox asked.

"Proof."

"What do you think? TEN got hacked?" Maddox asked.

"Doubtful. I know there isn't a system out there that is one hundred percent hack-proof, but the people behind TEN, they would be the ones that would come pretty damned close to boasting that accomplishment," Rose said.

"That's why I kept using the site," Maddox said.

"If the network is under siege, it has to be orchestrated from the inside," Rose said.

"I can buy that, but there is no way the administrator is doing this alone, he might be a genius with the tech stuff, but not with our line of work," Maddox said.

"He hired a TEN freelancer?" Rose asked.

"No. I can't see a TEN freelancer doing that to Fitzsimmons and Ramos. It violates the code," Maddox said.

"We've both seen good men turn bad, really bad," Rose said.

Maddox speared an olive from his Bloody Mary and popped it in his mouth.

"It wouldn't be the first time, that's for sure," Maddox said. He finished his Bloody Mary. "I need some coffee."

Maddox returned with a cup of java.

"I was thinking. According to the board, they've been getting uninvited requests to join, which is an automatic ban. Maybe it's one of them, pissed off that they hadn't been invited, then doubly pissed off at being banned for life because they took the initiative to reach out and ask to join," Maddox said.

"I can buy that. And the admin would know who has been banned," Rose said.

"And that would provide him with a nice pool of shooters to do his dirty work," Maddox said.

"Can you ask Troy if he can get a list of the banned from the hard drive? That way we don't have to ask the admin for it?" Rose asked.

Maddox nodded as he dug out his phone.

THIRTY-FIVE

SOCIAL OUTCASTS

Brussels, Belgium

AXEL WAS BACK AT THE SAFE HOUSE. HE WAS STRUGGLING to keep his anger and frustration in check. He wanted to smash every piece of furniture into smithereens. He went to the kitchen, grabbed a bottle of plastic water, and began to drink. He wanted to unleash his pent-up frustration on the dishes that were neatly stacked in the cupboard. But he fought the urge. He drained the bottle of water. He took deep long breaths just like the counselor had taught him to do in order to stay calm and in control.

It was progress for Axel. A year ago, he would have let loose on the inanimate objects of the house. But what would that accomplish? His targets would still be on an airplane to God only knows where, and he would have to deal with the repercussions of trashing the safe house, like a neighbor hearing the commotion and calling the police. Or the homeowner comes over to check on things and finds the house trashed. It wasn't worth it just to blow off steam.

The best thing he could do was figure out his next move. To figure out where the targets were going so he could kill them.

Axel was blowing off steam by doing pushups when the phone rang fifteen minutes later. It was Mr. White. Axel took the call.

"They're traveling together on British Airways Flight 98. The flight is already in progress, so they'll be landing soon. You need to get to London. I'll be setting up a safe house. There is a red-eye tonight. I have your ticket. By the time you land, the safe house will be ready and stocked for you," Mr. White said.

"How do you find that stuff out so quickly?" Curiosity had gotten the best of Axel.

"I'm a computer scientist with a master's degree and a Ph.D., I have my ways. You would need a few years of computer science training under your belt to understand what I do," Mr. White answered.

And there was the condescending arrogance Axel was used to.

But it bothered him less and less. *It didn't matter,* Axel thought. He was learning. They were gelling more and more each day as a lethal team with every operation. They made a good unit. Besides that, Axel believed Mr. White didn't even realize he was talking down to him. That he behaved like an ass most of the time. It was just how a lot of those geeks operated. Social rejects and Axel could appreciate that. He might not be a Ph.D. computer science genius, but had always been a social outcast with the personality of a honey badger.

In the end, they didn't really have to like each other. They just needed to work well together. And they were, with Mr. White handling everything behind the scenes, and Axel handling the fieldwork.

THIRTY-SIX

WENCESLAS SQUARE

Prague, Czech Republic

Wenceslas Square was one of the busiest city squares located in the New Town area of Prague. It was considered the business center of the Czech Republic.

The Kotera Building had been built in the early 1900s to be the headquarters of the First Nation Bank. The bank had long ago gone out of business, but it had left behind its beautiful building that oozed with Austrian Art Nouveau influences.

The building had that regal look banks had demanded in that era with its wide façade that hid its narrowness. The building hovered over the northwest corner of Wenceslas Square.

With lack of funds for upkeep and repairs, the building had fallen into disrepair by the time of the dissolution of Czechoslovakia.

The new Czech Republic emerged from those dark, isolated Soviet days.

It eventually joined the European Union, and the country began to modernize and transform itself. Its once decrepit buildings, like the country, went through their own transformation until the Kotera Building became a bustling office building with offices for lawyers, accountants, consultants, and tech companies like Cyber One.

Cyber One was a fully managed web hosting solutions company that provided dedicated servers and VPS hosting to their customers online needs with the promise of anonymity and security. Business was going well and they boasted over one hundred thousand customers from all over the world.

The company had built their own state of the art data center that was maintained on a 24/7/365 basis but they were not located in the Kotera Building. That was done at Cyber One's main headquarters, about thirty miles from Wenceslas Square in the city of Kladno.

The only office of Cyber One in the Kotera Building was a one-man office that managed cyber security and provided special consulting projects for the company, but in reality, it did the work for just one client: the Threat Elimination Network.

However, no one would find that name in any official business filings or in the roster of the smiling satisfied Cyber One customers splashed on their website. And no one would know that the one customer, TEN, was the whole reason Cyber One even existed. None of Cyber One's 125 employees in Kladno were aware that Cyber One began as a front for TEN. That their employer was owned outright by TEN—serving as the public face to the network.

However, TEN's servers were not located in the data center in Kladno with the rest of Cyber One's customers. The network had their own dedicated data center that had been built in the backroom of that small office inside the Kotera building.

Its access strictly controlled by Cyber One's Chief Information Security Officer, Edvard Danko, who—unbeknownst to the rest of the company—was the administrator of TEN's system.

Danko had been born in Revúca, Czechoslovakia—a village in the mostly forested region of the country that was now in Slovakia.

He had come a long way from the forests of the Revúca District. He sat at his desk. Worried. He wore his receding black hair short. His white skin had a pale translucent hue from spending most of his time indoors surrounded by servers and computer monitors. Two pairs of glasses seemed to always dangle from his shirt, one set of glasses for reading, the second pair computer glasses, crafted with special lenses made for those who spent most of their time staring into the digital abyss. And even though he worked alone in his one-man office, he dressed business casual in tan or black dress slacks and a blue or black dress shirt.

Cyber One might have been formed as a front for TEN, but Danko was proud of the multimillion dollar business that he had built from scratch and he resented the board's control over it and their ruling on all business matters. Down to who Cyber One could have as customers.

Danko found it ridiculous that a network providing mercenaries with work would prevent him from accepting the very lucrative online business from companies operating in the lucrative 3 Ps of business: pills, porn, and poker.

The board ruled that those businesses—which were notorious for spamming—would bring unwanted attention to the network.

Danko argued that he had TEN hidden so deeply that it would take a cadre of intelligence tech experts working around the clock to find it and even then, the odds were too low to worry.

When Danko was approached by Russian intelligence to set up a hidden server that would be used by the Russian SVR to launch their hacking activities, the board unanimously voted against that too.

It had humiliated Danko. Wasn't Russia a legitimate government, just like the United States or the United Kingdom? His humiliation had been compounded by the fact that the Russian business would have generated millions of euros for the company and a twenty percent referral fee paid directly to Danko. The board knew nothing of that private arrangement, of course.

Danko was incensed. If it wasn't for the board and their draconian ways of running the business, Cyber One would be the largest provider of web hosting services for the dark web and the entire internet, and Danko would be filthy rich instead of babysitting servers for the network. And although he was paid twenty times what a regular network administrator was paid, he wanted more.

Especially when it was right there for the taking.

Danko had grown tired of the board's sanctimonious oppression. He had his own long-term plans; a hostile takeover of sorts, but that was easier said than done when the network comprised the best private paramilitary operators in the world who were loyal to the chairman.

Danko picked up the dedicated phone he had set up to communicate with his man in the field. *He better pick up,* Danko thought, annoyed at his freelancer's flakey insubordination, and how difficult it was at times to get him on the phone. But after the third ring, Axel answered.

"Yes, Mr. White."

"Axel, everything is ready for you in London," Danko, who Axel knew as Mr. White said.

THIRTY-SEVEN

YOUNG GUN

Prague, Czech Republic

Axel only knew Edvard Danko as Mr. White and that's how Danko wanted to keep it. The less Axel knew about him and his business dealings, the better.

Danko had taken a chance with the inexperienced Axel, but he'd needed someone to do the fieldwork if he was going to get rid of the network's board of directors.

Danko needed someone he could control. In that line of work, it was a hard proposition to find the right prospect.

It had taken Danko over a year to finally find the right man for the job. He had gone through other prospects—men and women, all highly trained military people.

Danko wanted to find someone from the Special Forces branch, preferably from the former Eastern Bloc countries, America, or the UK.

He looked for soldiers with behavioral troubles. Danko figured that soldiers who performed their duties well, but had a difficult time coping with the highly regulated structure of the military, would make the best candidates.

But those types of candidates, by their own nature, were strong-willed and hard to control. It had made Danko's search difficult. However, he knew if he found the right one, the frustrations of managing such a person would be worth it for the work they would deliver on his command.

Ten months ago, Axel had caught Danko's attention. He was three months out of the Army. He was brash, overconfident, and cocky and he had approached TEN—he never revealed how he knew who to approach—but that had been his downfall in joining TEN.

Danko looked at his military service records. They were impressive with the right amount of reprimands for insubordination, failing to get along with fellow soldiers, and an eagerness to kill that raised flags with the Army.

The red flags would have negated the board from offering him an invite, but it was a moot point. Axel had approached TEN. That was it. He was banned for life.

Axel had wanted to join TEN, and he did the one thing that would prevent him from ever joining it. He contacted one of the liaisons directly.

That's when he first came to Danko's attention when he had entered his information into the system and issued the permanent ban as required by the board.

"How did he take it?" Danko remembered asking the liaison who Axel had approached after he had been banned.

"Not well. He went on and on about how we would regret banning him. He was going to make sure the network would pay. We made a big mistake. That he was going to become the best professional in the business. Then he would burn the network to the ground."

Danko looked deeper into the background of the pissed off young gun for his own purposes. He remembered how good he looked on paper.

Axel joined the Army at the age of seventeen. Since he was underage, his mother had to sign off on it. She had already downed a fifth of vodka by that afternoon, but she signed.

He began his Army Basic Training and Advanced Individual Training in Ft. Benning, Georgia on a muggy, humid June.

Axel was scrawny, but fit and eager to prove himself. Aside from a few scuffles with other members of his platoon, he made it through training with flying colors and he qualified for an expert marksman badge hitting all 40 of the targets.

Three months later, on September 11, 2001, he was stationed in Fort Carson, Colorado with the 4th Infantry Division when the Towers fell.

He knew he would be seeing combat and was excited. But he grew frustrated when all they did was train for a year and half.

It wouldn't be until January of 2003—over a year since the terrorists struck the homeland—that Axel was finally deployed into combat. His unit spearheaded the Army's advance into northern Iraq from Turkey.

Then Turkey fucked it all up when the country refused to grant permission for the US Military to pass through on their way into Iraq. And yet again, Axel was on the sidelines as the Marines and Special Forces unit went into Iraq instead of the 4th Division. Axel fumed.

He would have to wait three more months until April of 2003, when his unit finally moved into Northern Iraq for the Battle of Baghdad.

Axel killed his first man on his first day in Iraq. A balaclava-wearing insurgent scattering away with AK47 in hand as the Humvee approached with Axel manning the mounted M240 machine gun. He saw the man as he tried to duck behind a wall; Axel opened fire, killing him before he could reach it for cover.

It was something Axel had wanted to do since he was ten years old.

Even with all the video games, all the training, nothing really prepares you for actual combat. It felt as if time slowed down, even though in reality everything happened quickly.

Bullets flying everywhere, ricocheting off buildings as chunks of concrete shattered in the air, turning into dust. The ash from fires rained down like confetti, the acrid smell from the burning oil fields permeated the air and the sound of mortar rounds and IED's going off all around the perimeter.

The 4th Division was all over Northern Iraq for several months and Axel became the top M240 machine gunner in the division. As the killings piled on, they ate away at some of his fellow soldiers, but not Axel. He thought of that slogan, *Born to Kill*, which seemed to apply to him so well that he began to write it onto his gear and anywhere he could until ordered to stop by a PR-worried Major.

"We're here to liberate, not kill. Besides there is CNN-embeded journalists joining us so get rid of it."

Axel wanted to laugh in his face.

In the close-knit environment that is the Army, especially during combat, Axel stood out for being deadly with his M240. He was reliable, but he was aloof and indifferent when it came to his fellow soldiers. They got the sense he was there because he liked to kill not because of the mission, or to protect and support his brothers-in-arms.

He became the black sheep of the platoon family. When the company commander found a list of soldiers most likely to be fragged, he was the only enlisted man on it.

His combat skills did not go unnoticed by his commanding officers and he was selected to participate in Operation Red Dawn with United States special operations forces.

He was there when they captured Saddam Hussein who was hiding in a hole in the ground in December 2003.

The ego boost was short-lived for Axel. Although he enjoyed participating in the mission, he felt like a hired hand, there to only support the Special Forces soldiers who made him feel like a security guard at a mall in the background as the real cops did their thing.

By spring of 2004, he had rotated back to Colorado with his combat medals and a Bronze Star.

Colorado was a bore but three months later, he was excited to be selected for Ranger school. He was first sent to Airborne School in Ft. Benning, Georgia for three weeks.

Immediately following his graduation from Airborne School, he joined other volunteers and moved onto the Ranger Indoctrination Program to see if he had what it took to join the elite 75th Ranger Regiment.

He was just shy of his twenty-first birthday when he began RIP.

But nothing, not even combat, had prepared him for what he endured at RIP. Twenty percent of the class either quit or washed out in the first forty-eight-hours.

By the end of hell week, more than fifty percent of the starting class was gone. But Axel endured.

After eight weeks the hellish course was over, he was among those left standing.

Axel didn't care about the pomp and circumstance of being a Ranger. He scoffed at the notion of a brotherhood. He saw it as pabulum for brainwashing.

What mattered to him, was he was one of the few that made it to the end of selection.

He beat out jocks, college boys, fitness freaks to don the tan beret and the 75th Regiment Scroll.

He was a Ranger. Most washed out.

Eighteen months later, Axel went to Sniper School, where he graduated top of his class. He would serve two more tours in Iraq and in Afghanistan as a Ranger Sniper.

It was during his service in Iraq and Afghanistan that Axel began to meet and interact directly with Green Berets, Delta Force, and CIA paramilitary forces.

It was in 2008 that he first heard of a secretive, private, invitation only, organization that recruited Special Forces soldiers and intelligence officers to join their private network.

After eight years in the Army, Axel had enough. He loved having access to state of the art weapons and being lauded and given medals for killing, but he didn't like being told what to do during every waking minute as an active soldier by some douchebag officer or an asshole further up the noncommissioned chain of command than he was. So once his enlistment was up, Sergeant Brandon Jones didn't re-up and he was honorably discharged from the Army.

Banned by TEN he began his nomadic living as he drifted from country to country and job to job until he came to work for Danko exclusively.

THIRTY-EIGHT

SIX HOURS BEHIND

Prague, Czech Republic

DANKO WAS ON THE DIGITAL HUNT FOR THE TWO freelancers. Maddox and Rose were good at covering their tracks, but unless they were staying off the grid, he would find them.

He tapped on his computer pulling up a backdoor he had long ago installed. He was in.

All the big name hotels use software programs to manage their reservations so that a guest could seamlessly book a room online or on their mobile devices.

Three software companies dominated the business of providing hotels with their Hospitality Property Management Software.

That dependency was music to the ears of a hacker with Danko's skills.

By hacking just three software companies, Danko had untethered backdoor access to the reservation systems for thousands of hotels across the globe, including all the major hotels in London.

Getting into the hotel's reservation system was the easy part. Professionals like Maddox and Rose had access to experts that specialized in the forgery of identity documents, making it harder for Danko's search programs to find them.

Danko set up several search queries. Although unlikely, he couldn't just discount them not using their real names because sometimes the best way to hide was by doing it in plain sight.

So he typed in Tom Rose and Pete Maddox and ran a AND/OR Boolean search of their names—Thomas, Tommy, T, Peter, Petey, P., and so on.

He also ran an anagram algorithm he had written to search the guest names.

And finally, he ran a search based on time estimates.

Danko knew when Maddox and Rose's British Airways flight had landed at Gatwick Airport, so he figured best time estimates, allotting for best- and worst-case traffic scenarios.

Danko doubted they would stay in a hotel that was more than thirty miles from Gatwick, but he entered a search parameter of fifty miles just to be sure.

In the back of his mind, Danko knew if Maddox and Rose were staying at a safe house or a friend's house, which were possibilities since London was Rose's town, then the search would be a moot point, but it was better than doing nothing.

Danko unleashed his bots to crawl the hotel's reservation systems, as Axel was due to land at Gatwick Airport six hours behind Maddox and Rose.

THIRTY-NINE

GROSVENOR SQUARE

London, England

As Danko's bots crawled the hotel's reservation systems, Maddox and Rose were checking in at the Marriott on Grosvenor Square.

Maddox preferred that location near the historic garden square located in the swanky Mayfair district of London than the one by the London Eye.

After checking into his room, Maddox felt antsy, so he decided to go for a run to clear his head and reboot after the flight.

He went out the front of the hotel to a chorus of, "Have a good run, sir," from the hotel staff and a couple guests.

He started on a very slow, at an almost walking pace as he cut through Grosvenor Square. He picked up speed once he reached Upper Brook Street until he was held up at a traffic light where Upper Brook Street crossed over the congested Park Lane, a major road in Central London in the City of Westminster. Once the light turned, he continued jogging on a sidewalk paralleling Hyde Park.

At the first opportunity, he turned into Hyde Park and once inside, he was able to pick up the pace.

Maddox checked his Garmin Forerunner watch. His heart rate was decent; he was at the four-mile mark, and his head felt clear and void of negativity, so he turned and started to run back to the hotel.

Maddox was sweat-drenched as he made his way back into the hotel. The doorman dressed like Napoleon at Waterloo smiled and opened the door for him.

"Good run, sir?" he asked.

"Yes, thank you."

Maddox was making across the lobby toward the elevators when he spotted Rose reading a paper and drinking tea.

"Really, mate, a run, out in the wide-open space, all those sniper-friendly buildings looking down on you."

Maddox had texted Rose about his run as he'd made his way out the door. His phone had buzzed about a minute later, but he ignored it. He'd known what Rose was texting back to him.

Maddox smiled.

"Feeling much better," Maddox said.

Rose frowned and said, "I'll meet you at the restaurant in about thirty minutes. Is that enough time for you to get ready?"

"Sure thing. What's up?" Maddox asked.

"Nothing earth-shattering, but I spoke with the board. Some interesting tidbits," Rose said, turning his attention back to the paper. Maddox headed toward the bank of elevators.

Back in his room, Maddox took off his running shoes, stripped off his sweaty clothes, and stepped into the shower.

He let the warm water from the showerhead wash over him for a full minute. Then he soaped up and washed his hair.

Twenty-five minutes later, he was in the restaurant where Rose was waiting at a table toward the back with a view of the entire area.

Maddox told the hostess he was meeting his friend as he walked past her and sat in the chair opposite Rose. He had a great view of the back of the restaurant, toward the kitchen and staff area, and Rose had a great view of the front.

"Good spot," Maddox said as he sat.

Rose nodded. He was drinking more tea.

A spindly waiter in a white pique satin vest arrived to take their order.

Rose ordered the English breakfast with fried eggs over medium. Maddox said, "When in Rome, I'll have the same, except for the tea, coffee for me, please."

The waiter scurried away and Maddox and Rose began to talk business.

"I heard back from Troy," Maddox said as he glanced around the restaurant to make sure no-one was eavesdropping. "He found a spreadsheet with the banned members that's three months old, but that timeline should work. There is no way he hooked up with this guy to send him off on these jobs only in the last few months."

"I agree. It's a safe bet that these two connected a while back," Rose said.

"So, the bastard should be in here," Maddox said, tapping on a small keychain jump drive. "But it's not as easy as we thought it would be."

"How many are they?" Rose asked.

Maddox said nothing as the waiter arrived with his coffee. As soon as he was gone Maddox continued.

"This goes back from the inception of the network. Over two hundred names."

"What, seriously? How can that be?" Rose said.

"Word's getting out, I guess," Maddox said.

"Jesus Christ, so much for being ultra-secret and under the radar. If all these bastards heard about the network independently, no wonder we find ourselves in this situation," Rose said.

Maddox nodded and was about to say something when their waiter showed up again, this time with a helper to lay out their breakfast on the table.

"More coffee, sir?"

"Yes, please."

"How about you, sir, would you like more tea?"

"Yes, and a large orange juice."

The waiter scurried away to fetch their drinks.

"I'll tell you what, Tom. I don't see the network surviving this, no matter what. And regardless of what they do, we need to think long and hard about remaining part of it," Maddox said quietly.

"It does seem to be compromised, no doubt about that. And if two hundred blokes find out about it on the street, I must agree with you. It's tainted in more ways than I'm comfortable with," Rose said.

"Have they ever rejected someone after they invited them to apply for membership?" Maddox asked.

"Just three people," Rose said as the waiter arrived with more coffee, tea, and a large glass of orange juice, which Maddox had eyed all the way from the waiter's tray to the table.

"Is that freshly squeezed?" Maddox asked.

"Yes, sir."

"I'll have one too, please."

"Right away, sir," the waiter said, turning to head back toward the kitchen area.

Rose took a sip. "Oh, you're going to like it, tasty. I think they put honey in it."

"We should start with these three. I can imagine being approached to join the network, going through the process like we did, then to get turned down ... that would piss me off.

Not enough to go postal, like this dipshit, but still," Maddox said.

"Well, that happened toward the beginning of the network, they were still honing their process. Anyway, two are dead. One died doing contract work in Iraq in 2004, an IED got him and the other one died a few years ago from a good old fashioned heart attack. And the third one ... well he was rejected seven years ago, I doubt someone would hold a grudge for so long that he would wait to do something this drastic a decade later," Rose said.

The waiter arrived with Maddox's orange juice; he asked how was everything so far. Maddox and Rose said terrific even though they hadn't had a bite of their breakfast yet and off the waiter went.

"We should eat, tastes like shit cold," Rose said, grabbing a fork, and stabbing the yoke of one of his eggs so the yellow gooey goodness flowed into the baked beans like slow-moving lava.

Maddox eyed his plate. It was full. Two fried eggs, two sausage links, baked beans, half a fried tomato, a pad of fried hash browns. He winced at the black pudding.

"I can't eat that shit. Want mine?" Maddox asked Rose, nudging the black pudding with his knife like it was roadkill.

"What about when in Rome?" Rose said, laughing.

"I draw the line at fried blood."

"Hey now, that's a delicacy," Rose said, stabbing Maddox's black pudding with his fork and tossing it onto his own plate.

"Thank you," Maddox said as he went to town on the rest of his breakfast.

They ate in silence for a full minute or so, then Maddox said, "Makes sense about the one who's still living. Why wait this long? Do you have more details on him?"

"He's an American. A former Green Beret. According to Sennight's report, he landed a well-paying, civilian job and lives in California. Doesn't travel much. Unless it's just a legend and he travels under another name for the real work," Rose said.

"Anything is possible, I guess. We'll ask Troy to check him out further. He can sniff this stuff out like one of those truffle digging pigs," Maddox said.

Rose chuckled.

"So that leaves us with another two hundred or so possibilities," Maddox said.

"Bloody hell," Rose said.

"Well, let's check in with Troy to see if he can cook up an algorithm to speed up the process of going through all those names," Maddox said.

"I think the admin is the key. I pressed the chairman on that, but he's not ready to turn on him yet, so maybe Sennight can help us figure out who he is. Then we go right to the fucking source," Rose said.

"I like it. But will the board like that?" Maddox asked.

"No, but if we're right and it is that sod who is causing all this havoc in our lives, I'm sure he's creating plenty of havoc for the board too," Rose said.

"And if he's clean, they'll be able to say, hey, we didn't give you up. Those two went off the reservation and found you on their own. The relationship stays intact," Maddox said.

Rose nodded as he forked the rest of the black pudding into his mouth and said, "Win, win."

FORTY

KENSAL GREEN

London, England, UK

AFTER ONE HOUR AT GATWICK, AXEL COULDN'T TAKE THE boredom anymore, so he grabbed his backpack, shouldered it, and took the Gatwick Express to London Victoria station, a huge railway and London Underground station located in the city of Westminster.

He preferred to be mobile in the field than held up in an airport lobby.

Axel got off the train at the station. It was past the morning rush hour but as usual, Victoria station was bustling with pedestrians. Each one seeming to be in competition with each other as to who was in more of a hurry, and all needed to get to wherever they were going right away.

Since Axel didn't know where he was going, he moved in slow-motion in comparison to his fellow travelers, who seemed annoyed by his casual pace.

Axel walked out of the station. It was a nice day. He tried to breathe it in, but coughed at inhaling fumes from the traffic congestion.

"Fucking big cities," Axel muttered.

He made his way on foot from Victoria Station onto Grosvenor Place, a street that he knew would take him down to Hyde Park.

In a few minutes, Axel was walking down the west side of Buckingham Palace gardens.

He stopped—like any other tourist—and checked out the queen's digs at Buckingham Palace, then walked a bit further and marveled at the Wellington Arch.

Hunger struck him while walking along Piccadilly Street so he lit up in excitement when he saw a McDonald's down the block.

He went inside and ordered a Big Mac with fries, apple pie, and a Coke. He was eating when Mr. White called.

"Safe house is ready. You'll need to take the Gatwick Express," Mr. White said before Axel could stop him.

"Already did. I'm grabbing a bite to eat at the McDonald's on Piccadilly."

"You were supposed to wait at the airport."

"Got bored. What's the difference?"

It didn't really matter, but it annoyed Mr. White that he couldn't get Axel under control.

"Fine. How did you get down to Piccadilly?"

"I walked," Axel replied.

"Okay, good, I'm going to text you the directions to the safe house. Take a cab, but make sure you get off a few blocks from the actual address," Mr. White said.

"Yeah, I know that," Axel said, putting a few fries into his mouth.

"Once you get there, call me back. We have a lot of work to do," Mr. White said, and hung up.

Axel shrugged and finished eating. He then walked down Piccadilly for about a block and hailed a cab.

The cab was tiny. It looked like a black hunchbacked beetle. Axel got inside. The cabbie was an older white guy with a reddish face sporting a thick mane of gray and a bushy mustache that matched the color of his hair.

"Kensal Green Youth and Community Center," Axel said, and the cabbie was off to the races.

Kensal Green was a residential area in the southern boundary of London. Mr. White had texted to have the cab drop him off at the community center.

Twenty-five minutes later, the cab pulled over at the community center. Axel paid the driver and got out. He shouldered his rucksack and walked as if to go inside the center as the cab took off down the street.

Axel stood there for a few seconds until the cab was out of sight before turning away from the building entrance.

He began to walk in the opposite direction from the community center for almost a mile to the safe house.

It was a brick row house with white window trims and a blue door. The key was hidden inside a fake rock that had been placed underneath the shrubbery below the bay window.

Axel retrieved the key and went inside.

The place was small. Axel shrugged off his backpack, went to the bathroom and took a leak. He washed his hands and face. He was tired.

He was alone. He was always alone.

As always in the safe houses Axel used, Mr. White had stashed weapons for him. In this case a firearm, a silencer, and ammunition.

Axel opened the box and smiled at its contents. A Beretta M9 pistol. It was one of the official pistols used in the Army and was the same pistol he'd carried in the Rangers, so he knew it well.

He inspected the firearm. It was nice and clean, Axel could smell the Hoppe's oil.

FORTY-ONE

KILL SWITCH

MADDOX AND ROSE WERE SILENT AND BUSY ON THEIR laptops when Maddox's Sennight phone rang. He picked it up on the second ring and answered by saying, "Talk to me."

"Well, hello to you too," Sennight said.

"Yeah, yeah. Hi. What do you have for me?"

"I have it all, boss. The real IP of the administrator behind the hidden database is located in the Czech Republic, Prague specifically. I have it down to the building, but it's a commercial, office-type building with a lot of different tenants. However, I took a look at the current tenants and one piqued my interest— Cyber One, an internet web hosting company, so I figured they would have tech experts in this type of shit," Sennight said.

Maddox wrote down: *Prague, Cyber One. Internet. Web Host.*

"Excellent, Troy," Maddox said.

"I also got the report from the accountant and I just sent it to you, so you should have it by the time we hang up. Here are the crib notes: someone's been a naughty boy or girl with the network's coffers. Over two million euros siphoned from multiple escrow accounts," Sennight said.

"Shit," Maddox said.

After hanging up with Sennight, Maddox filled in Rose with the details from the call.

"Could the chairman or one of the board members be located in Prague?" Maddox asked.

"They could be anywhere in the world, no one knows," Rose said.

"I know TEN is all into their secrecy and not to be centralized or located in one location, but nowadays with computers, and servers, and even the cloud, everything has to be run out of a computer that's located somewhere. I don't care how good they are at covering their digital tracks, we pull on the cord long enough we'll find its physical location eventually," Maddox said.

Rose thought about it for a moment and said, "This smells like an inside job to me with the admin front and center."

"That is what makes most sense. It's the way of the world nowadays. An Army E3 or a contractor uploading classified documents to WikiLeaks that they should have never had access to begin within."

In the last decade, Maddox had witnessed something he'd never thought possible: former Green Berets, Deltas, SEALS, SAS, and intelligence officers from all branches were cashing in on their service with ghostwritten books, documentaries, and TV shows.

From being an expert guest on CNN, to showing your skills on the Discovery Channel, spilling tradecraft secrets as a consultant for HBO or to video game developers in Silicon Valley, it seemed that in the millennial social media generation, everybody talked.

It must be how the old-school mobsters had felt when

omertà had begun to crack, and its secret member's lips started flapping.

Rose placed a call to the chairman and left a message on the voicemail for Vincent Sinclair from Frank Glover and hung up.

"Okay, he usually gets back to me within ten minutes," Rose explained to Maddox.

Three minutes later the phone rang. Rose let it ring four times as had been prearranged to signal he wasn't under duress.

The greeting exchanged between the chairman and Rose involved a previously agreed passcode to ensure they were free to speak.

"Glover speaking."

"How are you old friend?"

"Mr. Vincent, how are things going for you in Cairo?"

"Splendid."

The charade and confirmation complete, he explained everything to the chairman, who remained silent.

"Hello?" Rose thought the call had dropped.

"I'm still here. You've given me a lot to process," the chairman said.

"I'll ask again," Rose said. "Is the network's administrator located in Prague?"

"Yes."

"And is he the one running the network?"

"Yes."

"Meaning he would have access to the escrow accounts, and the hidden database. All the information and bankroll to provide a contractor to catch us off guard for the kill."

"Yes."

"What is Cyber One?"

The chairman sighed. "I knew you two were the best. Cyber One has two sides. The public facing one is that of a legitimate and respected web hosting company. The private side is a front for TEN that manages the technical aspects of the network."

"And the admin runs that."

"Yes."

"Please tell me you have your own scorched-earth protocol to terminate the network," Rose said.

"We do. But he set it up," the chairman replied.

"Jesus, you put a lot of trust in this administrator," Rose said.

"Hindsight, Foxglove, hindsight."

"Well, now is as good a time as any to find out if it works. Hit that kill switch," Rose said.

FORTY-TWO

FISH AND CHIPS

London, England, UK

AXEL WAS WAITING IN THE SAFE HOUSE FOR MR. WHITE's call. It was the most downtime he'd had in a week. He slept for a few hours. Waking up believing that, as usual, he would have several missed calls and texts from Mr. White, but to his surprise there were none.

He was hungry so he picked up his blue jeans from the floor and smelled them. *Starting to smell funky, but not too bad,* he thought and he put them on. He then chose a new T-shirt that he had bought the day before whilst roaming down Piccadilly Street.

It was a white T-shirt with the Union Jack flag on it like Joe Elliott of Def Leppard wore. He slipped on his olive-green Army jacket and he put on his black Van shoes and headed out the door.

He walked a block through the residential neighborhood until he came upon Harrow Road, which appeared to be a major road with retail shops and places to eat.

He walked down Harrow Road for a couple of blocks to a fish and chips place.

It was a tiny setup that was for take-out only. It wasn't much to look at, but greasy deep-fried fish and fries—or chips as the Brits called them—looked good to him.

Ten minutes later, he was walking back to the safe house carrying a grease-soaked bag with his fish and chips in one hand and a one-liter bottle of Coke in the other.

Back at the house, he laid out the food, and noticed the fish and chips stuffed into a Styrofoam food container and the plastic utensils he had been given.

It's the stuff that drove the environmentalist crazy. Axel laughed.

Big cities back in the United States were banning plastic bags, Styrofoam containers, and politicians even wanted to ban sugary soda drinks while legalizing weed. Sugar is out. Weed is in. Axel didn't like the nanny-state ways of America on both sides of the aisles.

If someone wants to drink a gallon of sugary soda while smoking weed, so be it.

He didn't see much difference in some jerk-off Taliban government official enforcing Sharia law on its citizens and some jerk-off rich Berkeley politician legislating against a citizen's right to drink a soda chock-full of sugar.

"None of that shit matters anyway," Axel said out loud as he grabbed the plastic fork.

He viewed himself as more of a live-in-the-moment type of person. Living in the moment was what made sense to him. He seriously doubted he would grow old in the business he was in.

He didn't have kids and wasn't planning on having any, so he couldn't give two-shits about the environment or the ozone, or sugar, or religion.

Axel scarfed down the fish and chips—going through a thick

wad of napkins to wipe off the grease—and downed half the bottle of soda.

He belched and grabbed a bottle of water. He drank it and turned his attention to the M2010 rifle.

He reverently removed the rifle from the rucksack and assembled it.

It was clean, but a rifle could always use a fresh coat of oil, he thought as he reached for his cleaning kit.

He could clean a weapon with eyes closed. It was like meditation for him.

FORTY-THREE

THE RECRUIT

Czech Republic

Back in Prague, as Danko's bots crawled the digital world on the hunt for Maddox and Rose, he couldn't stop thinking that everything he had worked for could unravel.

He hoped his bots would sniff them out and he hoped that Axel would come through before Foxglove and the Board could strike.

He closed his eyes for a moment then he popped two Ativan pills which he washed down with a bottle of water.

He leaned back in his chair and he closed his eyes.

He waited for the pills to kick in and do their magic as his mind drifted back to when he began his recruitment of Axel hoping he hadn't made a mistake.

Thirteen Months Ago

Danko had done his homework on the solider banned by TEN for contacting a liaison directly to join the network.

On paper, the recruit had looked perfect. And of all the recruits he had considered, Sergeant Brandon Jones, the man who would become Axel, had the background that had impressed him the most.

He had been well trained by the US Army, an Airborne Ranger, and a sniper with plenty of combat experience after three tours in Iraq and one in Afghanistan.

When it came to on-the-ground skills, Jones offered more than enough for Danko to work with for his requirements.

But there were other less tangible skills that Danko needed from his freelancer. And those were skills that weren't easily ascertained from a soldier's DD-214.

Danko had hacked the military's TRICARE website and downloaded Jones's medical and psychological records. Those were the documents that had provided him with the information he needed.

Danko pored over Brandon Jones's records and the portrait of a skilled soldier with a huge chip on his shoulder had emerged. Reading about his candidate's troubled childhood and his difficulty at getting along with others in the Army was ripe for picking a personality trait that would make him easy to manipulate.

After almost two months of background checks and several telephone calls, it had been time for him to meet the recruit in person.

They met at small cafe in the southwest corner of the Žižka Square in Tábor, a quiet town on a hill overlooking the Lužnice River in the South Bohemian Region of the Czech Republic.

It was a sleepy village about ninety kilometers from Prague.

"Thank you for coming all the way to Bohemia, Sergeant. I am Mr. White," Danko said.

Jones looked at him suspiciously but said nothing.

"Please, join me," Danko said, pointing at the empty chair across from him.

There was a small wobbly circular table in between them.

Jones sat and looked around. He had never been to the Czech Republic.

"If you come to work for me, Mr. Jones, you'll need to sever all ties back home. How difficult will that be for you?" Mr. White asked, knowing the answer.

"Not difficult. I left when I was seventeen to join the Army and I haven't been back since," Jones said.

"You indicated you don't have siblings. What about your parents? Are they alive?"

Mr. White also knew the answer to that question as well. He knew Jones's mother was a drunk, living alone in a trailer park in Pennsylvania and the father was out of the picture since his birth.

"My mother is alive. Never knew my father. Mother said he's long dead, but I don't know one way or another, nor do I care."

"You're aware that you will need to disconnect from your mother, friends, any other family members, cousins, aunts. Anyone that might come looking for you, or file a missing person report with the police, or call the Army looking for you. Anyone that might feel inclined to hang up missing flyers with your picture on it. Anything like that. Do you think that might happen?"

Jones laughed at the notion that anyone from his life, including his mother, would care about him to go through all that.

"No. Look, my mother is a drunk. Probably doesn't even remember I was born," he said, his face turning harder. "And no one is coming around looking for me. You don't have to worry about that. I guarantee it."

"Excellent," Mr. White said, then stopped short and looked at him like he'd just spat in the punch. "Didn't mean—"

"I know what you meant," Jones said.

Mr. White cleared his throat and continued, "You'll need a new identity. I'll get you one. Clean. With all the paperwork: driver's license, birth certificate, and social security number. At that time, Brandon Jones will exist no more. Is that clear?"

"Good riddance," Jones said.

Mr. White was quiet for a full minute, and then said, "I know you have the skills, but I need to know that you're capable, willing, and dependable, do the jobs I give. Without question."

"I am. You have my military service records. I believe it speaks for itself," Jones said.

"It's impressive, yes, but I'm afraid, it does not speak for itself. You see there are many candidates that I've talked with, and they all have impressive military records like yours. Some, I might say, even more impressive, with more experience," Mr. White said. "What I need to know is if you're really in, one hundred percent. I need to know that if I give you a contract, I won't have to worry about you doing your job. I need to know that you will carry it out, no questions asked. That's the type of person I'm looking for. That if I ask you to terminate someone, you won't ask me, what he ... or she, did," Mr. White said, putting the emphasis on *she* because there would be men and women to terminate and he had already had to eliminate a prospect with an archaic *no women* moral code.

"There is no room for moralistic thinking in this business. It's a business, and that's all it is," Mr. White said. He leaned forward, "Do you understand what I'm getting at, Sergeant?"

"I do. That won't be a problem with me," Jones said.

"Then prove it to me," Mr. White said, sitting back on the chair.

"How?"

Danko smiled and looked around the coffee shop and out toward the plaza, then leaned in toward Jones.

They were almost face-to-face. So close that it made Jones pull back.

Then Mr. White spoke in an almost whisper, "Your first job. Here Tonight." He tapped on the table with his forefinger when he said tonight.

"Are you serious?" Jones didn't know if it was a bizarre test, or if Mr. White really wanted him to kill someone that night.

Mr. White slid a cell phone over to him. It was a small black flip phone. Unlocked. Prepaid. Untraceable and, for someone that night, deadly.

He picked up the phone and pocketed it without looking at it.

"You will find a calculator application on that phone. Tap it. Enter 9649 in the number field of the calculator, then press on the plus sign. That will reveal a hidden app with the information on tonight's target," Mr. White said.

Jones chewed the inside right cheek of his mouth. His one tell of nervousness that he had been trying to control. He stopped as soon as he noticed he was doing it.

He exhaled a sigh and shifted in his seat. So many questions, but he knew better than to ask about the target, and what they had done to deserve death so he said nothing.

After a moment, Mr. White passed Jones a small locker key.

"There is a public locker across the street by the bus station. That key opens locker number seven. There is a clean pistol in there. A Fort-12 9-millimeter. Untraceable," Mr. White said casually.

Jones took the key.

"When it's done, call me on this number," Mr. White said, giving him a napkin with a phone number written on it in blue ink.

Jones looked down at the key and the napkin but didn't say anything.

"Don't let me down, Sergeant. The fact I am here, meeting you in person, indicates I want you to join my organization. But, I need to know if you're capable of this line of work."

FORTY-FOUR

DO YOU WANT THIS, OR DON'T YOU?

Stoklasná Lhota, Czech Republic

BACK THEN, AXEL WAS STILL BRANDON JONES. HE CROSSED the street and walked to where the locker was located.

He still couldn't be sure that Mr. White was serious.

He kept thinking that perhaps it was all part of an elaborate training op, and that the supposed target worked for Mr. White.

Jones envisioned the three of them sharing a laugh about the successful mock execution that Mr. White had staged to test him.

Jones went to locker number seven. He put the key in and turned it. Jones was surprised that it worked.

He opened the locker door and saw a light-blue string gym bag inside. He didn't open it; he just grabbed it by its white drawstrings, shouldered it, and left.

Back in his hotel, he removed the items from inside the drawstring bag.

Wrapped in a white towel was the Fort-12 pistol Mr. White had told him would be there.

It was a black-framed 9MM handgun. Its handle was

wrapped in duct tape. Also in the bag were two magazines, fully loaded, and a black suppressor.

Jones neatly laid out the items on the bed and he stared at them. He picked up one of the magazines and, with his thumb, forced out one of the cartridges and caught it in midair. He looked at it closely.

It was a 9mm cartridge. Makarov stamped on it. Makarov was a Ukrainian firearms manufacturer, but Jones didn't know that.

He held the cartridge up to the light as if he could see inside to figure out if it was real or fake. He couldn't, but it looked real to him.

The Army used blanks for training, the only way you could tell them apart from real bullets was that the blanks had a red tip painted on. This bullet didn't have any type of color marking on it. That didn't mean it wasn't a blank though, but in his gut Jones believed it was real. Which meant this operation was real. The target was real.

Mr. White wanted him to kill someone in just a few hours.

Jones tapped on the fake calculator app on the phone that Mr. White had given him and entered the passcode, which revealed the hidden app.

He pulled up the target's photograph. A mustachioed man with black hair stared back at him. Also included was an address and the time to carry out the operation.

What was missing from the app was a name, bio, history, habits, or any of the other information he would have assumed would be part of a target's dossier.

Jones looked at the photograph of the nameless man again. He seemed to be in his forties or early fifties. *Just what the fuck did you do?*

Jones had done plenty of killing in Iraq and Afghanistan. As a sniper, he had fifty-seven confirmed kills.

Like most soldiers in the fog of war, he had some kills that were considered borderline, meaning he couldn't be certain if the man killed was a belligerent as recognized by international law. But in combat when you have seconds to decide, you always erred on the side of pulling the trigger. Better wrong but alive.

Since leaving the Army, he had done several freelance jobs in Iraq, Afghanistan, Pakistan, Colombia, and Thailand. But those jobs were tedious babysitting jobs—no wet work.

Just the one incident in Iraq, where he and two other contractors killed four Iraqis that were trying to either kidnap or rob them. They never found out what they'd wanted, but he hadn't had any second thoughts about killing those men. You don't ambush highly-strung, trigger-happy contractors and expect to walk away unscathed. It was a lawless Wild West of sorts during that time.

The local police had wanted Jones and the other contractors arrested, but they all snuck out of the country within hours of the incident. That pretty much shut out Jones from ever returning to lucrative Iraq for work.

This work was different. For all Jones knew, the target could be a terrorist. Or maybe it was just someone Mr. White had a personal beef with. Or maybe it was a poor random sap selected by Mr. White so that Jones could prove his mettle.

Axel thought about it. He wondered if Mr. White had gone that far with the other recruits. If he had, had they refused? Was that man alive because the others refused thus, failing Mr. White's test of commitment?

The question that Jones posed to himself was simple. *Did he have the balls and the moral morass to go through with it.*

Stoklasná Lhota was a small village about five kilometers from Tábor and it was the location of Jones's target. He parked a few blocks away from the target's address and walked. It was late at night and the village seemed to be asleep, right along with its inhabitants.

He walked along a stone wall that led to the house he was looking for. The village seemed quaint to Jones. That would change by morning.

Jones was soon standing in front of the address he had been given. He was looking at a home with white stucco and a red triangle-shaped roof that reminded him of a Swiss chalet.

Last chance, he said to himself. *Either you want to do this type of work, or you don't. What's it going to be?*

He walked toward the front door and looked around. The front door sat back from the road, obscured by shrubbery. Jones listened for a moment. Nothing but crickets, and the sounds of leaves brushing up against each other in the gentle breeze.

Do you want this, or don't you?

He turned the doorknob with his gloved hand and sure enough, as the instructions had indicated, the door was unlocked.

He left the door ajar for a few seconds and he peered inside. *Do you want this, or don't you?*

He removed the loaded Fort-12 pistol from the interior pocket of his black jacket. He then removed the suppressor from his other coat pocket and screwed it onto the barrel. He took a deep breath, then clicked off the safety and, with his free hand, pushed the door open.

Except for the soft hue of a night-light plugged into a wall socket, the home was dark. Jones stepped inside cautiously. For all he knew Mr. White had set up a trap for him. At least that's what his inner voice kept whispering. *What if this is some sting operation run by the Czechs, or perhaps the CIA, or Interpol?*

Jones took a deep breath and ignored those thoughts as he stepped further inside the home, closing the door behind him.

Do you want this, or don't you?

The instructions said to walk to the back room where he would find his target asleep, alone.

Jones did that. He stood outside the bedroom, its door open. He could hear the sounds of someone sleeping. No snores—just heavy breathing.

He looked around the house. It was neat, clean, orderly, and more importantly, empty. So far, the instructions were spot-on.

Jones stood there for a moment. Heavy curtains were drawn shut, and the room was pitch dark. He let his eyes adjust to the darkness for a moment until he could make out a bed and a lump under the covers. He went inside and got closer to the bed. He got close enough that even in the dark, he could see black hair, like in the photograph, sticking out of the covers and a man head's lying on a white pillow, fast asleep.

Do you want this, or don't you?

He crept in closer. The adrenaline was being pumped by his heart, which fueled him forward like gas through a piston.

Do you want this, or don't you?

He took one more step forward, raised the pistol and aimed at the sleeping man. He took another step forward. The floorboard creaked, the body in the bed stirred.

Jones pulled the trigger four times.

FORTY-FIVE
MCKEESPORT

McKeesport, Pennsylvania (Thirteen Months Ago)

MR. WHITE HAD BEEN PLEASED WITH AXEL'S FIRST assignment back in the Czech Republic. The target had been eliminated. Jones never knew who he had killed or why and Mr. White hadn't offered any additional details, only congratulated him on doing the job well and for proving that he was committed to the work.

A week after that he was back in the United States for the final step in joining Mr. White's special organization. He was to erase Brandon Jones from existence. and in order to do that, Jones had to go home one last time.

He hadn't been back to his hometown since he'd enlisted in the Army in 2001.

He flew into Cleveland, Ohio from Europe, even though that airport was 150 miles away from his hometown of McKeesport, Pennsylvania in comparison to the thirty or so miles from Pittsburgh. But he had former classmates that worked as baggage handlers and one for TSA. Even though he was traveling under a throwaway name Mr. White had provided, and he doubted those former classmates would recognize him, he felt uneasy flying into Pittsburgh. He rented a car at Cleveland Hopkins International Airport and drove down to Youngstown, Ohio, where he got a hotel room.

He showered, changed his clothing, and put on one of his fake beards—the fullest beard he had available. It made him look different enough at a glance, but it wouldn't raise suspicions if he were to run into someone he knew that might recognize him. They might say something about his bushy beard, but that would be it.

Jones left his stuff in the hotel and drove for about ninety minutes from Youngstown, Ohio to McKeesport, Pennsylvania.

McKeesport was a town located at the junction of the Monongahela and Youghiogheny Rivers. Like many towns in the county, it had once been a thriving mill town, until the steel-making industry packed up and moved elsewhere, taking tens of thousands of jobs with it.

Jones felt he would have decayed right along with the town if he had stayed. Moving back after his discharge from the Army was never something he had considered.

As a matter of fact, Jones hadn't thought he would ever come back, but this wasn't a homecoming. It was business.

He was coming home because he had chosen his path. It was work he knew he had been born to do. *What else could I do?* Axel would ask himself after leaving the Army.

He knew he couldn't survive in a traditional civilian job— not that they wanted him anyway. Most businesses play a lot of lip service about helping and hiring veterans, but as far as Axel could see, it was just that, lip service. Good PR. But to him, it was a moot point anyway. What else could he do? He had joined the Army at seventeen and it was what he did best. He joined Arminius International and they had provided steady work, but it was boring babysitting executives and journalists. What Mr. White offered is what he longed to do. He now needed to tie up a loose end to Mr. White's satisfaction so Brandon Jones could die and be reborn as Axel Gore.

Kilgore was a bit much, Mr. White had said.

The one loose end was Michelle Jones. His mother.

It seemed to Jones that nothing had changed in his mother's life.

She was still living the same shitty life she had always lived since he could remember.

Jones watched her for a while through binoculars. He wasn't sure what he would feel when he saw her again. He wasn't surprised that it wasn't a feeling of happiness or love. She seemed to have aged twenty years in the nine years since he'd last seen her.

It's amazing she's still alive, Jones mused as he watched her stumble out of her trailer. Squinting and turning away from the sun. She sat on her front step and drank from a cup. Axel figured the odds were about even whether or not she was having a morning cup of coffee, or the first of many cups of cheap vodka that got her through the day.

She went back inside. Jones sat in his rented car for another hour before breathing in heavily and getting out.

He walked up to her trailer and knocked on the cheap painted laminated veneer door. The door rattled as he knocked. He could hear faint noises from inside, but she wasn't coming to the door.

It was a vivid memory of his childhood—hiding from bill collectors, process servers, and lovers, with dear old mom telling little Brandon to be quiet as the knocking on the door became louder.

After about a minute of knocking, he shouted through the door, "Ma, it's me, Brandon, open up."

He heard her say his name then a loud crashing sound. He shook his head envisioning her stumbling drunkenly across the trailer to open the door.

"Brandon," she said again, opening the door. She hugged him and pulled him inside the trailer.

They sat on a ratty couch. She cooed about missing him and how great it was to see him again, the stench of cheap booze and stale cigarettes strong on her breath. She fussed over his beard and pulled at it, causing Jones to worry that she would yank the fake beard right off his face. He pulled away and looked around.

As usual, his mother lived in a pigsty of soiled clothing on the floor, cigarette butts, empty pizza boxes, dirty plates, and every nook and cranny stuffed with clutter. Jones saw the small glass pipe on the table.

Well, that's new, he thought.

"Jesus, Mom, meth?"

"Don't start with me, Brandon. I don't do it all the time. Do you have any money for your mother?"

Sometimes, in order to build something new, something old must be destroyed, Jones thought as he looked at his mother.

She had aged well beyond her forty-six years. He assumed she had the liver and lungs of an eighty-year-old on a steady diet of cigarettes and Skid Row vodka.

Time to erase Brandon Jones. I'd be doing her a favor. It's what you would do to a rabid dog. You put it down.

"Sure, I can give you some money." He smiled at his mother.

At three that morning, an explosion shook the entire trailer park from its deep sleep.

Firefighters arrived within ten minutes to a trailer that was engulfed in flames.

There was little that they could do but watch Michelle Jones's trailer burn into a molting heap of metal and plastic.

By the time it was safe enough for the firefighters to enter and sift through the debris, where they discovered the remains of Michele Jones, Brandon was sitting at the main terminal of Cleveland Hopkins International Airport, knowing he would never go back to McKeesport. Brandon Jones died in that fire with his mother. Axel Gore was born.

FORTY-SIX

PLACEBO

Prague, Czech Republic

Danko looked at the text message. It was the code that he knew would be coming, but he had hoped he would have more time before having to deal with it. He stared at the message from his partner: 999.

The board had voted no confidence in Danko and they were going to delete the network without him.

The plan was now being shoved into hyperdrive.

The way to shut down the network remotely was by using a special code that only the chairman had access to. It was a kill switch that he had insisted be put in place right from the start of TEN.

It made sense to him that the chairman would want something set up to delete the network in an emergency.

He remembered the chairman stating his case. "What would happen if there is a breach, and we can't get a hold of you or God forbid, you're dead. We must have an emergency contingency plan in place to be able to erase the network from existence without you."

But even back then, when the idea to double-cross the board hadn't even entered his mind, he'd known he wasn't going to give up control of his network. Danko had carved the network out of a single server. Coded from scratch, by hand.

There was no way he would ever turn over his creation to a cadre of diluted old geezers that before him, viewed the fax machine as cutting edge technology.

He had given the board a placebo.

When the chairman initiated the command line to delete the network as instructed by Danko, the board would get a dog and pony show that would make it look as if the network was being deleted. What would actually happen was a digital lockdown.

A hard encryption of the entire system and only he had the de-encryption code.

Danko snickered at the thought of the old fucks thinking that he would have given them the power to delete the network. All they had done was turn it into a brick. Not even a dedicated team of CIA technologists would be able to access it.

Danko knew the board would send someone to delete *him* from existence. That made him nervous, so he reached for the cell phone that he used to only communicate with Axel and punched the number to call him.

Axel was holed up in the London safe house waiting for the next move from Mr. White. He was bored so he had cleaned his already clean rifle. After killing time with that, he had plopped down on the floor with his laptop and was playing Call of Duty when Mr. White called.

"Axel, we have another problem. A problem that affects us both gravely," Mr. White said.

Axel couldn't help but notice that the usually centered Mr. White sounded frazzled. There was always a cowardly lion vibe Axel got from Mr. White. He tried to hide it with his arrogance and condescension. But he always spoke with Axel in a calm and reserved manner. It was the first time that Axel picked up on fear in Mr. White's voice.

"What is it?" Axel asked.

"It's the board. They know I'm involved in this, and that doesn't bode well for us."

"How do you know that?"

"I have my ways."

"Cut the shit, Mr. White. If my ass is on the line here and I'm the one who's going to have to do something about this in the field, then I need more information. If not, fuck this, I'll vanish and you can deal with the mess you've cooked up all on your own," Axel said. He felt good about it, too. It was the first time he had spoken that way to Mr. White.

Danko was quiet for a moment, weighing his options. Axel waited. He knew that the calculating prick was doing just that, calculating the benefits of giving in to Axel's demands.

Mr. White thought it over. He viewed Axel as a simpleton. A tool. Like a hammer in his toolbox. An inanimate object laying there until he needed to pound in a nail.

He was going to need more enemies neutralized if he was going to make it out of the situation unscathed. He was going to need the hammer that was mouthing off to him, Danko understood the shift.

At that moment, he needed Axel a lot more than Axel needed him.

It bothered Danko that the upper hand had tipped to Axel's favor. He would rectify that later, he thought, so what was the big deal?

So Danko, as Mr. White, told Axel about the kill switch that had been activated.

That the board wanted to burn down the network without consulting him meant he was out of the power loop, which meant they didn't trust him and soon they would send someone to terminate his employment with a bullet between his eyes.

Danko didn't tell him that he had been working with someone else all along and that they had warned him with the 999-text message. That, he didn't need to know.

"How do you go from that to they're going to kill you?" Axel asked.

"Why else would they try to permanently delete the network and not ask me to do it? The kill switch was for emergency purposes only. To be used if I was somehow incapacitated, or if I was dead. But here I am. If they still trusted me, they would have called me to do this. Instead, they bypass me and hit the switch. They're already acting as if I'm dead," he explained.

"The network ... it's really been deleted?" Axel asked.

"Of course not," Mr. White said. "But that doesn't change what the board thinks is happening and what they are planning to do to me."

"Okay, what's the plan, then?" Axel asked.

"Ideally, we would wipe out the entire board, but they're too smart for that. The members are located in different parts of the world. We take out the head."

FORTY-SEVEN

ACROSS THE MEZZANINE

London, England

AXEL PUT ON A BLACK WIG GIVING HIM EMO HAIR. HE WAS clean shaven and looked very different from the goateed base-ball hat-wearing disguise he had donned during the failed hit in Brussels. Happy with his appearance, he changed into darker colors. He couldn't go out into London in BDUs and a bala-clava, so he put on black jeans, a black dry-fit Under Armor running shirt, and a black long-sleeve jacket.

Dressed, he grabbed the rucksack and tossed in a pair of black running gloves and a knit cap. He then broke down the M2010 rifle and placed its parts into a hard carrying case. He tossed in the suppressor and four boxes of cartridges. Once packed, Axel grabbed the pistol. It was loaded. He checked to make sure the safety was on the Beretta and pocketed it in his jacket.

About twenty-five minutes after Mr. White's call, Axel left the safe house and was walking down to Harrow Street. From there, he took the bus to Oxford Circus. From there, it was a quick walk to Grosvenor Square, where Maddox and Rose were staying.

Axel arrived at his destination thirty minutes later.

The difference between the Grosvenor Square and Kensal Green neighborhoods was palpable. Tourists and the London well-to-do walked Grosvenor Square whereas the working class walked Kensal Green.

Mr. White was clear about not holding back on the hit again. Foxglove was the priority kill so even if Maddox and Rose pulled the splitting up trick like they had done in Brussels, it didn't matter. Axel would take the shot and terminate Foxglove.

Axel was nervous and excited. He had thought, more than once, how this job would be his masterpiece hit.

Foxglove was the board's go-to contractor, in Axel's head, he must be the best. And Maddox was with Foxglove, he must be just as good. Not only were Axel's targets the best of TEN; he had to kill them in a crowded luxury hotel in bustling London.

The logistics were daunting. The hotel was on a busy street with a public park directly in front of it, and a mostly residential area behind it.

The rooftop areas didn't offer the privacy and space Axel needed to set up a sniper's nest. And the park in front of the hotel was wide-open on a busy street. He couldn't just lie out there in the prone position with a rifle. Just about any scenario would have the police there in minutes. He needed to set up a shot from a room in one of the buildings across from the hotel where Rose was staying.

It was the move that made the most sense. Axel had already studied the location on Google Maps and on Google Earth and the best top candidate was the building right across from the hotel.

It was also part of the hotel, the bottom part used for events like weddings and conferences, and the top floors were more rooms for hotel guests. The two buildings were interconnected with the space between them being a mezzanine.

After a quick study, Axel picked three rooms that would be ideal for the shot.

He texted them to Mr. White. Thirty minutes later, Mr. White texted him back with the ideal room number: 712.

A businessman from Japan was staying there. He was traveling alone, had checked in the previous day, and had the room for two more days and most importantly, room 712 had a direct view into Rose's hotel room across the Mezzanine.

Axel made his way into the building via the staff entrance. If anyone challenged him he would play it off as if he were a lost American tourist. He made it inside and into the stairwell unchallenged.

Once inside the staircase, Axel breathed out deeply. He then took a moment to collect himself before heading up the stairs.

In a few minutes he was standing outside Room 712. He knocked and said, with authority, "Hotel security."

The businessman opened the door and looked at Axel cautiously.

"Sorry to disturb you, Mr. Ogawa," Axel said.

Referring to the businessman by name had the desired effect. The man's body language changed to relaxed, and he opened the door all the way.

"Yes, what is it?" he asked in well-spoken English.

Axel didn't say anything. He pushed his way inside as the startled man tried to shove the door closed, but Axel punched him once in the throat. It was a quick and hard punch that caused the man's body to go limp like a deflated balloon as he gasped for air. Axel gave the man another push into the room as he backed up with hands around his throat, trying to breathe.

Axel followed him inside, drawing out his knife. He sank

the blade into the man's stomach as the door slowly closed behind them.

Axel carried the dying man's body into the shower and tossed him in it. He then slit his throat. He grabbed a couple white towels from the rack and laid one over the dead man's head and the other one over the body, and then he closed the glass shower door.

Axel shrugged off the feeling of having killed an innocent civilian who just happened to have the bad luck of getting booked into a room he needed. He didn't want it to bother him, but it did. He figured those feelings would pass with more experience. As Mr. White had told him, *the more of these hits you did, the easier it got.*

He viewed it as collateral damage, which was something he had become very familiar with during the wars of Iraq and Afghanistan.

Axel washed the blood from his blade and his hands in the bathroom sink, then went back to the room. He cranked up the air conditioner as high as it would go since the chemical changes to warm-blooded animals start soon after death.

Next up he put the "Do Not Disturb" sign on the door hanger and looked both ways down the corridor. There was no one there.

He closed the door, turned the deadbolt over and engaged the door-jammer securing him inside. He then walked over to the window and peeled back the curtain across the mezzanine. He could see the windows of the hotel rooms. It took him a minute to locate Foxglove's room.

Axel removed the hard black case from his backpack and tossed it on the unmade bed. He unlocked it, flipped the cover open, and began to assemble the rifle.

FORTY-EIGHT

MR. OGAWA'S ROOM

London England

WHILE AXEL WAS PREPARING FOR THE SHOT FROM INSIDE Mr. Ogawa's room, Danko, from the comfort and safety of his Prague office, was inside the hotel's reservation management software, where he could monitor the keycard swipes associated with Rose and Maddox's rooms.

He didn't have visual confirmation, so he couldn't see that it was Rose swiping in and out; but he could tell if it was someone keying with a guest card or a master card. Danko would know if it was housecleaning or any other hotel staff. But wished he could set up a camera for visual confirmation, that way he would know with certainty that it was Rose, unfortunately that was a luxury he didn't have.

After forty minutes of staring at the monitor screen, the system signaled that someone was using the guest card to enter Rose's room. Danko set a text message to Axel.

After receiving Mr. White's text, Axel took position. He looked through the scope and he bit the inside of his mouth. Rose's curtains were drawn. It was those thick hotel room curtains designed to block daylight from disturbing the precious guests. An extra complication he didn't need.

Axel texted Mr. White.

Axel: *Curtains drawn. No view inside*
Mr. White: *Lucky coincidence or planned*
Axel: *not a mind reader*
Mr. White: *figure it out. Must happen now!*
Axel: *I'll figure it out*

Axel's eyes scanned his room and he went back to the telephone on the writing desk that was next to the window.

He had never stayed at this hotel before, but he knew that hotel room layouts were usually the same unless you had a penthouse or something like that. But Mr. Ogawa's room was the same type of room as Rose's room. If Mr. Ogawa had a desk with a phone next to the window, he figured the odds were in Axel's favor that Rose also had a writing desk with a telephone on it right next to his window.

Axel walked toward the desk and looked around. *It could work*, he thought.

The hotel room had two other phones.

There was one by the bed and another one in the bathroom. Why anyone would need a landline in the shitter was beyond Axel.

He thought it through.

If Rose is as cautious as Mr. White said, he'd take the call on one of the other phones and stay away from the window.

But in Axel's experience, his targets at the other side of the script usually made simple, brief mistakes. A momentary lapse in judgment of just seconds that would leave them exposed and that's all he would need to make his shot.

"It might work," he said out loud.

Axel walked to the window and inspected it. The window did not open all the way. "Another complication," he muttered. He undid the latch and the only option was to pull it toward the inside so only half the window could be opened, halfway and at a slant. He couldn't position the rifle from that angle so that wouldn't work.

Axel placed the palm of his hand on the inside and outside part of the window, feeling the glass. He knocked on it with his index knuckle like he was knocking on a door. It was thick glass to protect the guests from the city noises, but it shouldn't be a problem. He closed the window and locked the latch.

Axel went to the bathroom. He glanced over the red-soaked white towels covering Mr. Ogawa.

He grabbed a hand towel and put it under running water in the sink.

He then reached into his backpack and pulled out a nylon roll bag. He placed it on the bed and pulled on the strap. The sound Velcro made was louder than he remembered and rolled it open.

Inside were various pockets with knives, burglar tools, lock picks and what he was looking for: a thick glass circle cutter with a suction cup attached and a tin container of oil.

He wasn't worried about the measurement. He just needed a hole big enough for the barrel of the rife. He set up the suction cup for a 10" diameter cut.

Axel laid out an oil trail and scored the glass. The tool went through the glass like butter and he broke away the piece he was cutting out—he did this carefully and slowly, pulling the piece of glass he was removing toward him. If it were to fall below he would have to abort. Slowly, he pulled the cut glass inside until he was able to secure it by hand. He tossed it on the floor. Then he cleaned off the glass dust from the rest of the window with the towel.

In just a few minutes, he had made a hole big enough to fit the barrel of the rifle.

He maneuvered the rifle through the opening in order to test it and he smiled. *This works.*

From the sitting position, he would be able to make the shot. Axel texted Mr. White.

Mission on

As they had planned, the next stage was for Mr. White to confirm that Rose was in his hotel room so Axel could get into shooting position. When ready, Axel would alert Mr. White via another text message so Mr. White could call Rose's room via the room's landline telephone.

The odds of a success were mostly up to chance and luck. If Rose took the call on the bathroom phone instead of the phone on the desk by the window—or if he ignored the call—the mission would fail. If Axel could get Rose to that window he had a chance of killing him.

It was time to get into position for real. Axel took the rifle and carefully positioned the thin barrel out of the window, through the hole he had cut in the glass. He then sat on his butt and contorted his legs into a sitting position as he had been trained in Sniper School. It was a tricky position and not one he had used often in the real world, but he was able to cross his legs and angle his body toward the target window.

He moved the rifle's sling around until he had just the right amount of tension to make the shot. Once in position, he slightly rested his elbows over his knees. He aimed and waited.

London, England

Rose was in his room with the television on for white noise. He was meeting Maddox in ten minutes by the elevator. Rose was making their travel arrangements for the morning.

He was sitting on the edge of the bed with the laptop laying flat on the mattress when the room phone rang. He was facing the desk so all he had to do was look up and could see the phone light flashing as the phone rang loudly. It had actually startled him since all their communication had been done through drop phones and SIM cards. Only Maddox knew his room number so he texted him.

You calling me on hotel landline? ph ringing now.

Maddox texted him back:

NO. Be right there.

The phone kept ringing so Rose got up from the bed and picked up the receiver.

"Hello?"

Maddox entered Rose's room. He saw Rose standing by the window on the phone.

ACROSS THE MEZZANINE from Rose's room, Axel waited. He had propped the cell phone against the wall below the window so he could just glance at the phone's screen without disengaging the target. After a few minutes of holding the shooting position, he felt his body ache, but he had trained to ignore a foot that fell asleep, a cramp in the muscle calf, or a flared up back. Axel would not move until he could take a shot.

Even when his cell phone vibrated, Axel stayed in position as he glanced down at the text message from Mr. White in all caps:

ON PHONE NOW

That was Mr. White letting him know he had called Rose's room and someone—Axel hoped it was his target—had answered. Axel was now staring down the scope of his rifle. He could see the curtain, still drawn shut. Then the curtain moved —barely. It was subtle, like a soft breeze or perhaps a light brush from a forearm or elbow as the person one hundred meters away had picked up the phone.

Axel stared down the powerful scope of the rife for what felt was hours but was mere seconds when he picked out a shadow behind the curtain. He held his breath and squeezed the trigger.

Still holding his breath, he slowly squeezed the trigger a second time.

Maddox walked into Rose's room and he heard two thuds.

It wasn't very loud. Like the sound of a bird hitting the window.

Then Maddox heard a muffled sound of the thick glass cracking and the sound of a round whizzing inside.

"Sniper! Get down, get down!" Maddox yelled, but it was too late.

Rose's body twisted to one side as the bullet tore into it. His right leg went up instinctively like it could somehow deflect the bullet.

The telephone receiver dropped onto the desk hard and bounced like it was made of rubber, as chunks of plastic from the broken phone flew through the air.

Rose grunted and dove forward toward Maddox like a running back trying to stretch his body across the end zone for a touchdown as a second bullet found a home in the back of Rose's leg.

He tumbled onto the floor at Maddox's feet.

The rapport of the shot sounded like a laser to Maddox, who grabbed Rose by his wrist and pulled with all his strength as a third shot exploded into the room, hitting Rose on the foot.

A fourth shot proved too much for the thick glass of the window as it shattered into what seemed a million little crystal pebbles that rained into the room.

The fourth shot tore into the carpet, where Rose had been lying a second before Maddox had dragged him away and into the bathroom.

Then it was over. Silence.

It wasn't the first time Maddox had been at the receiving end of gunfire, but he still found the immediate silence that followed surreal.

He knew the silence meant the attack was over. Standard operating procedure would have the sniper quickly breaking down his equipment to get out of the danger zone as fast as possible.

Maddox was sitting with his back to the bathroom wall. It took him a moment to regain his bearings and realize he was holding Rose in his arms.

He looked down at his friend's body lying on top of his legs. There was blood everywhere and all Maddox could think of in that moment was the painting of Mary holding Jesus after the crucifixion.

Maddox then noticed bloody drag marks on the marble floor he too was covered in Rose's blood. He was afraid to look down when he heard Rose say, "Bloody hell."

Maddox looked down and said, "You're alive."

Rose grunted, "You sound surprised."

Maddox smiled and he laid out Rose flat on the cool floor. He lifted Rose's shirt and saw the wound on the right side of Rose's torso, blood gushing out. Maddox grabbed one of the white towels and placed it on Rose's wound. He applied pressure, which caused Rose to grunt louder. Maddox could see his body tense like it had a current of electricity flowing through it.

Maddox glanced at the leg wound—it wasn't bleeding as profusely so he was relieved that it appeared the bullet hadn't severed any arteries. The foot wound seemed like a nick—the least important one to worry about. The shot in the torso was his main concern because of the amount of blood, so he applied more pressure and hoped the bullet hadn't torn into any vital organs.

Maddox provided Rose with an assessment.

"He got you three times, side of the torso, almost to your back, lots of blood, but it's not thick so I don't think he got anything too important, buddy. And the leg wound seems like the bullet went in and out and the foot was just graze."

"Yay," Rose said sarcastically. He wheezed with each breath and every word. "I can't breathe, think I have broken ribs."

"Well, shit partner, if that's it, you're in the clear," Maddox said, trying to sound positive.

Maddox knew the shots were fired by a rifle with a suppressor, but those still made noise, and he and Rose had made plenty of noise dodging bullets, plus the window shattering. He figured help was on the way.

Sirens in the distance soon confirmed that.

Still, Maddox thought he better make sure.

"Can you apply pressure to your wound? I need to call for help," Maddox asked.

Rose nodded.

Maddox got up and saw his clothes and hands were bloody. He picked up the phone and began to dial 911 and stopped. "What's your 911?"

Rose laughed then wheezed in pain. "999, you Yank."

FIFTY

BAKERLOO

London, England

THE WHOLE ATTACK HAD TAKEN LESS THAN A MINUTE. Analysis and confirmation would have to come later. He had to get out. He wasn't about to be confronted inside the hotel room with a dead body in the shower.

Axel picked up his spent shells and shoved them in his backpack, then he quickly broke down his rifle and stowed it in its case.

He put the glass cutter and oil tin back into their corresponding pockets, rolled the carry bag shut and secured it tight with the Velcro.

He tossed the hard case and the rolled-up bag into his backpack. He undressed down to his underwear and removed a change of clothing from the backpack.

The room was freezing since the air conditioning was blasting, on its coldest setting, yet he was drenched in sweat.

He removed the wig and wiped his face, bald head, and armpits with the black T-shirt he had been wearing and tossed it and the rest of his discarded clothing and wig into the backpack.

Then he changed into a yellow Polo Shirt and tan slacks. He slipped on a light jacket. He patted to feel the Glock in the small of his back. He looked in the mirror and the transformation from emo to preppy was complete.

He shrugged on his backpack and slowly opened the door. He stuck his head out; the corridor was clear, so he left.

As he walked down the corridor—fighting the urge to run like hell—he removed his gloves and shoved them into a side pocket of his jacket. He took the elevator down to the lobby. It would be less suspicious than going down the stairs.

There were guests and hotel staff with worried looks on their faces. He asked what was going on; they said they didn't know but that something had happened in the adjacent building of the hotel.

Axel heard someone say nervously that they hoped it wasn't a "terrorist thing".

Axel could hear the sirens announcing the arrival of the cavalry.

He never got used to the weird sounding European sirens—they sounded like someone had stepped on a cat's tail. American sirens had a more menacing wail to them.

Dirty Harry versus Hercule Poirot.

He was worried about a lockdown, but Axel casually walked outside.

He quickly looked to his right, toward the building he had just fired upon and saw a bevy of police cars, ambulances, and firefighter trucks parking in front of the hotel and blocking the busy street.

The traffic was already jammed deep in both directions of the A4202 Park Lane road. Axel had already mapped his escape route, but he had to ensure he didn't make it seem like he was trying to escape anything, just another American tourist in London.

Axel turned away from the hotel, walked down Park Lane Road for about a minute, then turned left at the first chance he could, which was down Mount Street. He kept walking getting farther and farther from the hotel.

He could hear the sirens as he made his way down the street, but the commotion became fainter with each step he took.

He walked down Berkley Square Gardens Road and maneuvered his way on foot parallel to the park.

He cut through a couple of side streets until finally, about ten minutes later, he reached his destination—Green Park Underground Tube Station.

Axel walked down the stairs into the station and found that underground commuters were oblivious to any possible danger or police activity above ground.

They were just going about their business, getting on and off the tube going to-and-fro wherever they were going.

Axel made his way through the underground maze of white and blue tile walls until making it to the Jubilee Line, where he stood on the platform, his heart pounding.

He had to wait a few minutes for the next subway to arrive. He took that to Baker Street Underground Station, where he transferred onto the Bakerloo Line until, finally, he arrived at Kensal Green Underground Station about forty-five minutes after leaving the hotel.

The neighborhood was quiet, clueless to what had gone down in Grosvenor Square.

As he backtracked to the safe house, Axel mentally replayed the operation.

As usual with those missions, he felt detached. As if he were just an observer watching someone else pull the trigger.

He'd gotten off four shots. He knew two were hits. The other two were probably misses. The third shot would have been the money shot. But only if Rose lay where he fell. Since he didn't have visual confirmation, he couldn't know if the mission had succeeded or failed.

It was a poor setup. One he would not have undertaken had it not been for Mr. White's insistence.

The drawn curtains acting as a blindfold, the thick glass of the window would slow down the force of the bullet, or even cause it veer off. And the distance compounded the difficulty of the shot.

Axel's phone vibrated, pulling him from his thoughts.

A text message from Mr. White, who had been on the other end of that call to Rose during the hit.

Heard 2 voices after shot. Mission failed.

Axel knew that Rose would hit the deck, even if he hadn't been hit.

Crawling under the bed was always a good choice, but he had noticed the bed frame in his hotel room sat on the floor like a big box. He wouldn't have had the option to crawl under the bed.

He figured Rose would have gone for the door or the bathroom. The path to either of those options from the window were the same so Axel had aimed toward that space on the floor between the desk and the front door assuming Rose would crawl through there, and fired twice.

They were blind shots, but it was worth the chance that he would hit the target as he dragged himself across the floor.

But if Mr. White heard two voices that meant Rose would have had help getting cover and getting first aid. "Goddammit," Axel said out loud to himself.

From the station, it was less than a ten-minute walk. But it would take him a bit longer since he planned to stop at the fish and chips takeout place first. This type of work always left him famished.

Back in the safe house, he could finally breathe and decompress. He dropped his backpack on the floor. He felt lighter and not just from ditching the backpack. Axel tossed his greasy bag of fish and chips on the kitchen table and laid down on the floor for a full minute, recovering. He sat up, stayed sitting with his knees up for another minute. Then he got up and unpacked his gear.

He placed the rifle case and the rolled up bag with his miscellaneous tools in the hidden compartment behind the refrigerator.

He kept the pistol and his favorite knife nearby. He removed the clothing and gloves he had worn, grabbed some lighter fluid from the BBQ pit out back, and burned the clothing in the stainless steel kitchen sink. Then he let the water wash down what was left down the garbage disposal and hit the switch, letting cold water wash over it for about a minute. He opened the windows to air out the place.

Axel took a hot shower. Then changed into his favorite, most comfortable basketball shorts and a well-worn Metallica T-shirt.

He grabbed the pistol and the bag of food from the kitchen table. He plopped down on the couch in front of the TV like he had just gotten back from a long day at work—which he had—and ate his fish and chips as he went from one channel to the next, looking for the news.

FIFTY-ONE

TOUGH CROWD

London, England

Tom Rose was admitted to Royal London Hospital in the east of London. The trauma unit was waiting for him and within fifteen minutes, the team was performing an emergency thoracotomy to determine if the bullet he had taken to the torso had hit any vital organs.

The two police constables took Maddox down to a holding room in the hospital for the Metropolitan Police Service.

Maddox had asked if he could change clothes, but the police hadn't allowed it so he was still wearing his clothing with Rose's blood now caked on it.

"Wait here," one of the constables said as he closed the door. Maddox wasn't cuffed and it didn't sound like the cop had locked the door, so he figured those were good signs that they weren't arresting him.

A few minutes later, another uniformed police officer entered. He had three chevrons pointing down on his uniform. Maddox knew the layout varied from country to country, but three chevrons usually meant the wearer was a sergeant. That was confirmed when the police officer introduced himself as Sergeant Rogers with the Metropolitan Police. He was in his thirties. Black hair and eyes. Dark skinned.

"How's Tom doing?" Maddox asked.

"Two inspectors from CID are on their way. They want to talk to you, so you'll need to wait here," Sergeant Rogers said without providing the update. Rogers walked out, and closed the door behind him before Maddox could say anything else.

Maddox knew enough about the British police system to know that CID stood for Criminal Investigation Department and that was the department to which plain-clothes detectives belonged—the equivalent to an American detective.

Maddox sat in the room alone for ten minutes until finally the door opened and a parade of plainclothes cops walked in. Maddox was taken aback by it all.

"We're going to need a bigger room," Maddox said with a grin, but none of the others smiled.

The man who appeared to be in charge wore a gray suit and introduced himself as Chief Superintendent Walker with the Special Branch. He handled all the introductions. Chief Inspector Harrison with the Anti-Terrorist Branch, a doughy and balding man of about fifty, and two agents with MI5, the British version of the FBI.

One agent was female the other male; they were introduced as agents Robins and Haro, but it wasn't clear who was who, and Maddox figured it didn't really matter since Harrison would probably be doing most of the talking.

No first names were provided. Chief Inspector Harrison was about six feet tall, white with graying hair and mustache.

Maddox looked around the room. There were two uniformed policemen standing by the door. "Stuck with guard duty, huh?" Maddox said with a grin. They didn't acknowledge him, nor were they important enough to warrant an introduction by Chief Superintendent Walker.

Maddox turned his attention to the stoic faces gathered around the table. They were all looking at him.

"Well." Maddox stopped to crack his knuckles, producing a loud popping sound. The release of air bubbles from his joints felt good. "I hope there won't be a name test later, because I won't remember who's who and which agency you're with," he said with a smile. Again, no one smiled back.

Tough crowd.

Everyone seemed on edge, which of course they were. It made sense to Maddox. It was a normal reaction when you're covered in the blood of a former SAS soldier and MI6 agent who is undergoing emergency surgery after being shot by an unknown sniper. They weren't in Syria, sniper fire isn't supposed to happen in London.

By the looks on everyone's face Maddox deduced the sniper had gotten away.

"Look," Maddox said, putting both hands on the table, "I'm happy to provide any information that will help catch whoever shot Tom. But I'm afraid I don't know much," he wasn't going to give them any information about TEN or who he thought was behind the hit. *He* would be taking care of that business, not the police or MI5 or MI6. He handled his own business and he knew Rose would feel the same way. But he had to appear to play ball until they cut him loose.

Maddox figured they could not hold him long. It was obvious he wasn't the shooter. And he was the one who had saved Rose's life by dragging him into the bathroom. He was the one that called the authorities. Sure, he had done that because Rose needed medical care but that was a horse apiece, as far as Maddox was concerned.

No one said anything for a moment, then there was a knock

on the door. One of the uniformed cops opened it, and a man in a suit walked in.

"Sorry, I'm late," the man said with an American accent.

Chief Superintendent Walker turned around and looked at him. He seemed annoyed by the tardiness. It amused Maddox how punctuality seemed to be etched into British DNA.

"We didn't want to start until you were present," Walker said to the late arrival, then, turning his attention to Maddox he said, "This is Mr. Dale Shaw with the American Embassy. He's here as a courtesy." Walker glanced over at Shaw as if to remind him of that part.

Maddox didn't know much about British accents, but he could tell the difference from a working class and upper crust accent. He had Walker pegged for working class so he decided he must be okay.

Dale Shaw, on the other hand, reeked of Ivy League. Maddox looked him over. He was thin and was in his forties. Light skinned, white with brown hair and eyes. Clean-cut. He wore a bland bureaucrat's suit, off-the-rack, Men's Warehouse, if Maddox had to put a wager on it.

One glance and Maddox knew Shaw wasn't with the Department of State. He might as well have CIA stamped on his forehead.

Dale Shaw noticed that Maddox was assessing him and smiled sheepishly, "Hello, Mr. Maddox. I'm a Consular Officer with the embassy, and we like to be present when US Citizens are interviewed, especially concerning something like this," Shaw said, pulling a chair and sitting to the right of Walker.

Maddox and Shaw exchanged furtive smiles.

"Okay, let's get this over with," Maddox said.

"What are you doing in London?" Walker asked.

"Business," Maddox replied.

"What kind of business?"

"Tom Rose and I work together as security consultants."

"What kind of security?" Walker asked.

"Risk management."

"Risk management?" Walker seemed confused.

"I'm sure you've already checked our backgrounds. You know we're former military, intelligence officers, and we're now in the private sector. Risk management is our bread-and-butter. We assist companies, mostly from the US and the UK, that are doing business abroad, in some dangerous places. We help them mitigate risks to their executives, staff, property, and products. You know, so that their employees aren't kidnapped for ransom or that pirates in the Horn of Africa don't hijack their cargo. That type of work," Maddox said.

"Which countries?" Walker asked.

"Well, you'll get the picture by looking at my passport, which I'm sure you've already looked over. Check out the stamps," Maddox said.

"Indulge me," Walker was curt.

"Okay. The usual suspects: Iraq, Afghanistan, Pakistan, Venezuela, Colombia, Russia, Ukraine," Maddox rattled them off quickly.

The male MI5 agent and the antiterrorism police inspector took notes while the others listened.

Dale Shaw sat with his arms crossed. His expression that of a psychiatrist that was listening to a patient drone on about his childhood fears and judgmental mother.

"Those are dangerous places," Walker said, clearing his throat. "What were you doing in London?"

"Tom—Mr. Rose—he's based here. We meet a few times a year to discuss strategy, possible clients to target. We split the visits; I come here, he goes to the States," Maddox said.

"And you live in Florida, correct?"

"I do. Have you ever been there?"

Maddox's question annoyed Walker.

"Do I look like a sand and sun type?" he snapped.

Maddox pondered the question for a moment. "Now that you mention it. No, you do not."

He finally made one of the agents and the two guards crack a smile. Just for a second or two.

"Now that we've cleared such important matters, let me continue my line of questioning," Walker said.

"Shoot."

"I beg your pardon?"

"It's an expression for *go ahead*. I guess with what happened to Tom it's not the best choice or words," Maddox explained, looking for someone to agree but everyone was stone-faced.

Walker ignored Maddox and went on.

"What type of clients do you have?"

"Not the kind to sic a well-trained sniper to kill one of us. That's more government type work, don't you think, Dale?"

Walker's white cheeks blushed red. But he didn't acknowledge it. Shaw smirked.

"Just answer the question, please."

"Sure. Let's see ... we have clients in various industries, but mostly shipping, logistics types, oil companies pay well, journalists BBC, CNN, Fox," Maddox said.

"Companies from the UK and America?"

"That's why we make a good team. I leverage my contacts in America and Tom does the same across the pond. Well, I guess it's reversed now, isn't it, since I'm here, so across *my* side of the pond," Maddox said.

"Any government work?"

"Tom does some. I do not. Had my fill with government work," Maddox said, looking at Dale Shaw.

That line of questioning went on for about an hour. Walker

asked all the questions. Shaw just sat there, crossing, and uncrossing his arms and legs every few minutes.

The two uniformed cops stood by the door the whole time. They would bend their knees to ensure they didn't pass out. Maddox remembered that type of duty. It was no fun. Not that the questioning was a picnic at the beach for him, but Maddox had gathered some valuable intelligence. He now knew who was who in the investigation. He knew they didn't know jack shit. And he knew the CIA was sniffing around.

Walker sounded tired when he simply asked: "Any idea who shot your friend?"

"No," Maddox lied. Then he continued to lie. "But Tom had mentioned something from back in his time with SAS, something about a pissed off IRA family members wanting to get revenge over one of their loved ones who ended up on the losing end of a firefight with the SAS during the Troubles."

That caused everyone to exchange glances except for Shaw, who shook his head slightly.

"Are we done here for now? I've been cooperating, but I'd like to get out of these bloody clothes, take a shower, and visit Tom," Maddox said. Three times he had asked for an update on Rose, but Walker refused to provide any.

"Just a moment," Walker said, getting up. He left the room with everyone falling in tow, including Shaw. Only the two uniformed cops stayed in the room, bending their knees.

"I did a lot of standing around when I was in the Army. Feel free to take a seat, fellas. You've been standing for over an hour," Maddox said.

"We're fine, sir," one of the cops said.

Outside Dale Shaw, wanted to know what the next step would be. Walker told him there was no next step regarding Maddox.

"Everything he's told us is plausible. We know he wasn't

involved in the assassination attempt. He probably saved Mr. Rose's life by dragging him into the bathroom. He was clean when we searched him. No weapons not even a pocketknife. He's in the country legally. There's nothing to hold him for. So that's it. We're cutting him loose," Walker said.

A moment later, Walker was back and told Maddox he was free to go.

"What about Tom? Please."

Walker finally relented.

"Your friend is going to be fine. He'll be out of commission for a while, but none of his vital organs were hit."

"Can I see him?" Maddox asked.

"No. He just got out of surgery. And visiting hours will be over soon anyway, check with the hospital in the morning," Walker said.

"What if the person that did this tries again while he's laid up in the hospital?" Maddox asked.

"That was a concern of mine also. That is why an armed Special Branch officer will be posted outside his hospital room," Walker said.

Maddox thanked Walker for that and left.

He stepped outside into the early evening air. It felt much cooler than it had a few hours ago. He looked at his watch; it had been four hours since Rose was shot.

"Mr. Maddox," Dale Shaw yelled from the front entrance of the hospital.

Maddox turned to face him.

"Need a ride?"

"No, thanks. I'll take a cab," Maddox said.

"You're going to scare the driver with that bloody shirt," Shaw said.

Maddox looked down, shrugged, and walked away.

"We do need to talk, Mr. Maddox," Shaw yelled, as Maddox continued to walk away without acknowledging him.

Maddox took a cab back to the hotel. Tossed the bloody clothing in the garbage. He showered. Changed into a T-shirt and shorts. He ordered room service. Ate a $30 burger with fries. Drank a beer.

He planned to get good night's sleep and would visit Rose in the morning.

Then he would fly to Prague to kill the administrator.

After he got the name of the sniper from him.

The chairman and the board could go fuck themselves.

FIFTY-TWO

MORPHINE

DESPITE THE MADNESS OF THE LAST THIRTY HOURS, Maddox slept well. A feat accomplished due to sheer exhaustion and, to some extent, his experience and training.

It didn't matter that after the shooting, he'd had an adrenaline surge somewhere that felt like he had bitten into a hot power line. The aftermath of that surge was a drain just as palpable to the human body as the rush.

Sleep was the best antidote so Maddox had performed a set of exercises that he had learned during extreme duress training put on by the CIA's head shrink unit.

Sonia, who did yoga every day, called it meditation. Maddox would say, *"No it's duress diffusion training.* She would laugh. *Just keep doing it; it's good for you.*

Whatever it was, it worked. To him, it had the effect of powering down an overheated machine and rebooting at full capacity.

Powered back up from his rest, Maddox now needed coffee. He was delighted that the hotel had one of those Keurig machines in the room. He drank two of the little plastic cups marked "dark roast" while he caught up on email and checked the news.

The news covered a shooting at the hotel, but nothing about a sniper at large. The news had downplayed what had gone down. Maddox was impressed at how the government was able to put a lid on those events.

Hospital visiting hours didn't start for another two hours, so Maddox hit the hotel's gym for a quick workout. Afterward, he showered, packed, and checked out via the television set and went down to the lobby, figuring by the time the cab dropped him off at the hospital, visiting hours would have begun.

Maddox was pulling his suitcase behind him through the hotel lobby when he spotted him. Dale Shaw, sitting in a leather lounge chair on his laptop. He looked up and smiled at Maddox.

Maddox did not return the smile. He scowled back.

"You don't look happy to see me, Mr. Maddox," Shaw said as he got up and slipped a black laptop into a tanned leather messenger bag.

"Getting blindsided does that to me. Look, I'm off to the hospital anyway and I don't have anything to say to you," Maddox said as he walked past Shaw.

Shaw followed him, saying, "How about dinner? Tonight."

"I'm not up for dinner or company, or THE Company," Maddox said.

"We need to talk, Mr. Maddox," Shaw said, still following him.

Maddox stopped and turned back toward Shaw and asked softly, "Why is the CIA involved in this?"

Shaw smiled. "I figured you wouldn't buy into the counsel officer line. That was mostly for our British friends' benefit."

"I hate to break it to you, but I doubt they bought into your bullshit cover too," Maddox said.

"You're probably right. By the way, nice touch bringing up The Troubles. Northern Ireland and the IRA still gets their attention, doesn't it?" Shaw said.

"I have to go, Mr. Shaw," Maddox said.

"Please, call me Dale."

"I have to go, Dale."

"We do need to talk," Shaw said again, with more urgency.

"Oh yeah, about what?" Maddox asked, looking at his watch.

"The network. That is what this is all about now, isn't it?" Shaw asked.

"I have no idea," Maddox said, turning, and walking away.

"We'll talk later. It's important that we do," Shaw said.

Maddox didn't say anything, nor did he turn around as he walked out of the hotel and jumped into a waiting cab.

The cab dropped him off at the hospital. Maddox walked up to the information desk, which was being manned by a homely woman.

He gave her the special code and his name. She looked down for a moment and since it matched and his name was on the approved visitor sheet she directed him to take the elevator —*the lift*, as she called it— to the top floor.

Rose's room was down a long hallway. It was the last room on that wing of the hospital.

A bulked-up policeman with ruddy cheeks was sitting on a folding chair outside of the room.

Maddox felt the officer eyeing him as he got closer, rising when Maddox was a few feet away.

"Name, sir," the officer with a nametag of BATEMAN asked.

"Peter Maddox."

"Identification, please."

Maddox handed Bateman his passport.

The officer checked a notebook for about a minute then yipped, "Go ahead, sir," as he handed the passport back to Maddox and stepped aside.

"Is it okay if I leave my suitcase out here?" Maddox asked.

"That's fine," Bateman said, sitting back down.

Maddox walked into Rose's room as people always walk into a hospital room when visiting a patient—slowly. Like a cat burglar not wanting to make any noise.

Rose was lying on the bed. He was awake, but Maddox knew that face; Rose was lost in thought. The room was silent. The television was off. There were a few flower arrangements on the windowsill.

"Hey, Tom," Maddox said slowly as he tiptoed toward the patient.

"I'm not on my death bed, mate. No need to pussyfoot around," Rose said, grinning.

It might be a true statement, Maddox thought, but Rose looked like shit. His voice was groggy and weak. His breathing labored and his eyes were glassy from opiates.

Maddox hadn't seen his friend so vulnerable and was thankful that Walker had that meat-lug stationed on the other side of the door for his protection.

"Are they giving you some good shit for the pain?" Maddox asked as he approached the hospital bed. Rose was under the sheets. The upper half of the bed was tilted a third of the way up.

He had his head on a large pillow. The plastic tubes sticking out of his arms dangled from the bed and into the machines and IV bags next to him.

"This one's morphine," Rose said with a smile, holding up the dispenser button that he could press when he needed a splash of the powerful painkiller.

"Nice. You and windows," Maddox said, pointing at the window.

"Yeah, I won't lie. Freaked me out at first. I wanted a room down in the basement. But I'm not letting that fucker mess with my head," Rose said.

Maddox walked to the windowsill to check out the flower arrangement lineup.

"Nice flowers. I didn't know you had anyone that gave a shit about you," Maddox said, smiling.

"Hard to believe, eh? That one is from Tawny," Rose said, referring to Tawny Tree—a former SAS soldier who handled some of Rose's logistics, and helped him get the type of jobs, that on paper, would throw off someone like Walker if he were to get shot by a sniper in London.

Rose and Tree. Maddox chuckled every time he thought about their last names. *Sounds like a flower shop*, Maddox would tease them.

"Nice," Maddox said, peeking at the cards, and seeing the one from Troy Sennight.

"That bastard Troy, making me look bad," Maddox said, turning to sit down on the chair next to Rose's bed.

"Well, don't shed any tears, but you ain't getting any flowers from me," Maddox said.

"Cheeky bastard. I guess saving my life is enough then," Rose said with a weak smile.

"What's the damage?"

Rose spoke slowly and haltingly, "Broken tibia. Broken ribs." He took in a breath. "Nothing long-term. Bullets took to my bone like a hammer and chisel, but they missed the real important life-and-death stuff like my liver, spleen. It could be worse." Rose paused for another painful breath of air then continued. "Like Arnold would say, I'll be back."

"Excellent, my friend. Now stop talking so much. Looks painful," Maddox said, handing Rose a prewritten note.

Not talking business in case of bugs. I'm headed to Prague tonight to take care of business.

"When they letting you out? Keep your answers short, buddy," Maddox asked as Rose read the note then handed it back to him.

"Few days," he said as he shook his head. He didn't have to say it. Rose didn't want Maddox going after the administrator and his shooter alone.

Maddox smiled.

"No 10K runs for you for a while."

"Won't be long and I'll be back to kick your ass on a run," Rose said, then coughed and winced in pain.

He reached for the morphine button, but the pain passed so he didn't press it.

Maddox gave him a few seconds.

"Well, when you're ready for that. I just might let you win for once."

Maddox went to the bathroom, tore up the note, wrapped up the pieces of torn paper in a wad of toilet paper and flushed it down the toilet.

He walked back out to the room and sat next to Rose's bed. They sat there for a moment without saying anything. The two friends enjoyed each other's company, even though Rose couldn't do much with the broken ribs and the morphine buzz.

"If you don't mind, I'll hang out for a little bit before I take off, Maddox said.

They watched television for a while. The British cop show, *Luther*, was on.

"Good show," Maddox said.

FIFTY-THREE
RAILROADED

London, England

"You again," Maddox said as he saw Dale Shaw waiting for him in the hospital lobby, a younger redheaded man standing next to him.

"I'm sorry, but we really need to talk, Mr. Maddox," Shaw said.

"Who are you," Maddox said, looking at the other man.

"I'm Bob Guy," he replied nervously.

"Please, Mr. Maddox ten minutes. I have a car out front," Shaw said.

Maddox mulled it over. "We can chat here. I'm not getting my ass rendered to Lithuania by the agency," Maddox said.

Shaw and Guy exchanged an annoyed look.

"Let's go over there," Maddox said, pointing at a sign to a prayer room named "The Sanctuary."

Shaw and Guy hesitated when they arrived.

"Don't worry, it's probably empty," Maddox said with a grin before he opened the door. He glanced inside before entering. It was empty.

"See, told you. After you," Maddox said, holding the door open.

Dale Shaw went inside and told Bob Guy to wait outside. Maddox followed.

"What do you want?" Maddox asked. His voice coated in exasperation.

"Like I told you earlier. I want to know about the network," Shaw said.

"Why? Are you worried it's taking business away from the CIA?" Maddox said.

Shaw smiled and said, "To avoid events like yesterday with Mr. Rose. This is the sort of thing that happens with these private for-profit networks operating like in the Wild West."

"A lot worse happens with official CIA contract work. I would think you would be concerned about cleaning your own house first. Are things that slow at the CIA?" Maddox asked.

"Oh, we have plenty of things to keep us busy. And at first, my chain of command thought this was a waste of time. I was grounded from moving forward with this until the little gun show yesterday. Sniper fire. Right in the very heart of affluent London, no less. And two men with MI6 and CIA backgrounds in the mix. It's a very sticky situation that got a lot of people's attention. And not just in government. The CEO of the hotel was not happy with what went down at his place. He called Senator Barrett and the Senator called the DI directly, demanding to know if this was one of our operations gone to shit. Now, thanks to you and Mr. Rose, I have some wiggle room," Shaw said.

"I'm happy for you, but this has nothing to do with me," Maddox said.

"I'm asking for your help. Don't you want to help us to bring the persons responsible for trying to kill your friend to justice?" Shaw asked.

I'll be taking care of that, Maddox thought, but said, "First of all, since when does the CIA deal in justice? You seem to be confused with the FBI. You're not law enforcement. And they can't do shit about this on foreign soil. Let the Brits do their thing. Second, did you look at my file? I'm blacklisted by the agency. For ten fucking years, the agency has shut me out of those juicy contracts you dish out, and now you just want me to thank you and jump into your arms? I don't think so."

"I know your history. And I'm sorry you got railroaded, but that was a long time ago. The people behind that are long gone. You just had bad timing; another year, and you would have received a promotion for what you did in Caracas," Shaw said.

"What the hell are you talking about?" Maddox asked.

"It's in our history. How the agency operates, changes every couple of decades between the two camps struggling for power —the information-gatherers, who just want to recruit foreign agents and not get their hands dirty. The Yale spymasters from the beginning of the agency. Then we have the paramilitary camp. They got their power in the 60s—Vietnam, Laos, Cambodia, and the Yale boys hated them. But just like that, they were out and the paramilitary camp is in and so is direct action. Then they screw up with Vietnam, carpet-bombing the shit out of Laos, and our messy hands-on approach in Latin America, Chile, Argentina. Then the peanut farmer becomes president, and we're back to having intellectuals running things. Paramilitary is out. Yale boys are back in. I don't have to tell you about the conflicts between the paramilitary and the scholarly officers since you lived it. 9/11, of course, changed all that and by 2003, we were back to having the paramilitary force back in the driver's seat. But that was about a year or two too late for you," Shaw said.

Maddox laughed. He actually agreed. "You've really put some thought into that."

"It's just history. And looking at the big picture is my job," Shaw said.

"Where did you go to school?" Maddox asked.

Shaw blushed. "Harvard."

"Well, that's a big difference from Yale," Maddox said with a smirk.

"I just want information from someone on the inside of the network," Shaw said.

"Well," Maddox said, turning toward the door, "your interest in history is admirable, but I'm not one to look back. I only look forward. I don't dwell on "what ifs". And I don't give two shits who was in and who was out. The CIA fucked me by firing me. Then they kept fucking me by blacklisting me from government contract work. That's been an albatross around my neck to this day. So, Dale, let me be frank, I'm not interested in helping you, or providing you with any information. As to the network you have a hard-on for, I neither confirm nor deny its existence."

Shaw stood there, arms crossed. "I'm sorry to hear that. Just remember the consequences of acting as a civilian. These European countries would love to toss an American cowboy into jail for being involved in these types of shenanigans on their soil."

Maddox walked out of the meditation room. Bob Guy looked confused as Maddox stormed past him. Shaw came out, and stood there next to Guy as they watched Maddox leave.

"What happened?" Guy asked.

"As I expected. He told us to shove it," Shaw said.

"You think he's going home?" Guy asked.

"No. He's pissed off. He wants revenge. And he's going to lead us right to the network," Shaw said, dialing the number of the surveillance team leader he had on standby.

The team leader picked up on the first ring.

"He just came out the building. Follow him. Carefully. The man is well-trained to spot tails. And keep me posted. Every ten minutes," Shaw said into the phone.

Shaw hung up staring down the empty hallway.

FIFTY-FOUR
PIGEONS

London, England

Maddox was sitting on a crowded short wall that surrounded the water fountain in Trafalgar Square. He sat across from Nelson's Column, which had been built to commemorate Admiral Horatio Nelson who hadn't made it out of the Battle of Trafalgar alive.

It didn't matter how often Maddox visited old cities like London—he was always amazed at being surrounded by all that history, from the remnants of a third century Roman wall to an almost five-hundred-year-old pub nestled in a small alleyway.

A pigeon strutted up to him, looking for food and broke his thoughts.

The pudgy bird was a survivor of London's war against the Trafalgar Square pigeons. There were far less pigeons now, but despite the city's best efforts, which included criminalizing feeding the birds, kicking out the seed sellers, and even unleashing predator Harris hawks after them, the pigeons remained, begging for food, and shitting on everything in defiance to city leaders. Maddox liked the little rebels.

Without food, the pigeon quickly lost interest in Maddox and strutted away. Maddox went back to contemplating the events that had unfolded since he'd arrived in London.

Dale Shaw was going to be a problem, Maddox thought as he kept watch on the crew of impish young CIA officers Shaw had sicced on him.

Luckily for Maddox, the crew was utterly oblivious to how bad they were at their surveillance job.

Maddox had spotted the tail a block from the hospital.

It was a five-team tail. Maddox was flattered. There was the waif-looking female agent. There was the lean, athletically built African-American in full Nike running gear who kept running around the same loop for some reason. Then there was the man and woman team pretending to be a couple they were dressed as tourists—from the Midwest with their Iowa Hawkeye gear. And there was a tiny, matchbox-looking FedEx minivan that seemed to always be parked within a block of Maddox's location.

Maddox wondered if there was at least one agent doing their job well enough to not be picked up by him. He doubted it. Regardless, he would need to lose them all. And it shouldn't be too difficult with that crew, Maddox thought. But it would still make him waste time he didn't want to waste dealing with Shaw's nonsense.

He didn't think the Special Branch or MI5 was watching, but they might be as well. Maddox cracked his neck then twisted his back until he heard it pop. Then he called Sonia and provided her with an update on Rose.

She was beside herself with worry, and was making arrangements to come to London. As resentful and angry she would be at Rose for involving Maddox in their odd jobs, she loved Rose like a big brother. So she wanted to be there for him. And despite their problems, she missed her husband and wanted to see him too.

At first, Maddox was against it; he was worried about her safety, but he really wanted to see her after a week of strained phone calls and FaceTime videos.

Maddox and Rose had been in agreement that it was unlikely the sniper would strike again so soon and in London. Especially with the Special Branch detail assigned to protect Rose. And Rose's friend, Tawny Tree, was on her way down from Northern England to help Rose out. She was just as handy with a SIG Sauer and an MP5 as Maddox and Rose were.

"Did you get your ticket?" Maddox asked. The square was noisy with tourists, traffic congestion, and the water fountain splashed behind him.

"I did. Where are you?" Sonia asked.

"Trafalgar Square. It's so beautiful here," Maddox said.

"I love London. We haven't been there together in years," Sonia said.

"Once I'm done with this, we should plan another trip here, just for fun. A few days in London then a few days in Paris," Maddox said, excited about the thought.

"I'd love to. When will you be done with work?" Sonia knew not to ask too much about Maddox's odd jobs, especially on an open line.

"A few more days," Maddox said. He hoped it was true.

FIFTY-FIVE

ROOM SERVICE

London, England

WHATEVER WORRIES MADDOX HAD ABOUT THE STATE OF
his marriage, or her safety in coming to London, evaporated like
water on a Phoenix sidewalk when he saw Sonia walk out of the
arrivals gate at Gatwick Airport.

It had been over a week since he had seen each other so they
held embraced tightly to the annoyance of arriving travelers
behind them.

They kissed. And they walked quietly holding hands to the
baggage claim area.

"How was your trip?" Maddox finally asked.

"Long. But it was fine. *Skyfall* was one of the movies on the
flight, so I watched it," Sonia said with a mischievous smile as
she bumped Maddox with her hip.

"Cute," Maddox said, and bumped her right back.

He collected her bag and they took the Gatwick Express to
London. From there they took a cab to the hotel.

They ordered room service and spent that evening, and
morning, making up and making love.

They were lying on the bed naked, recovering. She was lying on his chest, sideways, her legs hanging over the bed, dangling in the air.

"I'm glad you came," Maddox said as he leaned over and kissed her forehead.

"Me too. And I'm glad I'm here in London, too," she said, giggling.

Maddox was packing, Sonia watched him from bed.

"Two, three days tops," Maddox said, even though she hadn't asked.

"You've said that already," she said.

"I know you're not going to believe me. But even if this network doesn't implode or something else takes its place, I'm done with the odd jobs."

Sonia smiled. She didn't say anything. She wanted to believe him, but she had come to believe that the work Maddox did was soldered into his DNA. But after seeing Rose in the hospital, she knew he couldn't just walk away.

There was someone out there killing freelancers and if Maddox didn't find this person first, they couldn't reasonably expect to go home without worrying that the shooter wouldn't try to kill him too. She nodded. She smiled. She just wanted him to come back home to her, safe. Then they could discuss, plan, and argue about the future.

"I'll be back in a few days. You can help Tawny with Tom while I'm gone," Maddox said. She smiled, tears welled up in her eyes and he left.

FIFTY-SIX

ROSE'S PLAYGROUND

London, England

MADDOX WAS TRAVELING LIGHT WITH JUST AN OVERNIGHT bag with a change of clothing and toiletries. He felt a bit at a loss without Rose.

Europe was Rose's playground, not his.

He was in the hotel lobby, making calls before heading out to take the Gatwick Express back to the airport.

His first call was to Troy Sennight.

"I'm getting ready to head out to the airport," Maddox said.

"Once you're on the ground in Prague, turn on the cell phone with my tracking app so you can find that son of a bitch."

After hours of data churning, Sennight had tracked the administrator's real IP address to the Cyber One Company.

The IP address wouldn't show Maddox who, out of the hundred or so employees of Cyber One, was the administrator. But once Maddox was in the actual building pinging to that IP address, he would fire up Sennight's custom app.

If the admin was logged into the network, Sennight's app

would turn Maddox's phone into something akin to a metal detector.

Digitally, the admin would be that buried penny in the ground, ready to be dug out by Sennight's app.

The administrator was good at covering his tracks, but Sennight was better at the tech game.

He had written a program that would execute relative distance measurements to facilitate the triangulation that would pinpoint the admin's exact location. It was the technology that the FBI used to hunt its cyber criminals.

It was how the FBI had tracked down the illusive admin of Silk Road, Dread Pirate Roberts to a public library in San Francisco. The FBI had caught him red-handed logged on as Silk Road's admin.

As long as Maddox was in the same building as the administrator of TEN and he was logged in, Maddox would be able to do the same thing to get his hands on him.

Then he would get the identity of the sniper from the admin.

Maddox's next call was to Tom Rose's hospital room. Rose told him he was doing better, and was down to just once a day with the morphine drip and that he might be discharged as soon as the next day, maybe the day after. Rose then passed the phone to Tawny Tree.

"How is he?" Maddox asked.

"He's fine, really. It'll take more than a few three-aught-eights to bring that tough old bird down," Tree said, referring to the .308 Winchester military-grade NATO rounds used by the sniper.

Maddox laughed, as did Tree. Then she turned serious.

"I've made the arrangements with your contact in Prague, Jaromír Lux. He goes by Jar, which is good since it's a hell a lot easier to pronounce than Jaromír," she said with a laugh. "Jar will be carrying a white dry erase clipboard that will have 'Welcome Mr. Prince' on it. Welcome will be misspelled: W-E-L-C-O-M. And there will be a smiley face drawn in blue. He will know you by your codename: Harry Prince."

"He has black hair. Worn short. He'll be clean-shaven and about 172 centimeters in height. He will drive you around. He knows the entire country, and Prague especially, like the back of his hand. He'll also provide you with a weapon to use while in country. Don't worry, I trust him. The guns will be clean. He's reliable and trustworthy."

Maddox thanked Tree for her help and hung up.

Twenty-five minutes later, he was on the Gatwick Express, a nonstop train that took him from London's Victoria Station to Gatwick Airport.

Maddox was approximately halfway to the airport when his phone rang. He didn't recognize the number. "Hello."

"Hello, Larkspur. I'm the chairman of the board," an old man's voice said over the line.

Maddox was surprised.

But he was also skeptical about the caller's identity. For all he knew it was the administrator pretending to be the chairman to get data from him.

"What can I do for you?" Maddox said curtly.

"Seems like you're already doing plenty. Foxglove has filled me in on your plans. I just wanted to call you to personally thank you for picking up the baton for our fallen friend. I've been told Foxglove wouldn't have survived had you not been there to drag him to cover."

Well the caller certainly had all the details down, Maddox thought.

"How can I help you, sir?" Maddox asked, not wanting to say, or confirm anything to a voice on the phone.

Maddox could hear the old man give a faint laugh then the voice crackled over the phone.

"I want to apologize. It's such a shame. If professionals behaved and did what they were supposed to, we wouldn't find ourselves in such a predicament."

Maddox didn't know what to say so he said, "It's the nature of the beast, I suppose."

"I also wanted to let you know that I've transferred the escrow monies from Foxglove's account into your own to cover your operational expenses."

"Thank you," Maddox said.

"Is there anything else you need?" the chairman asked.

"Anything you can tell me about the administrator would come in handy right about now. It's pointless protecting him any longer. He's waist-deep in this," Maddox said.

The call had ended by the time the train pulled into the airport railway station at Gatwick. Maddox exited the train with the throng of passengers. Some of them—cutting it too close with their flight departure time—took off from the train like Sea Biscuit at the starting gate.

Maddox always gave himself plenty of time at airports. He called Troy Sennight as he made his way to the terminal. It was little after 5:00 p.m. in Virginia.

"I have a new name for you to check out," Maddox said.

"Shoot," Sennight said.

"Edvard Danko. That's Danko, Delta-Alpha-November-Kilo-Oscar. And Edvard. Echo-Delta-Victor-Alpha-Romeo-Delta."

"Got it. Who's that?" Sennight asked.

"According to the chairman of the network, that's the name of the administrator," Maddox said.

"Holy shit, I'm on it," Sennight said.

"Hey, hold on. Anything on that other name?" Maddox asked.

"Yeah, hold on, let me get that report."

Maddox could hear the sound of a chair rolling on the hardwood floor then paper shuffling. Something made a loud noise and he heard Sennight's voice. "Shit."

Maddox shook his head, envisioning Sennight's workstation cluttered with stuff as usual.

Sennight came back on the line. "Okay, got it. I agree with Tawny about Jaromír Lux. He checks out."

Maddox didn't know Tawny Tree as well as Rose did, so although he did trust in her capabilities, he felt it wouldn't hurt to have Sennight double-check things.

He went on. "He's Forty-four years old. Married. Two kids. He started out as a Paratrooper in the Czechoslovak Army. Got out as a platoon leader for the Army of the new Czech Republic then joined the National Police force. He's been there since 1994. He's a lieutenant. Works for the Agency for Special Activities of the Criminal Police, just the type of cops that TEN loves to have on their payroll. So dirty in that respect, but nothing alarming popped up with his background. No ties with Russian mobsters, terrorists, or any groups like that. He seems legit for our purposes."

"Okay, sounds good. My flight leaves in ninety minutes. It's about a two-hour flight to Prague. Let me know what you find out about Edvard Danko as soon as possible," Maddox said.

"Already running some queries. I should have some preliminary info pretty damned quick."

FIFTY-SEVEN

THE ORDERLY

London, England

AT SIX IN THE MORNING, AXEL WAS WALKING AMONGST the tombstones of a London cemetery with a bouquet of bright yellow button pom flowers in his hand.

He was doing that against his better judgment. *I should be as far away way from London as possible*, he kept telling himself.

He walked to a predetermined headstone which had a granite flower vase built into its base. He bent down and shoved an envelope into the empty vase then put the flowers in the vase, concealing the envelope.

The flowers also signaled the drop was ready for pickup. Inside the envelope were ten fifty-pound notes.

An hour later, from a safe distance, Axel watched a young Indian man wearing blue hospital scrubs walk up to the same headstone. He looked around nervously for almost a full minute.

Can you be more fucking obvious?

He knelt and cringed as he felt the wetness of the morning

dew on the grass, then he sprang to his feet to inspect the wet spot on his knee.

The man wiped at it for another full minute as Axel seethed at the man's lollygagging.

Finally, he bent down again, but that time he took the flowers and the envelope. He tore it open right there and, after a quick glance, folded it and shoved it into his pocket with a wide smile.

He removed his own sealed envelope and placed it and the flowers back in the vase. Then he meandered away, glancing around awkwardly.

Axel watched for another ten minutes after the man in the blue scrubs left, and he walked back to the headstone.

He tossed the flowers on the ground, removed the envelope and shoved it in his coat pocket without looking and walked back out onto the sidewalk, heading toward the London Royal Hospital.

After a couple of minutes, he took the envelope from his pocket, tore it open and removed a folded piece of white paper and a key.

Written on the piece of paper was the address to the man in blue scrubs' residence a few blocks away from the hospital. The key was to his apartment.

Axel arrived there in ten minutes. He used the key and went inside.

As instructed, the man had left a blue gym bag on the kitchen table, which Axel opened. Inside was what he had paid for—an orderly uniform in his size and an ID badge.

The orderly had warned him that the hospital badge was an old one but, at a glance, it shouldn't be an issue. However, if stopped or confronted and someone gave that badge a closer look he would probably be found out as an imposter.

Luckily for Axel, the badge did not have a photograph since he would have a hard time passing for an Indian man.

Axel was fine with those odds. He wasn't planning on spending too much time inside the hospital anyway.

Axel put on the blue scrubs with the hospital name embroidered on it over his own clothing and clipped the white ID badge to his belt.

He checked himself in the mirror. He was wearing his blond wig. He made sure it was snug to his bald head. He checked the fake beard he had glued on earlier in the morning. It looked good.

Axel left the orderly's apartment and made the fifteen-minute walk to the hospital in less than ten minutes.

He was going to Room 351. He knew where to go thanks to Mr. White's accessing the hospital's computer system like he had done the hotels system. He hadn't found a patient admitted by Tom Rose's name but that hadn't surprised Mr. White, who scanned admissions looking for patients suffering gunshot wounds that had been admitted within the last forty hours. He found a John Doe who had been shot three times, once in the torso, leg, and foot.

Axel was surprised how untethered he was able to roam the hospital. But he knew that half the battle of walking into places you don't belong is to act like you belong.

He avoided the elevators and took the stairs to the floor where Rose's room was located. He felt nervous. The Beretta with its suppressor felt bulkier and heavier than usual, but he chalked it up to nerves.

He walked down the corridor. There was the typical activity that would be expected in a hospital with staff and visitors here and there, but overall, less than he expected.

Axel roamed the floor for a moment, grabbing a food tray

cart full of trays with dirty plates with partially eaten meals on them along the way. It made him feel less out of place.

He was about halfway to Rose's room at the end of a long hallway when his heart sank.

"Orderly, come here, please," a female voice called out to him. Axel ignored her and kept pushing the trolley.

"Hey, you, I'm talking to you," she said louder, sounding angry. Axel stopped and looked at her. He was relieved she was a nurse and not police or security. He pointed at himself gave a *"who me?"* look.

"Yes, *you*," she snapped. "There's a dirty bedpan in Room 312. Please see to it."

He nodded but didn't speak. He didn't want to give away his American English accent. She scurried away.

Axel walked into the room. There was an old man sleeping with a silver bedpan on the floor next to the bed. Axel gagged. It was full of thick, brownish urine. He was already wearing blue latex gloves, so he picked up the bedpan and shivered at the smell.

This old dude must have eaten a pound of asparagus, Axel thought, disgusted. *The fuck am I supposed to do with this?* He carefully picked up the pan to ensure he wouldn't spill piss on himself.

He dumped it down the drain of the bathroom sink and he let warm water run for a few seconds. He tossed the now empty pan back on the floor and walked out of the comatose old man's room. He glanced to the right and left and, to his relief, the nurse that had put him to work was nowhere in sight.

He resumed pushing the food tray carrier along the long skinny corridor looking, at the room numbers until he saw what he was looking for. Room 351.

He stopped short and surveyed the situation. It was quiet with most patients still asleep. A few hospital workers in scrubs and white coats kept popping in and out of patients' rooms, but they were too busy to pay attention to Axel.

They wouldn't be a problem, Axel thought, but the uniformed police officer sitting right outside the door to Rose's room would be trouble.

The cop seemed bored but alert. While most police officers in the UK were unarmed that one was part of the Special Branch and he *was* armed. That would make things more challenging for Axel.

Axel was trying to figure out how to get into Rose's room to finish the job when the door to Rose's room opened and a woman stepped out, closing the door behind her. She stretched and yawned. She was a short-haired brunette, svelte and dressed well.

Axel was mesmerized by her and he felt that surge in his groin area again. And again, he tried to will it away. *That feeling is nothing but weakness,* he thought.

She had a brief conversation with the police officer who had stood when she came out. Axel was too far away so he couldn't make out what they were saying but her accent didn't sound British from his vantage point.

He tried to look away, but it didn't work. No matter how much he tried to ignore it, the excited tingle in his groin was growing. He felt embarrassed. Weak.

"Sure thing, Miss Collins." That Axel heard from the guard. She smiled and turned and went back into Rose's room.

The police officer remained on his feet for a few seconds with a goofy smile on his face. It seemed the woman had the same effect on the guard too.

Axel knew Rose was single. Divorced three times, so he figured she might be Rose's girlfriend or friend. He felt jealous at the thought she might be Rose's lover.

He was jolted back to reality with that nurse again yelling

out to him.

"Oi, are you just going to hang out there all day, orderly?"

Axel turned and glared at the nurse; his scowl changed her facial expression from anger to fear. So he smiled and pushed the cart down another corridor, away from Rose's room and the nurse.

He ditched the cart and took the stairs down to the lobby and walked back outside, he knew there was no way he was going to make a move against Rose in the hospital.

The armed cop stationed by the door, the Collins woman—and he had no idea who else could be inside the room with Rose and there were too many hospital staff around.

As he walked he tried to figure out who the Collins woman was. She was perhaps a friend, a family member, or another cop.

Back at the safe house Axel called Mr. White and shared the details of his scouting mission.

"You sure the last name wasn't Tree?" Mr. White asked.

"Tree? No. I can tell the difference between Tree and Collins for chrissakes. Who's Tree?"

"That would be Ms. Tawny Tree. Another of TEN's favorites," Mr. White explained. "She was British Army. One of the first members of the Special Reconnaissance Regiment and she probably would have made one hell of an SAS soldier if they allowed women to serve in that capacity. She's been independent for a few years and works closely with Mr. Rose. It makes sense she would be there," Mr. White explained.

"Well, it doesn't matter who she is. Needless to say, it's a no-go moving in on Rose there. Too many people, too public, too risky," Axel said.

"What about the American?" Mr. White asked.

"I didn't see him there," Axel said.

"Okay. Let me do some checking on this Collins woman," Mr. White said, disconnecting the call.

FIFTY-EIGHT
LEVERAGE

London, England

Sonia Maddox walked back into Rose's room with a smile. "I asked Officer Bateman outside your door about his shift. He's there until midnight. Then an officer by the name of Jessica Ashby will take the midnight to eight shift. As far as he knows, they'll continue on a one-man detail. I told him we're not expecting anyone tonight or tomorrow morning," Sonia said, sitting down in the chair next to him.

"Thanks for checking. You don't have to hang out here all day, love. I'll be fine. Plenty of nurses and orderlies coming in and out and Tawny will be back soon," Rose said.

His voice sounded weaker than normal, but it was getting stronger.

It wasn't the first time Rose had been shot, but at fifty-two years of age, he'd thought those days were behind him, especially in London. And that was what the sniper had counted on. That was how he'd gotten Fitzsimmons and Ramos on their home turf at the tail end of their career with their guards down to DEFCON 5.

Cowardly piece of shit, Rose thought. The anger made him wince in pain and Sonia saw it.

"Don't be so stubborn, Tom, push the damned button," she said, pointing at the morphine dispenser.

"Don't want to become a junkie," Rose said with a smile.

"You'll become a sadist trying to endure the pain," Sonia said.

"Too late for that." Rose said. "Now, go back to the hotel. Rest up. You've been running around non-stop since you got to London. I'll be fine."

BACK AT THE SAFE HOUSE, Axel was thinking about that woman he saw outside of Rose's hospital room when Mr. White called back. It had been fifteen minutes since they last talked and it had dawned on Axel he had been sitting there daydreaming about her that whole time. Snapped from his trance, he answered the phone. "That was fast."

"I'm that good. And a gift has just landed on our lap." Mr. White sounded downright giddy.

"Okay," Axel said slowly.

"The woman's last name, Collins, well that just happens to be the maiden name of Peter Maddox, the board's own Larkspur's wife. Sonia Collins Maddox."

"Foxglove's partner?" Axel asked.

"That's right."

"That is a gift. So what do you want to do?"

"I want leverage. She'll give us plenty of it," Mr. White said.

"How do we do we get that?" Axel asked.

"We take her."

FIFTY-NINE

THAT DISTRACTION

London, England

AXEL MADE HIS WAY THROUGH THE BUSY STREETS OF London in a stolen white van. Driving on the left hand side of the road added more stress to the operation at hand.

The van was small. It was really a minivan. He wished he had an American-sized vehicle, not one that looked like it had come out of a Matchbox Blister Pack, but he had make do with what was available.

He had never kidnapped anyone before, but it felt like at a minimum, it should be a two-man job. But it was all up to him. Mr. White would come up with the plans, but he never wanted to get his hands dirty.

"That's what I'm paying you for," he would say when Axel complained about it.

Axel was double-parked kitty-corner from Whitechapel Station when he saw Sonia emerge. She was as beautiful as she had been the day before outside Rose's hospital room.

He was too nervous to get sexually aroused at seeing her, which was good, he thought. He didn't need *that* distraction.

Axel had followed her from her hotel to the hospital to nail down her route. He didn't have much time since Rose could be released from the hospital any day now, and he only had a small window of opportunity to pull it off.

Axel followed her as she walked down Whitechapel Road—a busy intersection with pedestrians, cars, and buses jockeying for position on the road and the sidewalks.

She was dressed casually in black yoga pants and a gray jacket, which she had zipped up all the way to her neck.

As she had before, Sonia headed toward the Starbucks that was about a five-minute walk from the hospital.

He was on the other side of the street when she walked past the van; *now or never*, he thought as he pounced from behind with a handheld Taser in his right hand.

He wrapped his left arm around her waist as he shoved the taser gun to her neck and pulled its trigger, which unleashed a jolt of electricity that surged through her body.

A spastic Sonia crumbled into Axel's arms. She was slender. Maybe 110-115 pounds, so he was able to easily pick her up before she hit the ground and in mere seconds he tossed her limp body into the van.

He tasered her one more time for good measure, then quickly duct taped her mouth and secured her arms behind her back at the wrists with plastic Speedcuffs.

He grabbed a large English flag beach towel that he had bought at one of the many novelty kiosks around London and wrapped it around her head so she couldn't see.

He tossed the duct tape to the floor of the van, stepped back, and slid the door closed as hard as he could.

He glanced around as he ran to the front of the van and jumped into the driver's seat.

He had left the van running. He looked around again and it

didn't appear that anyone had noticed the abduction so he merged back onto the road and drove toward the safe house.

Once back at the house, he carried her into the master bedroom and tossed her on the bed like a coat.

He locked the door to the bedroom and ran back outside, where he had left the double-parked van.

He drove a few miles to a nearby cemetery. He parked and wiped down the van with disinfectant wipes. He locked it and tossed the keys in a nearby trashcan.

Then he walked back to the safe house. He wouldn't be staying there much longer so he didn't care about ditching the stolen van so nearby the safe house.

He double-timed back to the house. His nerves were frayed and it took him almost five minutes to get his breath back. His body trembled. He had never done anything like that before.

He drank three glasses of water, then went to check on his hostage.

He unlocked the door to the master bedroom. He stood there for a moment watching her. She had regained consciousness and had managed to sit up on the bed. She was wriggling and struggling to break free from the Speedcuffs.

The towel was coming loose but was still wrapped around her face so she couldn't see.

Axel picked her up from the bed and moved her over to a chair. He tied her to it with nylon ropes as she kept grunting and struggling.

Once he had her secured, he removed the towel from her head. Her hair was tousled. Black mascara ran down her cheeks.

She looked beautiful, Axel thought.

It was curious to him that she wasn't sobbing uncontrollably as he had envisioned. She looked scared but also angry. Defiant even.

She was trying to speak but all that came out were muffled sounds from the duct tape.

Her wrists were still bound by the Speedcuffs and her upper body and arms were tied to the back of the chair tightly, which caused her breasts to lift.

Axel stared at her breasts and he felt that sensation again and licked his lips.

Then he realized what he was doing and he wondered if she could see the lust in his face. The terrified look on her face confirmed that she had seen it.

He felt ashamed and abruptly turned and left the room, slamming the door shut.

He stood there for a moment with his back to the door. "I'm no fucking rapist," he shouted through the closed door.

He was still standing with his back to the door when his phone rang.

It was Mr. White.

Axel had texted him that the extraction was a success.

"Hello?" Axel answered, welcoming the distraction from the feelings he was having about his kidnap victim.

"Any problems so far?" Mr. White asked.

"None. I ditched the van. She's here. Everything is fine," Axel said.

"Where is she?"

"In the bedroom. I have her tied up and gagged so she won't be going anywhere, and she won't be able to make a peep either," Axel said.

"Okay, great. Good job, Axel," Mr. White said.

"What's next?"

"Hold tight for now," Mr. White said.

"Don't take too much time. I've been at this safe house too long, and now with the van and all," Axel said, sounding worried.

"You said no one saw you take her and I've been monitoring the police scanners. Nothing about a kidnapping and I have the feeling that Maddox will want to address this himself without getting the police involved, so we have that in our favor," Mr. White said.

"Still. It's not safe to stay here anymore," Axel said.

"It won't be long. I'm making the necessary arrangements to get you both here as soon as possible. Now, I need you to take several photographs of her and email them to me, then destroy that phone," Mr. White said before hanging up.

Axel walked into the room. Sonia's restraints were holding nicely, as he'd known they would.

He took pride with how quickly and effective he was with a rope and knot tying.

She screamed, but the duct tape muffled the sound.

He was holding the cell phone. He turned it on and navigated to the camera, then held it out at arm's length and began taking photographs.

Sonia seemed to scream and wriggle more with each photograph he took. After about a dozen photographs, Axel pocketed the phone.

He got closer to Sonia, like a child cautiously approaching a wild animal at the zoo.

Sonia bucked trying to kick him. He was impressed. He liked her spunk. But the muffled screams were getting on his nerves so he leaned in closer to her and said, "With that tape over your mouth, I'm the only one who can hear you scream and it's getting on my nerves. If you don't cut it out, I'm going to shove my dirty underwear that I've worn for two days into your mouth and tape your mouth shut. If you think your current situation is bad, it could get worse. A lot worse. So. Shut. The. Fuck. Up."

Axel walked out of the bedroom and the muffled screaming stopped. He smiled.

It had been an hour and Axel felt like a caged animal. His threat with the dirty underwear as a gag had worked. She'd stopped the muffled screams and groans, but he could still hear crying and whimpering.

The phone rang. He picked up at the first ring.

"Excellent pictures, Axel, excellent. Here is what I want you to do with her."

SIXTY

I'LL BE WATCHING YOU

London, England

INSIDE THAT LOCKED ROOM, SONIA FELT LIKE SHE HAD gone through all five stages of grief in one hour. She had lost track of time but guessed it had been a couple hours since was kidnapped from the street.

After his dirty underwear threat and photo session, her kidnapper had left her alone, bound and gagged, for a while when she heard the door being unlocked.

He walked in with a bag from McDonalds.

"Brought you something to eat," he said. His voice sounded normal. She didn't know what she expected it to sound like, but not ... *normal*.

He continued to speak, "I got you two cheeseburgers, large fries, an apple pie for dessert, and the largest cup they had of Diet Coke. I figured you for a diet soda type."

Sonia nodded. It was about all she could do with the restraints and the duct tape over her mouth.

"I forgot to get you ketchup and I don't have any here. I hope you don't mind," he said, sounding sincere.

She couldn't believe it. This man that had kidnapped her, tasered her several times, put duct tape over her mouth, and tied her to a chair, leered at her, and threatened to shove dirty underwear in her mouth suddenly seemed to feel bad that he'd forgotten to get her ketchup.

What the hell?

But Sonia figured it was a good sign though. He was thinking about her as more than just a thing to keep locked up.

She watched how he handled himself. Taking mental notes. He was soldier-like. She didn't know how to describe it, but being married to a former Army Ranger and having been around so many of Maddox's military friends and colleagues, her real estate clients from the Pentagon, she picked that vibe up. It was a tell that military people seemed to have.

He told her he would remove the tape from her mouth if she didn't scream. She agreed. He was an American, no doubt about that. From the accent or lack of accent, Midwestern, she thought.

If she was going to make it out of this alive, she needed to be smart.

Panicking and being frantic wasn't helping. He wasn't going to let her go because she screamed. It only made him mad.

She thanked him for the food. He nodded but didn't say anything. He removed a black knife from a leather sheath. She flinched but remained calm. It looked like one of Maddox's knives and she actually took comfort thinking about him.

He reached behind her and cut off the plastic Speedcuffs.

Her arms felt like they were floating in the air. Her shoulders, elbows, and wrists were sore. She rubbed her forearm and wrists.

He stepped back and sat on the floor with his back to the door, watching her.

"Eat," he said.

"Thank you." Sonia smiled, reaching for the food in the bag. She couldn't recall the last time she'd eaten fast food.

She was so hungry that she didn't care that she was eating pink slime. She scarfed down both burgers and the fries, then the apple pie. She was surprised that she could eat.

She ate everything in about ten minutes.

"Thank you. I was starving," she said.

He stood.

"I can tell you're a soldier. Does this have anything to do with my husband's work?" She asked.

"Was. A solider. And yes. This is about his work," he said without looking at her.

She felt reassured about that. He wasn't some deviant kidnapping women to be his sex slave, or a serial killer.

She told herself that her situation was just a business transaction.

From her years as a Realtor, she knew a lot about dealing and wheeling. She convinced herself this is what this was, and she was obviously worth more alive than dead. She would do what he said, because eventually he would take her to Maddox to close the deal, and then Scarface over here would be fucked.

Sonia smiled at the thought.

"Look, lady," he said, snapping her from her thoughts. She looked up, and he was standing in front of her, holding the ropes and a new set of plastic Speedcuffs.

"I don't want to have to tie you up again and duct tape your mouth shut, so I won't. As you can see, there are no windows in this room. I'll be right on the other side of the door. There is no way out. So just hang tight for now. I'm putting this camera right here," he said, holding out a small, white, wireless camera.

Maddox had several of those small Bluetooth cameras set up in their home. She knew they recorded clean crisp video images and recorded audio too, which could be viewed and listened to on any computer or smart phone.

"I'll be watching you. If at anytime I look at the video feed and I can't see you, I will tie you up and duct tape your mouth shut again. No second chances. Same rule applies if you shout, scream, or make a fuss. If you need the toilet, leave the door to the bathroom open. Remember, if I can't see you through that camera or I see that bathroom door closed, or you fuck around in any way that makes me not trust you, I'll tie you up again. Don't test me," he said.

"I won't. Thank you for not tying me up."

He didn't say anything.

He grabbed a chair, put the camera on it and placed the chair in front of the door so that the camera could keep watch over her.

He checked the position of the camera with his cell phone. Satisfied he turned and looked at her.

"Look. We'll be on the move soon. How you travel will depend on how you behave now. You can go under your own volition or I tie you up and transport you like a hog. Option A is easier, so I hope you make the right choice," he said.

"Are you taking me to my husband?" Sonia asked.

He stood there for a few seconds, thinking about how much he should say.

"That's not important right now."

He turned to walk out of the room before she could say anything else.

He closed the door and locked it from the other side.

"I'll be watching you," she heard him say once again from the other side of the door.

Prague, Czech Republic

MADDOX'S FLIGHT ARRIVED ON TIME AT VÁCLAV HAVEL Airport in Prague. It was a quick flight from London—less than two hours.

As the plane taxied, Maddox looked at his watch. Prague was one hour ahead of London so it was close to one in the morning local time and six in the morning in Virginia. It made sense that he hadn't heard back from Sennight about Edvard Danko yet.

The downtime would give Maddox an opportunity to get his bearings. He had only been to Prague once before. That had been decades ago so he felt like a fish out of water.

He deplaned shouldering his bag as he made his way out to the terminal. He looked around the airport. All the shops, bars, and restaurants were closed.

There weren't many people waiting for passengers in the meeting point area right outside the gate, so it was easy for Maddox to spot Jar Lux right away. He was holding a white dry erase clipboard just like Tawny Tree had said and on it was written in black: WELCOM—welcome was misspelled as agreed upon. Underneath WELCOM was the formal name he was using. MR. PRINCE, also written in black ink, and in blue ink next to MR. PRINCE was a badly drawn smiley face.

Maddox smiled, walked up to the man and said, "I'm Mr. Prince from Denver."

"I was in Denver once in 1999," the man said, lowering the sign. Their codewords confirmed the man put out his hand toward Maddox. He took it and they shook.

"I'm Lieutenant Jar Lux. Welcome to Prague," Lux said, still shaking Maddox's hand.

The description of Jar Lux that Tree had provided fit to a T. The Czech cop was dressed in blue jeans, a black dress shirt with a fashionable sports coat over it.

"This way," Lux said, waving toward the exit.

"Thank you for agreeing to come get me at this ungodly hour."

"No worries. I'm a bit of night person anyway," Lux said in very good English.

Outside the terminal, the late evening air felt cold. Maddox zipped up his jacket.

"It gets cold at night in Prague," Lux said with a smile.

Lux led Maddox to his black Škoda Octavia, which he had parked on the curb, where passengers were dropped off for their flights.

Lux took Maddox's bag and tossed it on the backseat. Both men got into the car and Lux removed a white placard he had laying on the dashboard and handed it to Maddox, saying, "Please put this in the glove box."

Maddox glanced at it, but the writing was in Czech so he couldn't read it. He opened the glove box and put the laminated sign inside.

"It lets the traffic police know I'm with the police so they don't ticket or tow my car," Lux said, smiling as he pulled out of the terminal fast, causing Maddox's neck to snap as he reached for the seat belt.

Lux drove at breakneck speed during the whole journey from the airport to Prague, even as he played tour guide for Maddox, pointing out this and that of the historic city. It was a blur at that speed. Maddox smiled nervously and nodded, and hoped the man would slow down a bit.

The airport was located eleven miles west of the city center. Traffic was light at 1:30 in the morning so twenty minutes later Lux was speeding across the Hlávkův bridge—"One of the thirteen bridges that crosses over the Vltava river into the city of Prague," he explained without slowing down.

As they drove through the city, Lux pointed out Wenceslas Square. "Our famous square," he said.

A couple of minutes later, he pulled over abruptly, stopped in front of a building and said, "That is the Kotera building. Cyber One location. Five-minute walk from the apartment I have arranged for you."

Maddox took it in. The sidewalk was quiet and the building was dark.

"By morning, this area will be very busy with rush hour. People going to work," Lux said.

Maddox nodded but didn't say anything as he thought about Sennight's geolocating app, and hoped it would work to lead him right to his target.

Lux pulled back onto the street like a bat out of hell, and in a few minutes, he pulled over again and parked in front of another building.

"We've arrived at your apartment," Lux said, getting out of the car. Maddox did the same. He got his bag from the backseat. Lux opened the trunk of his car and removed a shoebox, which he tucked under his arm.

"I'll show you in," Lux said.

He pressed 4628 and the pound sign into a keypad located by the main door of the apartment building. The double doors buzzed and clicked. Lux grabbed one of the door handles and swung the door open.

"After you," he said to Maddox.

"Thanks." Maddox stepped inside.

They took the elevator to the second floor. "Apartment 201," Lux said, removing a key from his pocket. He unlocked the door, opened it, and they stepped inside.

Lux flipped a switch and after a brief flickering, the lights came on.

The apartment was small: one bedroom, one bathroom, and a kitchenette, but it was cozy and the location was ideal for the job at hand.

Lux handed Maddox a keychain with the Epcot Center Spaceship logo dangling from the loop along with a single key. Maddox looked at it.

"Epcot Center," Lux beamed. "My kids love Disneyland in Orlando. You gone to Disneyland?"

"Yes, I have. It's nice," Maddox said, lying. He hated the overcrowded Disney and Epcot Center where the bulk of the visit was spent waiting in line for everything from the rides to the bathroom.

"Place is clean, quiet," Lux said, looking around the tiny apartment. "The neighbors mind their own business. Popular rental for tourists, students. Airbnb. You know it?" Lux asked, sounding excited.

"Yes, the website place to find non-hotel places to stay," Maddox said.

"Yes, that's the one. Good for this type of stay," he said with a wink. "And most importantly, it's not unusual having an American here for a few days. The stove and microwave work, but there is no food in the apartment. Lots of restaurants nearby."

Quite the host, Maddox thought. "Got it, thanks, Jar," Maddox said.

Lux handed the shoebox to Maddox.

"It's clean," Lux said as Maddox looked inside.

There was a Glock 23, two magazines and a box of 40 caliber Underwood Ammo.

"The ammo box is half full. Best I could do on short notice. It's hard to get ammo in city," Lux said.

"This is great. Thank you so much."

The box indicated it was a one hundred count size, so if Lux was right, the box should have fifty rounds in it.

Too light for going in heavier, but he didn't have any other choice since he would be at Danko's building first thing in the morning.

"If the gun becomes hot, Mr. Prince, I would suggest dumping it into the Vltava River. Easy access to the river all over this city," Lux said.

They chitchatted for a few minutes, then Lux said good-night with a warning.

"If you get in trouble. If you're shot. Anything ... call this number and I'll see what I can do. But don't mention my name to anyone and if the police arrest you — I will not be able to help you. I hope you understand."

"I do. Thank you, Jar," Maddox said. The men shook hands and Jar left.

It was two thirty in the morning. Maddox changed into a T-shirt and sweatpants and crashed for three hours of sleep.

SIXTY-TWO

MALA STRANA

Prague, Czech Republic

THE U.S. EMBASSY TO THE CZECH REPUBLIC WAS HOUSED in the Schönborn Palace in the Malá Strana district of Prague. The palace went back to the 1640s. It was built on the site of another home that had been destroyed during the Thirty Years War of 1618-1648.

An heir to a plumbing fortune from Chicago had bought the palace from the royal Schönborn family, and eventually sold it to the US government in the 1920s. The American embassy had been located in the princely looking building ever since.

The embassy was on Vlašská Street, about three miles from Wenceslas Square across the river.

Dale Shaw arrived at nine in the morning with Bob Guy. The meeting was a courtesy check with the CIA Station Chief, Richard Montiglio.

The Marine guard ushered Shaw and Guy inside the embassy where Dennis Beattie, a thin and tall African-American case officer for the agency on his first foreign assignment, met them. Beattie escorted them to the third floor that housed the CIA Station in the Czech Republic.

The three men arrived at a locked door. Beattie entered his access code into a digital touch screen that was fully integrated with fingerprint security. After a few seconds, the door clicked, Beattie opened it and held it open for Shaw and Guy.

"Follow me, gentlemen," Beattie said as he led them down to a windowless conference room at the end of a long corridor. Another biometrics reader was required to gain access to the conference room.

"We have coffee over there and it's not bad," Beattie said, pointing to a coffee machine. "I'll go get the others so we can start the meeting."

Shaw and Guy were left alone and both men made beeline for the coffee machine. After a few minutes, Beattie returned with the Chief of Station and two others, a man, and a woman.

Full introductions took a couple of minutes. Richard Montiglio, the Station Chief, was there, along with Jim Durban, the Assistant Regional Security Officer for Diplomatic Security, and Carey Beachy, a Special Agent with the Diplomatic Security Service.

The DSS was the law enforcement branch of the Department of State and it handled all diplomatic security spanning the globe.

It was a little known law enforcement agency that surprisingly was one of the largest US law enforcement and security organizations in the world.

"Thank you for meeting with us," Chief Montiglio said. He was a beefy man with large hands and a round, shiny, shaved head. He had a high-pitch voice that didn't seem to belong to such a large man.

"I received your report and spoke with your director. My concern is the safety of my station and of our current operations in the field. And with your safety and that of all embassy personnel, which is why I invited Assistant RSO Durban and Agent Beachy to this meeting. To assess if there is anything that might be a security issue for the embassy," Montiglio explained in a friendly but stern demeanor.

"Well. Firstly, thank you for your concern. We're from the analysis side of things, so we welcome your input when it comes to security," Shaw said. It was his "I'm just a data-crunching geek" shtick that he used when he wanted to be left alone in someone else's playground. And in the CIA hierarchy, the Czech Republic was Montiglio's playground. It behooved Shaw to be nice and get his blessing to play in it, unfettered.

Shaw continued, "We have a report detailing why we're here." Shaw nodded at Guy, who handed out copies. "The gist of it: one of the paramilitary private networks is going through what appears to be some sort of civil war. Or at a minimum some serious internal strife that has left at least two of their free-lancers dead, and another one barely survived a sniper hit in broad daylight in London. His partner, an American and a former member of the Agency, has flown to the Republic. We want to know why. We have no plans to get in any of your officers' way, or step on anyone's toes," Shaw said.

"That would be Pete Maddox?" Montiglio asked.

"Yes, sir," Shaw said.

"You're positive he is in the country?" Assistant SRO Durban asked. He was in his late forties. He was a slight man with a bit of a hunch in his back. He didn't look like the typical alpha types in law enforcement that Shaw usually encountered. With his thin black hair parted to the side, Durbin looked more actuary than security officer.

Special Agent Beachy on the other hand, looked the part. Shaw could tell under her black suit and white dress shirt that she was physically fit. She had short blonde hair. Firm hand-shake. Looked you in the eye. Alpha.

"I'm certain. That's why we're here. We suspect that Mr. Maddox belongs to that private network that pimps out their services to the highest bidder. The network is highly secretive. Operates deep in the dark web. We've been trying to infiltrate it for several years. It appears the network might be run from Prague, at least the digital part of it. It's a good opportunity to see who is behind it. How many of these hired guns work for it. And the jobs this network has carried out. We're hoping Mr. Maddox can lead us to uncover this information. That's our purpose here," Shaw said.

Montiglio and Durban exchanged worried glances.

"I don't know why Langley is sticking their nose into this. We work with similar networks like you've described, *a lot*," Montiglio said.

"Our concern is if it's being used, or could be used, against our own interests. Against our assets. For the most part, Langley agrees with your assessment and has had a laissez faire approach to this subject. But this possible infighting has them worried. Frankly, I've never agreed with this type of setup, and we've never been able to get inside one, as you know, a network like this is very good at being tight-lipped," Shaw said.

"Waste of time in my opinion. But as long as our field work isn't disrupted and you don't step on any of our agents' toes, then I don't care what you two do," Montiglio said.

Bob Guy remained quiet. He was the new kid in school, on his first CIA trip abroad. But inside he was awestruck at meeting station chiefs and DSS special agents, and tracking down mercenaries, and the network in exotic Prague. And all that activity was born from his reports, written after months of research in a cube, thousands of miles away in Northern Virginia. He had to bite his cheek to not smile.

"Thank you," Shaw said to Montiglio.

"I will be assigning Special Agent Beachy here to be your contact while you're in Prague. I want to make sure the overall embassy's interests and people are safe," Durbin said.

Shaw pouted. "That would be fine," he said, trying hard to muster a smile.

Montiglio wrapped his knuckles on the conference table. Once he had everyone's attention he spoke, sounding like a cannonball. "If you're going to be out on the field I need to make sure you're unarmed."

Shaw and Guy looked at each other. Shaw seemed offended. He was an intelligence officer not paramilitary. He never carried a weapon when he was abroad.

"We aren't even issued firearms," Guy said.

"I know that's how it's supposed to be. Six years ago in Turkey, my first station. One of my case officers decided to carry a piece. He was arrested on his way to meet a contact. What would have been standard moves in the game turned into a cluster fuck because one of my officers decided to carry his personal firearm out in the field, unauthorized. It gave that asshole nutjob Abdullah Gül leverage he would have never had. We had to work twice as hard to get our man out. I personally recommended his firing. I won't be burned that way again, so I always ask. Don't take it personally," Montiglio said.

"Besides, Agent Beachy is authorized and registered with the local authorities to carry a firearm, so she'll be handling security," Durbin said.

The meeting broke a few minutes later. Shaw and Guy agreed to meet in Beachy's office that afternoon to go over logistics.

Dale Shaw and Bob Guy crowded into Special Agent Beachy's office. DSS was also on the third floor, but they were on the other side of the biometric-protected door that housed the CIA section.

Beachy didn't know what to make of her strange assignment. It was a basic babysitting duty, which was a big part of her DSS job, but it was unusual to do that for CIA officers, especially Langley-assigned analysts. The agency usually preferred to handle their security in-house.

Dale Shaw was curt and dismissive toward her. It was nothing new to her. She knew he didn't want her in his business. Most didn't until the shit hit the fan; then they came running for her help.

It was the same bullshit she'd gone through as an Army MP, and in five years with the Houston Police Department before she'd joined DSS. People love to hate the police until they needed the police to lay their life on the line for them.

The Czech Republic was her third embassy assignment and, of all the embassy personnel she had to deal with, the CIA was the worst.

The Agency was known for not cooperating with other federal agencies. If it bothered Beachy, she never let it show. She was a thick-skinned professional that didn't rattle easily, who wasn't intimidated by anybody, inside or outside the embassy. She would do her job and she would be pleasant with the two spooks, but she wouldn't trust them, especially Dale Shaw. Bob Guy was just a kid with the rookie sheen still on him. She wasn't too worried about him.

"If Maddox is in Prague, he entered without his own passport. I guess that's not too surprising in your line of work, but it's unusual to me," Beachy said.

"These contractors change identities as easily as socks," Shaw said.

"I looked him up online. Law enforcement only databases.

Google. Not much there about Maddox. A bit unusual for someone with his reputation," Beachy said.

"Men like Maddox have experts that specialize in keeping his online persona clean, and skimpy on the information side of things," Shaw said, sounding annoyed.

Beachy pursed her lips. She was impressed.

"We were always told a record is a record. It stays with you forever," Beachy said.

"Not when you don't play by the rules. One of the reasons I find these private networks troubling," Shaw said, stepping up on his soapbox.

"Okay," Beachy said, sitting back in her chair. "What now, then?"

"We wait."

SIXTY-THREE

43 ROUNDS

Prague, Czech Republic

MADDOX WOKE UP FROM HIS THREE-HOUR SLEEP, showered, and dressed. He did an ammo count before heading out the door. Lux said the 100-count box was half-full, but it came up short. Maddox counted forty-three rounds, not fifty. He loaded the two magazines. He pocketed one and inserted the other magazine into the pistol and loaded a round in the chamber. He checked the safety and placed the pistol at the small of his back.

He scrounged around the apartment for something to put the remaining rounds in. *That will work,* Maddox thought as he pulled out a box of ziplock sandwich bags from the pantry. He took out one of the plastic bags and dumped the remaining seventeen rounds he had into it. *Not a lot of firepower, but it would have to do,* Maddox thought as he shoved the little bag into his coat pocket.

He checked his phone to make sure Sennight's app was still there. It was. He was holding the phone in his hand and looking at the app when it rang, startling him. It was an incoming call from Sennight.

They exchanged hellos.

"What did you find?" Maddox asked.

"For starters, Edvard Danko is not his real name," Sennight said.

"No shit?"

"No shit. The National identification number he's using is from an Edvard Danko born in Slovakia. It's the birth number recorded on the real Edvard Danko's birth certificate, but that Edvard Danko died at age three. Then he resurrected at age nineteen with a new Citizen's Identification Card Number and he was back among the living, praise Jesus," Sennight said with a laugh.

"What else?"

"Well, for one thing ... he is your administrator, so you're on the right track, but I'll be damned to find out his real identity. I don't even know if he's really from Slovakia or the Czech Republic or Detroit for all that matters. I'll need more time to figure out his real identity," Sennight said.

"Not sure that matters anyway. If he's the administrator, he's the one I want. I don't really care how he came into this world—just who he is now as Edvard Danko," Maddox said.

"Makes sense. But I got more," Sennight said. "Edvard Danko 2.0 made his bones as a well-known hacker that went by the handle of Rizzer. Hell, I remember Rizzer back in the day. Dude was famous in the hacker circles and infamous to law enforcement. He was listed as the top spammer in the world. He would ghost machines to send millions and millions of spam emails every single day, pushing the 3 Ps of pills, porn, and poker. He made beaucoup bucks doing that. Then he moved to carding. Ran the biggest carding forum in the dark web. Sold credit card numbers by the millions. Made even more money doing that. US feds had a hard-on for him, but could never get him since he was so good at covering his tracks. Didn't hurt that he worked from that neck of the woods, Slovakia, Bulgaria, and Russia. Anyway, he then he pulled a Keyser Söze and, just like Rizzer, was gone. His legend and myth grew, but he never resurfaced again. But now I got the motherfucker," Sennight said boastfully.

"How?"

"Followed the money and connected the dots but, what really has me vexed is, why the board would have someone like Rizzer onboard. Surely they knew about his background? I mean, it took some work, but the information is there if you know where to look and they should know where to look," Sennight said.

"That's a good question," Maddox said.

"Well, I poked around the community looking for more recent info on Rizzer and all that's left were rumors that he had taken his skills to work for the Russian mafia or that he joined the Russian FSB or SVR hacking unit, no one knows, but there is about a six-year gap between Edvard Danko as Rizzer and Edvard Danko the administrator of TEN," Sennight said.

Maddox made the short walk to the Kotera building on Wenceslas Square.

Everything Sennight had told him bounced around his head. *But in the end,* Maddox told himself, *None of that matters.*

Danko was behind the murders of Fitzsimmons and Ramos. He was behind the hit on Rose. Whatever his motivation, it didn't seem as important to Maddox as it was to the chairman.

He was in Prague to get the identity of the sniper from Danko.

Maddox suspected the sniper wouldn't be too far away if he

was Danko's muscle. Either way, he was there to eliminate a threat.

Let the board figure out the whys over the administrator and the sniper's dead bodies. After that, he was going home.

SIXTY-FOUR

TEN PHOTOGRAPHS

Prague, Czech Republic

It was a quarter past nine in the morning. The streets and sidewalks were a lot busier than they had been a few hours ago.

Maddox could see the city better in the daylight and was impressed by what he saw.

The traffic, though heavy, was nothing compared to the gridlock of London or Miami.

The city streets and sidewalks were clean, and the architecture of the buildings surrounding him was amazing—that was the first impression he had whilst standing in front of the Kotera Building.

Architecturally, it was a beautiful building designed by Czech architect Jan Kotera. It was only seven stories tall and oozed that Art Nouveau look from the late nineteenth and early twentieth century.

Maddox walked inside and was surprised there wasn't a desk with a security guard serving as a gateway into the building. He just walked inside unchallenged.

He found the elevators, but he was looking for the stairwell. It took him about a minute — made more challenging by him not understanding a lick of the Czech language—he finally saw a sign with squiggly red lines forming into what looked like stairs above a door kitty-corner from the elevator. Maddox casually walked over, slowly opened the door, and peeked inside, sure enough, there it was: the stairwell.

He stepped inside and let the door close behind him. The stairwell was empty. He removed the cell phone and fired up Sennight's Geolocating app.

The app icon was simply the letter "G". He tapped on it, and it began to pulsate and glow as it loaded.

After a few seconds, the app was ready. There was only once choice—to tap on a blue button with a single word in white text: START.

Maddox tapped the start button. It took about a minute for the app to do whatever it needed to do, until finally, a blurry depixelized image of a map appeared. After a few seconds, it sharply focused into a clear image of a map with two horizontal hashmarks—one white, the other red.

The white hashmark represented Maddox and there was a dotted green line leading to the red hashmark. A small blue transparent circle was over it, pulsating.

The red hashmark represented Danko, or at least his computer, which meant he, or at least his computer, was inside the building.

Maddox breathed in deeply and began to go up the stairs. He held out the mobile phone like it was a Geiger counter.

Sennight had explained that the closer he got to the target's location, the larger the pulsating blue circle around the red hashmark would become.

Once he was within a few feet and within striking distance of his target the red hashmark would turn green.

Maddox still marveled at the mobile technology. A phone that could be purchased anywhere by anyone had been turned into a target-tracking device by activating a software program.

Beats the hell out of a room-to-room sweep.

Maddox kept going up the stairs as the blue circle began to get bigger and bigger.

After the sixth floor, the circle was larger than the red hashmark. When he reached the seventh floor, the blue circle covered the entire map.

At the seventh floor, he opened the door and stepped into a carpeted corridor with several doors dotting a nondescript hallway.

Maddox made his way down the hallway until the red hashmark turned green.

Maddox looked up. He was standing outside of a brown wooden door with a small plague that read: Suite 7-201. There wasn't any other signage to indicate what business was behind that door.

Maddox looked up and saw a small camera perched above him. Shit. He was going in anyway.

He turned the knob, but the door was locked. He was contemplating his next move when he heard a buzzer go off, and the door lock clicked.

There goes the element of surprise, he thought as he stood there for a moment then he tried the door again. It was unlocked.

His first instinct was to get the hell out of there, but he figured if there was an army in there they would have pounced already.

He removed the pistol from the small of his back, he flicked off the safety and he went inside.

The door shut behind him. He looked around. The office seemed empty. It was poorly lit. Aside from the hum of machines that Maddox figured were computers, it was eerily quiet.

"What now?" Maddox yelled out.

"I'm unarmed, Mr. Maddox," a voice said, coming from the back.

Maddox slowly made his way toward the voice and saw an office with its door open. Maddox peered inside with the pistol still leading the way, ready for action.

He could see a man sitting behind a desk. He moved forward, the gun pointing at the man like an accusatory finger.

The man had both hands up in front of his chest, palms out.

"As you can see, I'm not armed," he said, sounding calm.

"You go by the name Edvard Danko?" Maddox asked. The pistol still trained on the man.

"Yes. It's a pleasure to finally meet you, Mr. Maddox."

He was still holding his hands in front of his chest.

Maddox looked around the office, but he kept the pistol pointed at Danko's head.

"Is it okay if I put my hands down? We need to talk, Mr. Maddox."

"Put your hands on the desk. Palms down. Keep them flat on that desk," Maddox ordered.

Danko complied with a smile, and said, "As you wish."

"Edvard Danko. Or do you prefer to go by Rizzer?"

Danko laughed out loud. "Wow!" he said excitedly. "I haven't heard that name in years. It does bring back memories of much simpler times."

"Just a small-town boy spamming boner pills and porno sites," Maddox said, still in a standing shooting stance.

"You really are good. I now understand why you're one of the board's favorites. Any well-trained goon can pull a trigger, but here you are with my dossier no less, bravo, Mr. Maddox," Danko said.

"What have you been up to with this whole shitstorm you're behind?" Maddox asked.

"First, it's just business. Secondly, I'm one of the people behind it. And please understand I don't take any joy over the violence that took your friends and almost cost Mr. Rose his life. But as you well know in this business, bloodshed is sometimes unavoidable," Danko said. He sounded perversely sincere.

"The chairman wants you alive. Bad news for you, I don't give a shit what the chairman wants. I would put a bullet in your head right now, but you're in luck because you have something I want," Maddox said.

"You have no idea," Danko said.

Maddox glared and cocked his head and said, "I don't play games. Where's the sniper?"

"Good. I don't like to play games either. But I'm afraid we're going to have to meet at another location tonight," Danko said.

For a man with a gun pointed at his head, he was calm. Cocky actually, and that worried Maddox.

"I actually need you for one of your odd jobs," Danko said.

Maddox scoffed. "You must be delusional."

Danko got up slowly, hands back up and said, "I'm not delusional. Everything will be explained three hours from now. But you now work for us."

"How do you figure?" Maddox asked nervously.

Danko sighed. "I do admire you, Mr. Maddox. I'm not bullshitting you. I really do hate this part of the business. But I need to show you something. May I turn this monitor around so you can look at it?" Danko said pointing a laptop on his desk.

Maddox felt his heart pounding. What could they possibly have over him that would make him meet them at that other location? And how could they be so sure he would work for them?

Maddox nodded but didn't say anything. The gun still

pointed at Danko, who slowly turned the laptop around so that Maddox could see its monitor.

Maddox legs felt wobbly. The gun felt like a strongman's anvil in his hand. He felt tears welling in his eyes as he looked at a montage of ten photographs of Sonia.

SIXTY-FIVE

THREE MINUTES

Prague, Czech Republic

Sonia Maddox was tied to a chair.

Maddox stepped forward, and leaned in until his nose was practically touching the monitor screen.

Danko could have shot him in the head, and he wouldn't have noticed.

His mind tried to assuage what he was feeling. He wished what he was seeing was some elaborate photo manipulation. But he knew it was real.

In one of the photographs she was holding a British newspaper with today's date.

And in one of the photographs he could see a gloved hand holding a pistol with its barrel touching Sonia's right temple. Her eyes shut tight.

Maddox felt as if he were watching a movie of him leaping over the desk. He cleared it in one bound.

In seconds, he was on top of Danko shoving him to the ground hard, his left hand around Danko's neck as he squeezed as hard as possible. With his other hand, he shoved the barrel of the Glock right between Danko's eyes and dug in until he drew blood.

Maddox stuck the barrel of the pistol under Danko's chin and he leaned in until they were almost nose to nose.

Maddox seethed, "I'll blow your fucking head off, right now."

Danko's face was sprayed with Maddox spit.

Maddox realized he was acting like a rabid dog. He began to regain his composure, loosened his grip, and pulled the barrel from the man's forehead.

He was still on top of Danko, who was gasping for air.

Maddox snapped out of that blind rage. He let go of Danko's throat and got up.

The administrator stayed on the floor for a moment breathing heavily, rubbing his neck, and putting his fingers to the cut on his forehead.

Danko sat up. He looked at his shaking hands. "I'm bleeding," he said, sounding surprised.

He got up slowly. "I must admit, I didn't see that coming." He patted his hair and looked at Maddox.

"I understand your reaction. You love Sonia and—"

"Say her name again you piece of shit, and I'll kill you right now."

Danko sighed heavily. "Listen to me. You're wasting critical time with these unprofessional outbursts. If I don't call my man holding your wife in three minutes, he will kill her. Three minutes and counting," Danko said, looking at his wristwatch.

"How about I start taking a finger. One at a time, until you tell me where she is. Believe me. I know your type, you don't have what it takes to endure pain," Maddox said.

"You're correct in your assessment. But please, we are well beyond any of that," Danko said, pointing at his watch. "You're down to two minutes and thirty seconds. If I don't call with the code, they will kill her. Even if you were to kill me and get the code, my man will know it's not me and he will kill your wife. If you kill me now and head off looking for her, you're ensuring her death because if you or I don't show up by five in the afternoon, they will kill her. You have no other choice. And now you're down to less than two minutes."

Maddox felt helpless and he was.

Danko stares at his watch. "One minute and forty-five seconds, Mr. Maddox. Tick. Tock."

After another ten seconds Maddox blurted out, "Okay, okay, I'll do whatever you want. I'll be wherever you want me to be. Just call it off. Please."

Danko seemed relieved, and the smug look returned to his face, as he tugged at his clothing and patted off the dust from the floor from it.

"I really need to have a word with the cleaning lady. The floor is filthy."

"Please, call it off," Maddox sounded more desperate.

Danko looked at his watch. "You're quite right," he said as he picked up the phone. It took a few seconds that felt like an eternity to Maddox.

"Yes, it's me. Everything is fine. Nine-Four-Echo-Seven-One-Bravo," Danko said, staying quiet for a few seconds afterward.

"Okay good. Mr. Maddox will be there tonight," Danko said, looking at him with a smile.

"Let me talk to her," Maddox pleaded.

"Hold on. I'll put you on speakerphone."

Danko pressed a button and hung up the receiver.

Maddox could hear background noise.

"Sonia, are you all right?" he shouted.

"Pete. I'm fine. I love you." She sounded hoarse and stuffed up.

"I love you too and don't worry. I'll come and get you. Trust me," he said.

"I trust you." Sonia's voice came over the speakerphone sounding stronger.

Danko cut her off, "okay, that's enough." He disconnected the call.

"I told you she's alive. We just need you to do a job for us, then we'll release her to you safe and sound. Be at this address," Danko said, handing Maddox a piece of paper.

Maddox glanced at the address.

"Remember. Don't be late or she dies. Now get out of my fucking office," Danko said, rubbing his neck and blotting the blood from his forehead with his shirt sleeve.

Maddox spilled out of the building and onto a sidewalk of busy pedestrians unaware what had just happened inside. He was in a fog as he meandered down the sidewalk bumping into annoyed people. Everything and everyone around him carried on as usual, whilst his world was crumbling.

He turned and looked back at the building, thought about going back inside and making Danko talk, but it was risk he wasn't willing to take. He didn't need to take any risks with Sonia's life at stake and by agreeing to the meeting he was buying her time. Maddox doubted they would let her and him live, regardless of what they want him to do and if he did it.

He kept walking in a daze, the vibrant city abuzz. *Get it together* Maddox told himself. Wallowing in grief. Wandering Prague aimlessly wasn't doing him or Sonia any good. He called Sennight and brought him to speed.

"Motherfuckers," Sennight said. Maddox could hear him tapping away furiously at his computer keyboard. "I'm going to look around his servers, see if I can dig up where they have Sonia."

Maddox's next call was to Tawny Tree and Tom Rose. Rose

had been discharged from hospital that day and was staying near Richmond Park, about ten miles from Central London.

"We can check to see if she is still in London," Rose said, sounding stronger.

"I'm on it," Tree said.

"Goddamn, Pete, wish I could be out there with you. My mess and all," Rose said.

"Don't even go there, Tom. See what you guys can find out from that end."

SIXTY-SIX

TROUBLESOME

Prague, Czech Republic

Maddox walked out of the apartment building and saw Jar Lux leaning against his car, working on what was left of a half-eaten Misa ice pop.

They made eye contact and Lux waved him over. Maddox nodded and walked up to him. Lux dropped the popsicle in a trash bin and said, "Sorry not to shake your hand. Sticky."

He reached into his car from the open passenger window and he removed several sanitizer hand wipes from a portable pack that was on the dashboard. He wiped his hands and looked at Maddox embarrassingly. "Sorry."

When he first saw Lux he got sick to his stomach. Was he there to tell them they had found Sonia's body?

That can't be it, Maddox thought. Who would take the time to finish a treat before giving him the worst news possible?

Besides, Lux was alone. Another good sign, Maddox figured there would be a cadre of police if that was the case.

"I wasn't expecting to you see so soon. What is it?" Maddox asked, not knowing what Lux knew about Sonia's kidnapping.

"Tawny Tree contacted me. She told me what happened to your wife. I'm very sorry, Mr. Prince."

"Thanks. Call me Pete," Maddox said.

Lux nodded, not questioning why Harry Prince wanted to be called Pete. He had known it was a cover name. His dealings with the the network were always via code names.

"I assume you want to keep this off the official channels. So right now, the police are not involved. I'm the only one who knows and I'm here to help. Off the books," Lux said.

Maddox considered the offer. He had just met Lux, whilst he had been helpful and reliable so far, he couldn't really trust him unequivocally. Still, having someone who knew Prague and was well-connected locally would come in handy. It was an offer Maddox couldn't pass up.

"Thank you, I appreciate your help," Maddox said.

Lux offered a thin smile. "Animals. It's what we have devolved into. In the past, it didn't matter how black-hearted and vicious these gangsters were, they didn't mess with a man's family." Both men sighed and nodded. "Let's go inside. We can chat," Lux said.

On the way to the apartment, Maddox filled in Lux with what he knew. Lux was a member of TEN, so Maddox didn't have to hold back on its existence.

Once inside, Maddox showed the address where he was supposed to meet Danko and whoever else he might be working with in just over two hours.

Lux looked at the piece of paper with the address and sighed. "Boží Dar," he said.

"Who's that?" Maddox said.

"Boží Dar. It's not the name of person. It's a place. It means 'god's gift'. Hardly," he explained, still looking at the address.

"Why is that?"

"It's a relic from the past. It's an old Soviet airstrip and

Army base. Used to have thousands of Soviet soldiers stationed there and a city sprung up around the base and then wilted away during the winter of 1991, when the last of the Soviet troops pulled out of the country. The area sat in limbo for years until it was finally completely abandoned. It was left to the weeds. Now it's a ghost city. The airstrip, hangers, barracks, school, gym, hospital, heating plant, parking lots, even a cinema, all abandoned to rot near the village of Milovice. About forty kilometers from Prague," Lux explained.

"Sounds like a charming place," Maddox said.

"It's a troublesome location. Isolated. Abandoned for twenty years. Overgrown by vegetation. A lot of old buildings. Large ones, warehouses, hangars. A lot of places where they could hold your wife undetected. And there are a lot of locations to set up tight parameters for security. They will be able to spot anyone coming in or out, easily. Troublesome. Very troublesome ..." Lux said, trailing off.

"Any idea how many people will be there?"

"No. There is Danko and the man that has been doing his dirty work. I don't know who he is, but he's a well-trained sniper. Danko made it sound like there was someone else in charge. I thought it might be bullshit, but I detected fear when he spoke about that person," Maddox said.

"When you and Foxglove told the chairman about your suspicions, he had me look into Edvard Danko," Lux said.

"We checked him out too. It's a fake identity," Maddox said, then proceeded to share what Sennight had dug out.

Lux was impressed.

"You would make a good policeman," Lux said with a laugh, "I can fill in the gaps."

"Pavel Nossik was a powerful man in Russia. Very rich. Very connected all the way to the Kremlin. He had a brutal reputation. You know like, Al Capone, in your country or John Gotti," Lux said.

"So Nossik was a mobster?" Maddox asked.

"Russian mafia, yes. The Bratva. Nossik became even more of a powerful man after the Soviet Union collapse. Danko worked for Nossik's organization but tech crimes only. Not muscle."

"Explains why he needed to find a muscle to do that work on his behalf."

"Edvard Danko's real name is Mikhail Chernykh. He was born in the USSR, in what is now Azerbaijan. He worked for a Nossik front called Federal Capital Partners that was a fund run by a financier in Moscow that was a close personal friend of the president of Russia.

The fund did a lot of legitimate business investments, but it also cleaned the dirty money of the Russian Mafia. Nossik did that work for years earning hefty commissions along the way. He had other businesses as well, and was one of the first in organized crime to jump into cybercrimes using the best hackers in Russia and the Eastern Bloc."

"Such an entrepreneur," Maddox scoffed.

"Danko was still going by his real name and he was Nossik's best hacker. Made his way into his inner circle. Hacking into the computers of his enemies and friends in order to have something over everyone he encountered. It didn't matter if that person was a lowly drug dealer or the president of Russia himself. He had dirt on everyone. It was the reason he got away with everything he did for a very long time. As usual in that world, he must have pissed off the wrong people because Nossik was killed in a very public way. Gunned down along with his driver and bodyguards inside the Lefortovo Tunnel in 2005."

"Not very subtle," Maddox said.

"The hit was during the middle of the day and it was

captured by the tunnel's many CCTV cameras. You can still find the video of it on YouTube. It was a way to send a message to the mafia by the oligarchs," Lux said.

"I thought those two groups were one and the same," Maddox said.

"This is true. A reason why Nossik's murder remains unsolved. Only someone more powerful than Nossik could have gotten away with killing him. No one says it but everyone knows you don't kill a man like Nossik without the president's blessing. After the hit, Mikhail Chernykh goes dark for several years, before reappearing here in Prague as Edvard Danko. At first, he seemed to be a legitimate IT executive for an internet hosting company called Cyber One, but of course, we now know that was a front company created by TEN to manage and protect its network."

"I can't figure out how in the hell the chairman would get involved with someone like Danko. He had to have known. I found out about him. You found out," Maddox said.

"I asked him just that. He said Danko was brought into the network by another member of the board. And, since he didn't know anything about the technical aspects of putting together a network such as TEN, he trusted in the board member's recommendation and let that person be in charge of the tech aspects of the network. Which he now says was an obvious mistake, but he trusted that person," Lux said.

"Who was the board member?" Maddox asked.

"He would not tell me," Lux said.

"Why not?"

"He says divulging the identity of anyone in the network, myself included or you, without absolute proof, like in Danko's case, would violate everything that the network stands for. In order to do that, it would require a board majority vote," Lux said.

"Seriously? He wants the board to vote about exposing one of their own?" Maddox shook his head.

"He said that was the problem he was trying to get his arms around," Lux said.

"Sounds convenient. How do we know the chairman isn't behind all this? He knew we were in London. He contracted Foxglove. He could have provided this information to Danko and his triggerman," Maddox said.

"I wouldn't discount anything right now," Lux said.

Maddox looked out the window and up to the sky.

"Do you think an airplane could land on that old Boží Dar airstrip?" Maddox asked.

"Sure. The entire town is crumbling, but a few years ago, drug smugglers patched up one of the airstrips so they could land their planes filled with heroin from Pakistan. Why do you ask?"

"My wife was kidnapped in London. The only way to get her here quickly and quietly would be via a private airplane," Maddox said.

"You're under the assumption she is here, though. She might still be in London," Lux said.

"When Danko showed me a photograph, she was tied to a chair in what looked like a small loft. She had duct tape over her mouth. But when he called his shooter and he let me talk to her for proof of life. Although it was audio only over a landline, she wasn't gagged and when she spoke, I picked up an echo, it sounded like she was being held in a large location. I was thinking warehouse or a storage facility. For sure not a small apartment from the photograph. The way you describe it, Boží Dar would be perfect. Isolated so they didn't have to worry about her talking loudly. They could be holding her in an old, empty hanger or any of those abandoned buildings you described. It makes sense that they would bring her here, versus

London. And the sniper, I'm sure he was itching to get out of London after he shot Foxglove," Maddox said.

"That makes sense. What do you want to do?" Lux said.

"I have no choice. I'm going to show up at the meeting location. They have my wife."

SIXTY-SEVEN

THE TECHNICAL SIDE

United States Embassy, Prague, Czech Republic

DALE SHAW AND BOB GUY WERE SHARING A SMALL OFFICE on the CIA floor in the embassy.

As promised or warned, depending if looking from Montiglio or Shaw's perspective, the Station Chief didn't offer anything but the one office for them to share.

That was fine with Shaw. This was his operation and he would make sure Montiglio didn't receive any credit for its success.

Shaw looped in Melody Andrews, a Technical Intelligence Officer and his Senior Analyst, Tanya Girard back in Langley to assist them.

Their focus was on the technical details that Guy had provided in his reports, to use that to find more actionable intelligence on the ground in Prague whilst looking for possible gaps in the intelligence gathering done so far.

Guy didn't mind knowing that Shaw wanted Girard riding shotgun. He was too green to come off overconfident and cocksure in his analysis. He demurred to the sixteen-year veteran and the computer wizardly of Andrews.

It was Shaw's contention that the key to getting inside the network was from the technical side because, regardless of how deep inside the dark web, TEN had to have a home on a server somewhere. Just follow digital breadcrumbs, Shaw kept insisting. Not that simple, Guy thought but kept it to himself.

It was eleven o'clock at night for Melody Andrews in Langley. She had been working for close to twenty hours straight. Her eyes were bloodshot, her vision blurry, and her neck and back ached from being crouched over a bank of computer monitors.

She was getting ready to head home for a few hours, but as she was packing up she remembered something from earlier that day and got her second wind.

She logged back into her computer and began tapping away. Two hours later, she called Bob Guy in Prague.

"I might have found something. Are you in a secure location?" she said excitely.

"I'm at the embassy it's secure. Do tell," Guy said.

"Well, Mr. Shaw had me tracking flights from London to Prague. As you know that didn't turn up anything. And I went down to the smallest puddle-jumping airlines out there, and still nothing. Then I started thinking about private planes. Maddox is a licensed pilot. How difficult could it be for him to get his hands on a private plane, even if it's a small, single propeller type craft? I started looking into that possibility. I didn't find anything to tie it to Maddox, but there was a flight that I haven't been able to get out of my head. It originated in London. The destination was a small town not too far from Prague called Milovice. Population around 10,000. The timeline fits what you gave me," Andrews said.

"How far away it is?" Guy asked, taking notes.

"Not far from the embassy. I was doing fifty-mile sweeps. It's about twenty-five miles from Prague. They don't even have a municipal airport or landing strip there. Why would anyone fly there? And where would they land? As I was trying to figure that out I learned that there is an old Soviet military base there with landing strips. MIG fighter jets used it back in the Soviet days. It was abandoned decades ago, after the dissolution of the USSR and it's now a popular spot with the off the beaten track tourists, but that airstrip is still there and if a MIG could land there, so could a small plane. I used the GPS data that I have on that airfield and began to pull some real-time satellite imagery and, well, something is going on there," Andrews said.

"Hold on, let me see if I can find Shaw," Guy said, sounding excited. He stood up and opened the door, but Shaw wasn't within earshot, so he closed the door and sat back down.

"He's not around. What did you see?"

"I have a satellite honed in. I'm seeing a small aircraft and several vehicles," Andrews said.

"At what time?"

"Real time. I'm looking at live satellite video."

"Holy shit, fantastic," Guy said.

"Don't get too excited. For all we know it could be sightseers or a drug deal going down, it doesn't mean this is related to Maddox or the network," Andrews said cautiously.

"Yes, but what are the odds? A London flight. That town. Like you said, off the beaten track. I'm certain Shaw will want us to check it out on the ground here," Guy said.

"Can't hurt," she said.

"I'm going to find Shaw and let him know what you found," Guy said. He hung up to find Shaw.

"That would be a hell of a coincidence for it to not be about the network," Shaw said, looking at a thirty-minute video clip Andrews had sent of Boží Dar.

Shaw called Special Agent Beachy on the telephone and asked her if she knew that location.

"I know it well. It's a fantastic hiking area, especially with the Soviet ruins out there. A lot of fun to go exploring. It's also well-known to the DEA since it has been used in the past for drug and even human smuggling. I haven't heard of anything going down there along those lines since I've been stationed here though, but Boží Dar would make a phenomenal spot to meet clandestinely. The closest village near there is small, a one-horse kind of town. And they're used to people going up to the ruins and trespassing. Just about every inch of concrete has been tagged by graffiti, the locals probably wouldn't think twice seeing anyone heading out there. And a small plane could discreetly land without raising any suspicions."

"Do you think we can go?" Shaw said.

"Tonight?"

"The sooner the better. We have strong evidence there is some activity going on there right now, I'd like to check it out before they're gone," Shaw said.

"I'll be ready in ten minutes. Meet you in the parking lot. It's about a forty-minute drive up there," Beachy said, and hung up.

SIXTY-EIGHT
EVERYONE DIES

Czech Countryside

Maddox drove a rented white Volkswagen Golf out of Prague and onto the D10 autostrada highway toward the Czech countryside.

Once he was out of the city, the traffic was light.

The highway was in great condition and the landscape passing Maddox by was serene and peaceful. He was surrounded by the green countryside, and expansive mountain ranges that seemed to keep a watchful eye for him.

Weather-beaten homes and farms dotted the countryside. He felt a twinge of jealousy for the people living there peacefully and quiet, simple lives. At least, that was how it seemed from the highway. He wanted that life for him and Sonia without odd jobs.

He tried to stay positive thinking about their future. Maybe it was time to get out of hectic Miami. Buy a small farmhouse like the ones he was seeing in a blur as he drove passed them. Maybe somewhere in Europe. Or Central America. Or Wyoming. Maddox smiled, thinking about that. More importantly, it pushed the dark thoughts about his wife being killed out of his head.

It didn't matter for how long his mind would drift away from those thoughts it would circle back to that and he knew what he would do.

If anything happens to her, everyone dies. Myself included.

"Stay positive," he shouted out loud. He would say that over and over during the drive out to Boží Dar.

Jar Lux followed Maddox in his car as Bach's Brandenburg Concerto No. 4 in G Major hummed from the CD deck.

The sounds of the violins and recorders of Allegro soothed his mind from thinking about what they were driving into.

He could say no. What good was a bundle of money paid by the network if he was dead?

He had just met Maddox. Why did he care what happened to him or his wife? He'd made his bed, let him lay in it. But Lux had done the same. He had taken money from the network. It didn't matter if a cop took money from the Russian mafia or a network doing what he believed was good in the fight against terrorism and extremists. The bottom line was simple: he was corrupt. Good cause or bad.

He was involved in the criminal world. That was his bed. And he wasn't going to leave Maddox and his wife out in the cold to face these troubles alone. He also felt certain that Maddox would do the same for him if it were his loved one being held hostage.

They had agreed that he would stay far back. They didn't believe they were being followed. Danko held all the cards. But it was best to play it safe.

Besides, there was no need to follow closely. Lux knew where Maddox was going. The key for him was to remain unseen while Maddox met up with Danko and his people in Boží Dar.

SIXTY-NINE

BOŽÍ DAR

Boží Dar, Czech Republic

MADDOX DROVE INTO MILOVICE. IT WAS A QUAINT LITTLE village that only took a few minutes to drive through.

From there, he had another ten-minute drive to reach the abandoned Soviet military village of Boží Dar.

The approach road into Boží Dar was bumpy and curvy. He turned a corner and suddenly there it was up ahead.

He slowed down to a crawl. He looked at the crumbling buildings, every inch of them covered in graffiti and overgrown vegetation.

It was an eerie sight that reminded him of the photographs he had seen of Chernobyl.

He drove for a few more minutes, looking at the abandoned buildings until he saw a shiny new black Cadillac Escalade. The front of the SUV was facing Maddox, blocking his way.

Maddox stopped and the SUV lights flicked on and off three times. Maddox did the same.

The passenger and driver side doors opened. The passenger stood behind the open door, using it as a shield. He was in the crouching position, his elbow on the car door panel, and he leaned forward, sticking an Agram 2000 submachine gun out through the rolled down window.

The man didn't say anything. He didn't have to. Maddox could see the stubbed-barrel of the submachine gun pointed at him.

The driver approached Maddox slowly with a pistol drawn, but it was not aimed at him. He didn't have to with Agram man covering him. He held the pistol down to his side. Maddox noticed it was cocked and ready.

The driver didn't say anything as he walked toward Maddox. All he could hear was the road gravel and broken glass from the ghost town crunching under foot with each step the man took.

He was short and stocky. He looked like a fat bullfrog. Black hair cut short. He was dressed in black from head to toe. He wasn't dressed in tactical gear. He wore a stylish Hugo Boss quilted windbreaker jacket.

Finally, the man spoke. "Mr. Maddox, I need to search you. Don't do anything stupid. Understand?" the man said with a Russian accent, but his English was very good.

"I understand," Maddox said.

The man got up within arm's reach. He had a flat face and a boxer's nose. Small red bumps covered his cheeks like broken blood vessels.

The man glanced over to his partner to make sure he was still there, then pocketed the pistol as Maddox raised his arms out. The man put both of his meaty hands on Maddox and began to pat him down.

Maddox noticed he had a small eight-pointed star tattoo. And he recognized it. Danko had the same tattoo in the web of his hand between the thumb and index finger. Just like this guy. Maddox hadn't made much of it when he noticed it on Danko, tattoos being so common now days. But the tattoo had taken a whole new meaning to him.

The Russian mafia was big on tattooing their people. *Is that who was behind all of it?* Maddox thought. *But why?*

The man stopped and flinched when he felt Maddox's pistol tucked in the small of his back. He looked up making eye contact.

Maddox noticed the black nothingness in the man's eyes.

He had made no effort to conceal the gun. He knew he would be frisked. But you learn a lot from these encounters. Maddox took it all in. Filing it for later use.

The man took the pistol, looked at it, then used it to wave Maddox toward the Escalade, saying: "Let's go. Get in the passenger side, in the front."

Maddox did as he was told. The man with the submachine gun, who had kept it trained on Maddox the whole time his partner had frisked him, stepped back a few steps and followed Maddox with the barrel of the weapon as Maddox climbed inside the SUV's passenger side.

"Close door," the machine gunner grunted. With just those two heavily accented words, Maddox could tell the triggerman didn't speak English as well as his partner.

The triggerman was taller and bulked up, muscle-wise, in comparison to the bullfrog. *A weight lifter and steroid user Maddox thought.* He also was dressed all in black. He peeked at his hands, but he was wearing gloves. No doubt he would be sporting the same tattoo on his hand as the bullfrog and Danko, Maddox thought.

Once Maddox was seated inside the SUV. The triggerman climbed into the backseat. Right behind Maddox and said, "No fuck round. I shoot. Kill you."

"Yeah, I got that," Maddox said flippantly. He heard the man grunt from behind.

The driver got in. He looked at Maddox then at the trigger-man. Said something in Russian or some Eastern Bloc language.

He started the SUV. The bullfrog made a U-turn and drove through the ghost town.

Maddox stared out of the window. After a few minutes Maddox saw a cylinder-shaped concrete building that looked like one of the old hangars that the Soviets had built. It looked like an empty can of cranberry sauce turned on its side.

As the SUV got close, the driver turned the wheel and slowly backed into the front door of the hangar.

The bullfrog parked the SUV. He removed his pistol and said to Maddox, "Get out, slowly."

Maddox stepped out of the SUV, slowly.

The triggerman was already outside the SUV. His subma-chine gun still pointed at Maddox. He hadn't stopped pointing it at him since they'd met. No doubt they had been warned that Maddox was not a man to be taken lightly.

"Let's go, toward the back of the building," the bullfrog said, waving his pistol like a wand.

Maddox did as he was told while the triggerman and the bullfrog walked behind him keeping enough distance to keep their weapons from Maddox's reach.

The building had been built to house fighter jets so it was a huge space.

Maddox looked up and noticed the broken glass and its crumbling façade. There was graffiti everywhere inside too. Even on the ceiling. He wondered how in the hell a kid had gotten up there to tag it. *Impressive. Must be Spiderman.*

The sun was setting. It was dark inside the hanger so they had set up a bank of floodlights toward the back.

"Keep going. Toward the light," the bullfrog said.

Maddox hoped he was being literal.

The floodlights blinded Maddox as he approached.

"Stop," Bullfrog croaked.

Maddox blinked in an attempt to get rid of the white spots from the scathing lights. Slowly, his eyes began to autofocus and he saw another black Escalade SUV parked sideways next to a card table that had been set up. There was a well-dressed woman sitting on a folding chair. A table was between them. The triggerman and bullfrog split up to flank Maddox.

He turned toward the SUV. Its windows were tinted so dark he couldn't tell if anyone was inside. A third black-clad, steroid-taking thug, was leaning against the passenger door of the SUV, holding an RPK machine gun in the ready position.

"Right on time, Mr. Maddox," Danko said.

Maddox's eyes had now adjusted. He turned to glare at Danko who was sitting next to the woman at the table. Maddox turned his attention toward her. He had never seen her before.

"Let me guess, you're Danko's puppet master," Maddox said. It was now Danko glaring at Maddox.

The woman smiled.

SEVENTY

KING ARTHUR'S NEPHEW

Boži Dar, Czech Republic

She was in her mid fifties. Good-looking. She seemed rich in her gray Armani pants suit. A 19-karat gold Omega De Ville watch peeked from underneath the Armani sleeve of her right arm, resting loosely on her wrist.

A black Chanel bag was on the table next to her. She wore bright red lipstick that seemed out of place with her power suit and light makeup.

It was a surreal moment for Maddox as he looked around the dilapidated hanger surrounded, by well-armed and well-dressed thugs and that woman, dressed like a Fortune 500 executive.

It reminded Maddox of a board meeting.

Then it began to dawn on him. *Fuck. A board meeting.*

He knew one of the Threat Elimination Network's board members was a woman. He couldn't recall her codename. It was one of King Arthur's knights or some shit like that, but the name escaped him. *It had to be her.*

She looked at him and, realizing Maddox was starting to

figure out who she was. She smiled wider than before and nodded.

"It seems you know who I am," she said cheerfully with a trace of Russian accent.

"You're one of the board members of TEN," Maddox said.

"I am. Gawain."

"Gawain. I knew it had something to with King Arthur's Knight, right?"

She kept on smiling.

"Indeed. He was King Arthur's nephew and a Knight of the Round Table. Not as well-known in the Arthurian legend. I like that. In the background but still in the circle of power."

She removed a pack of Dunhill Menthol Lights from her coach bag. She pulled out a cigarette and lit it with an 18-Karat Gold Cartier pocket lighter.

Very rich indeed, Maddox thought.

"Would you like a cigarette, Mr. Maddox?"

"Where is my wife?" Maddox said.

She took a drag, and slowly put the pack of cigarettes and lighter back into her bag. She then sat up straight and took another drag from her cigarette.

"I must say, it's such a pleasure to meet you. An honor really, a man of your skills," she said, eyeing him up and down.

"Where. Is. My. Wife."

Gawain grinned and nodded at the RPK machine gun-holding thug by the SUV. He nodded back, stepped aside, and opened the passenger door that he had been leaning against. Inside was Sonia. Her clothing was disheveled and sweat-stained. Her brown hair was a mess, and a red bandana gagged her. Her arms were tied together in front, bound by plastic hand restraints. She looked like she had been put through hell, and she had, but she was alive.

Her eyes widened when she saw Maddox, and she smiled

wide despite the gag in her mouth. Maddox smiled back and without even realizing it, he stepped toward her, causing the thug with the RPK to point his weapon at her, while the bull-frog and triggerman aimed their weapons at Maddox.

"I wouldn't do that, Mr. Maddox, the men are a bit jittery. Your reputation precedes you," Danko said.

Maddox stopped.

"As you can see your lovely wife is fine. She has not been harmed. Now, we have business to discuss," Gawain said.

He turned to Gawain and said, "Please, take that gag from her mouth. She won't scream, and we're out here in the middle of fucking nowhere anyway. There is no need for that."

Gawain mulled it over for a few seconds and nodded at RPK thug, who brusquely removed the bandana so it hung around her neck.

"Thank you," Sonia said. She was breathing heavily, but she was trying hard to be strong and to not show her captors the fear that was consuming her inside. She looked at Maddox. Her green eyes boring into his soul. It was strange even though she had been put through hell she had never seen such pain on his face before and it hurt her. She smiled at him and mouthed: *I love you*. But before he could do the same, the RPK thug slammed the door shut. He smirked at Maddox.

Maddox yelled out, "I love you!"

The three black-clad thugs laughed at the perceived sign of weakness.

"Bulletproof vehicle. Soundproof. I'm afraid she couldn't hear you, Mr. Maddox," Danko said with a shit-eating grin on his face.

Maddox wanted to kill them all, but he was powerless. He hadn't felt that helpless in his life, and he had been in plenty of sticky situations during his professional career.

He'd been shot at more times than he could count, a few

rounds finding their way into his body. That pain paled in comparison to what he felt right now inside.

He stood there without a weapon. Without any power. Without any leverage. He felt naked. The only backup a lone Czech cop that Maddox wasn't even sure had followed through with his promise to help.

He turned and faced Gawain. She sat there stoically, smoking her cigarette.

"What do you want?" Maddox asked.

"My fellow board members and I haven't always been on the same page when it came to running the network," Gawain said, brushing off dust from her Armani lapel.

"And?" Maddox said impatiently.

"It's nothing personal, really. It's just a differing philosophy. Creative differences. You see, Mr. Maddox, I view the world from a business perspective only. I don't really care how the money clients pay us is made. Whether it comes from the CIA or a drug kingpin. It's irrelevant to me, as long as they pay. And as you can imagine, those in that world of running drugs, guns, and women, pay much, much better. I never understood the board's insistence of leaving all that money on the table. And to deal with freelancers such as yourself with these archaic moral codes to justify what you do. It's silly really, darling. To me, all decisions should be based strictly on business decisions. Not morals or politics. The tobacco companies haven't shut down and they kill millions of people," she said looking at her cigarette with a smile, "I stopped caring about the politics when that pig in the Kremlin double-crossed us and had my husband killed," Gawain said.

Maddox sighed. "This is just rich. Let me guess. Your husband was Pavel Nossik?"

Gawain looked genuinely surprised. Danko fidgeted in his chair.

"Well. You are good, Mr. Maddox. He was my husband. Believe me I don't want to have to put you through what I went through. It's not nice being a widow," Gawain said, glancing over to the SUV where Sonia was being held.

Maddox shook his head, "Okay. What does this have to do with me? With my wife? What do you want from me?"

"Direct and to the point. I like it," she said, holding out the butt of her cigarette in the air. The man with the submachine gun stepped forward taking the cigarette and he flicked to the side.

Gawain interlocked her hands on the table. She looked at Maddox directly in the eyes and said, "I want you to kill the Chairman of the Board."

SEVENTY-ONE

LARKSPUR

Boží Dar, Czech Republic

THE REQUEST TOOK MADDOX ABACK. HE LOOKED AT around and he scoffed. "It seems to me you're pretty damned capable of doing that yourself," He pointed at her armed thugs.

Gawain laughed. It was a throaty smoker's laugh.

"The chairman trusts very few people. As you can imagine after what has happened here in the last couple weeks, we are no longer trusted. He's always been very careful. Did you know he was one of the first Mossad agents?"

Maddox shook his head.

"He was there at the birth of Israel. Keeping the Palestinians in check. Surrounded by Arab enemies that wanted nothing more than to destroy them all into oblivion. He's extremely capable. And I'm convinced, clinically paranoid, but that's my uneducated personal assessment," Gawain said, smiling.

"The chairman trusted three freelancers: Adonis, Dogbane, and Foxglove. He loves to assign his assassins code names after poisonous flowers. Did you know that, Mr. Maddox?"

He shook his head and sighed. "I really don't care about any of this."

She ignored him. "That's why he gave you the code name of Larkspur. Such a silly old man with his love of poisonous flowers. He is quite an accomplished gardener, a botanist at heart who focuses on growing the most poisonous flowers in the world in his garden. Appropriate, I guess. Death is such a part of our business that even when he grows beautiful flowers, he makes sure they're deadly," she said with a laugh.

"You knew Dogbane as Malcolm Fitzsimmons. Adonis your friend, Hermes Ramos. And of course, Foxglove, unfortunately, is your still alive dear friend, Tom Rose. Adonis and Dogbane went down easy. Foxglove got lucky, thanks to you. The plan was easy. Kill the chairman's three freelancers then we were home free to kill the chairman and take over TEN. Since you messed up our plans, *you* will now kill the chairman. As payment, I let your wife live. And if you can get Foxglove to agree to stand down, I let him ... and you live. Seems like a fair price to me. One old man for your three lives. Don't you agree?"

"Just how—" Maddox began to say, but was interrupted by Gawain.

"There is no debate, Mr. Maddox, no further explanation. I don't care how difficult it will be, or how you have to do it, but you will kill the chairman. You've proven to be extremely resourceful. Tracked down Edvard here, even though he assured me he was so good that no one would ever track him down or put our past and us two together," she glared at Danko who fidgeted some more. He looked down but did not speak.

"I'll give you one week. Don't worry. Your wife will be under my care. No one will harm her. I promise you that. Kill the chairman and your wife lives. That should be your only concern. The only information you need to have," Gawain said, rising as her three thugs shuffled around in the background with their weapons aimed at Maddox.

"Wait, wait, one week? I don't even know where he is," Maddox said.

"You're resourceful. I know you have contacts. Like that CIA tech person in Reston, Virginia at your disposal. I'm sure you can track him down. And I'm giving you a whole week. Shouldn't be difficult for a man with your skills," Gawain said.

He tried to bargain and to stall her, but she stopped him cold.

"That's it, Mr. Maddox. We're done here. You have your assignment. Go do it. If you fail ... your wife dies. It's simple."

SEVENTY-TWO
AMERIKANSKIY

Boží Dar, Czech Republic

OUTSIDE OF THE HANGAR, AXEL WAS IN THE PRONE shooting position. He was viewing the proceedings inside of the hangar from his rifle's scope. He could have put a bullet into Maddox's head whenever he wanted. He liked having that power over life and death. It made him feel important. Especially after the way he had been treated by the Eurotrash inside.

Mr. White, who Axel now knew as Edvard Danko, had always treated him with condescension, but they had bonded the last few days and Danko had been impressed with his work and the way he had taken Sonia off the streets of London without anyone noticing.

No manhunts. No police. Nothing on the news about the pretty Venezuelan-American girl gone missing. His best work.

But that had all changed when that Gawain showed up. *And she's the one in charge?*

Axel couldn't believe it. Every single woman he had ever encountered, starting with his mother, had been nothing but a disappointment and torment in his life. And now she was the one charge?

Danko cowering to a woman? And she was so smug, dressed to the nines and her men all dressed sharply. He knew they laughed at him, in his blue jeans and Judas Priest T-shirt.

They laughed and called him Amerikanskiy. He didn't speak Russian, but he understood the Russian word for American. Sounded like Amerikans-key to him. He'd heard it before. He knew they were mocking him.

Tough guys with their shitty Russian machine guns. They couldn't do what he had done alone. With his rifle and his bare hands. Killing top echelon freelancers from TEN on Danko's orders, which he knew, had really been that bitch's order.

He seethed, watching them through his scope. "All those steroid fuckers can do is spray and pray when they pull the trigger."

Axel was consumed with that disrespect. How Danko was back to treating him like hired help. Suddenly he found himself aiming the rifle at Gawain's head.

Then he aimed at each of her thugs' heads. Then at Danko. *It would be so easy*, he thought. He was certain he could hit all five targets before they even knew what had happened.

They would hear the first retort, but by then it would be too late.

He grinned then put the crosshairs back on Maddox's head as that was what he had been told to do—lay out there in the dirt where he belonged and shoot Maddox if he tried something.

After a few seconds, Axel once again aimed at Gawain. *I'd like to show her what this* Amerikanskiy *could do to you.* "Boom," he said softly and smiled thinking about blowing her head off.

SEVENTY-THREE
RIFLESCOPES

Milovice, Czech Republic

Jar Lux parked in front of the small grocery store in Milovice—the only one in town. He removed his official police placard from the glove compartment and tossed the "I can park anywhere" pass on his dashboard.

He got out. There was a chill in the air and it would soon be dark. He put on a jacket, went inside the store and started to ask the clerk if he had seen vehicles heading up toward Boží Dar.

"Yes. I've seen a few vehicles drive by heading in that direction. Very unusual for this time of the year, the sightseers and tourists usually go earlier in the morning," he said, scratching a scruffy grey beard.

"What type of vehicles?" Lux asked.

The cashier's eyes lit up. "Oh, nice ones and more than one. Shiny. They looked brand new. These big black trucks. Expensive. They looked like fancy tanks."

"Anything else unusual?" Lux asked.

"Well, we heard an airplane, one of those small ones. Landed a few hours ago. I mean it's not that unusual since more of these small planes are landing at that old airstrip. But usually it's on the weekends. The day and time, that's why I say it's unusual. Plus those nice trucks," the cashier said, then asked, "Any troubles? We've had problems in the past up there with criminals." The cashier leaned in and whispered, "Drugs."

"It's an official police investigation," Lux lied.

"Just you alone? One policeman?" the cashier said incredulously.

Lux barked, "Don't worry about my business. Besides, I can't share any information about an active investigation. Just make sure to tell your friends and family and anyone who comes to your store to stay out of Boží Dar until I say so, okay?"

"That, sir, won't be a problem. Place gives me and all us locals the creeps. I wish the government would bulldoze the damned thing down. Attracts riffraff."

Lux told the cashier that he was leaving his car parked at his store. He stepped outside and walked to his car. He opened the trunk, looked around and saw the cashier snooping at him through the window. Lux glared at him, making him flinch, and the old man stepped away from the window.

Lux removed his pistol from the holster clipped to his belt. It was a CZ 75 P-01.

It was a powerful Czech-made pistol that was the official service firearm for the police, as evident from the letters spelling POLICE stamped on the slide of the gun.

He removed its extended capacity magazine to make sure its cartridges hadn't evaporated into thin air—a nervous tick cops around the world have of triple and quadruple checking ammo before heading into danger.

The rounds were still in the magazine so he slapped it back into his pistol.

He grabbed two more fully loaded extended magazines and shoved them both into his jacket pocket.

Then he reached for a soft nylon rifle case. He unzipped it and removed a Sako 85 Finnlight with a Leupold scope. It was his personal rifle used to hunt deer and mouflon wild sheep.

He loaded it with .308 Winchester cartridges. He pocketed the ammo box, then slung the rifle over his shoulder.

He closed the trunk of the car and he began to make his way up to Boží Dar on foot.

Lux cut through the woods instead of walking up the road. He figured they would watch the main road but not the woods.

It added time for him to get there but remaining unseen was the most important aspect of him being there to backup Maddox.

If challenged, he would pretend to be out hunting.

After hiking for twenty minutes, he saw the abandoned village off to his left. He was still deep in the woods.

After a few more minutes, he located Maddox's rented car about fifty feet down a wooded embankment.

The car was not on the main road that was still maintained by the Czech Republic, but one of the crumbling, potholed roads that used to be the hidden road into Soviet-era Boží Dar. Like the rest of the village, those old roads had been abandoned by the Czech government around the same time the Soviets had pulled out of the country.

Maddox's car was parked in the middle of the buckled road near the outskirts of the village.

Lux couldn't see Maddox or anyone else. He seemed to have just stopped right there and just taken off.

He saw tire tracks in front of Maddox's car. Lux followed the track marks, which seemed to head deeper into the village, so he kept walking parallel to the road, still in the woods to avoid detection. He kept looking over to his right to follow the tracks.

After about five minutes, Lux was on top of an embankment, looking at a flat surface and a gravel road leading into one of the many Soviet-era hangars.

He then spotted one of the fancy trucks the cashier had mentioned.

It was a black Cadillac Escalade SUV, parked at the entrance of a hangar.

It had been backed into the hangar's large barn-like doors, but the driver had stopped and parked halfway into the hangar so the front of the Escalade stuck outside. The rear was inside the hangar and out of his line of sight.

It appeared that it was parked that way to block the only way in, and out, of that hangar.

Lux cursed himself for forgetting to bring binoculars; he used the scope of his rifle to check things out.

He couldn't see any other vehicles or people around. It was quiet. He began to scan the area around the building. He quickly stopped and popped his head up for visual confirmation, to make sure he'd seen what he'd thought through the rifle's scope.

It was a man downslope about one-hundred yards. He was lying on the ground on his belly in a prone position, holding a rifle that he was pointing at the side of the hangar.

"Shit," Lux whispered, looking again through his scope.

The man didn't know Lux was directly above him at the top of the embankment.

Lux followed the man's rifle with his rifle's scope and could tell the man was aiming into the hangar through one of its large windows that had long ago become glass free.

It was a surreal experience for the city detective to peer down the scope of his rifle to watch a man doing the same to someone else.

Lux studied the man's rifle. It was not like his—a simple

deer-hunting rifle. That man was holding the type of rifle used by the Czech police special tactics team members.

That's when it dawned on Lux who that man was: the sniper that had tried to kill Tom Rose in London.

It was the shooter that Maddox was after.

Shit. Lux swallowed hard.

What the fuck have you gotten yourself into?

He couldn't call for backup. He couldn't make this official. Doing so would alert his superiors that he took on work off the books.

That he worked for the network. Like picking up their contractors from the airport and setting them up in a safe house. Providing them with illegal firearms and backing them up, like he was doing right now. No. He was on his own.

The thought of sneaking back down to Milovice and getting into his car and going home to his family danced around his head, but he had told Maddox he would help.

He told the same thing to the chairman. And if someone had kidnapped his wife, he would hope someone like Maddox would help him.

There he was in the woods surrounding Boží Dar. Armed with a hunting rifle and a pistol. Up against ... He didn't know what he was up against. But they had much more firepower than he could offer.

He swallowed hard again.

SEVENTY-FOUR

A FIST TO A GUNFIGHT

Boží Dar, Czech Republic

Danko motioned toward the bullfrog and said to Maddox, "It's time for you to go. *Now.*"

Maddox could only helplessly watch, as Gawain walked toward the Escalade where they were holding Sonia.

She waved a well-manicured finger in the air. "One week, darling."

The bullfrog shoved Maddox hard with his left forearm, pushing him toward the door while holding his pistol in his right hand.

Maddox glared at him and the bullfrog grunted, "Come on, move it, asshole."

He started making his way toward the door that was blocked by SUV, which was about thirty feet away in that huge hangar.

It was Maddox, the bullfrog behind, shoving him, and the triggerman bringing in the rear with his Agram 2000 pointed at Maddox's back.

The thug with the RPK stayed back by the other SUV with Gawain, Danko, and Sonia.

Maddox was trying to figure out what to do, but his options were limited. *You don't bring a fist to a gunfight.*

He tried to stall.

"Come on let's go, faster." The bullfrog would bark and shove Maddox hard every time he looked back at the Escalade.

Sonia was so close. She was right there.

Maddox put the odds of Gawain keeping her word and letting Sonia go if he killed the chairman right up there with peace breaking out in the Middle East, and Israel and Palestine happily sharing land in the next century or two.

It wasn't going to happen. He needed to do something to ensure that the Escalade did not drive away with Sonia.

He had no way of communicating with Jar Lux and he didn't even know if he was out there. But the Czech cop was his only hope.

Maddox side-squeezed in between the first SUV and the hangar's rotted out doorframe and stepped outside.

He stopped to look around, hoping to see a cadre of police vehicles out there. There were none.

It was dusk out. The orange tinged sky was barely holding on.

The bullfrog barked: "Go, now. Walk to your fucking car." And he shoved him hard, with both hands this time. He caught Maddox off guard and soft-footed, which caused him to fall to the ground near the front driver's side of the SUV ending up on all fours.

The bullfrog and his triggerman found that hilarious as they both laughed out loud.

Maddox was humiliated. He was like a dog at the feet of his masters. He looked up toward the woods and saw a glint from afar. He knew what that was—a sniper's tell. A mistake from the reflection of the rifle or from the scope itself.

He knew who that was.

The shooter that had killed Fitzsimmons and Ramos and almost killed Rose. Maddox stayed down on the ground, rolled to his side, got up into a squat and double-timed toward the back of the SUV, which was still parked inside the hangar.

The bullfrog was no longer laughing. He looked befuddled and angry as he raised the pistol and pointed it at Maddox's head, "Stop playing games."

A shot rang out and Maddox cringed, thinking he was being shot when he felt a warm spray of red mist on his face. He watched as the bullfrog collapsed onto the ground with a chunk of his skull missing.

Before Maddox could even process that, the triggerman began to scream and fire his submachine toward Maddox.

Dirt and debris flew up into the air as Maddox rolled over the bullfrog's dead body, grabbing his pistol in midroll. Then he rolled again, right underneath the SUV that had been blocking the entrance to the hangar.

The sniper couldn't shoot him under there and Gawain's two remaining thugs would have to crawl down on the ground to get to him, so it was the safest place for him to regain his bearings.

Maddox lay flat on his stomach as he looked toward the woods but there was no activity from there. Then he looked toward the hangar and saw the legs of Gawain's men.

All Maddox could make out from under the SUV were four legs running around the vehicle in chaos as they screamed in a panic.

Both men unleashed a barrage of machine gun fire toward the general direction of the gunshot that had killed the bullfrog.

RPK man had joined the triggerman and both men were firing into the woods indiscriminately.

They weren't paying any attention to Maddox so he took

aim from underneath the SUV at the only target he could see —
the legs of the two thugs.

He pulled the trigger of the bullfrog's GSh-18, a Russian-
made 9mm semiautomatic pistol.

Maddox didn't know it at the time, but the bullfrog liked to
use armor-piercing rounds, which tore into the two men's legs
like it was tissue paper.

The men seethed and screamed in pain as the bullets shattered their fibula and tibia bones like twigs.

Both men collapsed in agony, their faces reddened and
contorted in pain, their broken and bloody legs akimbo as they
screamed in a language Maddox didn't understand. But their
screams and faces relayed their message clearly.

Now that were on the ground he could see their faces, so
Maddox took aim from the prone position underneath the SUV
and shot each man once in the head.

Their screaming and spasmodic jerking bodies stilled.

It suddenly became very quiet.

SEVENTY-FIVE

CRUNCHING METAL

Boží Dar, Czech Republic

THE MEN LAID THERE, DEAD.

For Maddox, the silence seemed as loud as the gunfire had been. He tried to do an ammo check but lost count and he didn't know if the bullfrog had had a full magazine and he didn't want to remove the magazine with the sniper out there.

He also figured Gawain and Danko were still inside the hangar with Sonia and he was certain they were armed. He had to get to them.

Maddox looked around and he saw the solution to his ammo problem lying beside the two dead men.

He had to move. For all he knew, Gawain and Danko were killing Sonia as he had lain there pontificating his next move.

He crawled out from underneath the SUV. He made his way, crouched low, toward the two dead bodies and picked up the triggerman's Agra 2000 submachine gun.

He slung the submachine gun across his chest. He thought about shooting the gas tank of the SUV to keep the sniper off his back, but he didn't want to waste the ammo and gas tanks didn't usually explode as easily as shown in the movies.

He placed the pistol into his waistband and proceeded to go back inside the hangar, with the Agra 2000 leading the way.

He began making his way toward the back of the hangar where the other SUV, the one with Sonia inside, had been parked. He walked slowly, in the crouched position. *Good*, he thought. It was still parked there. He couldn't see Gawain and because of the tinted windows, he couldn't tell if she or Sonia were inside. Suddenly Danko came around the back of the SUV, holding a pistol. He took a shot that missed Maddox by a mile.

Maddox fired a warning shot at Danko's feet kicking up dirt and concrete. He hoped to scare Danko since he didn't know if Sonia was still inside the SUV, he wasn't going to take the risk of firing anywhere near it.

Danko took two more running shots in Maddox's general direction, but he wasn't aiming, just shooting wildly as he ran over to the driver side of the SUV and jumped inside.

Maddox aimed but held back. He was working on the assumption that Sonia was still inside that truck, so, mostly out of desperation, he ran right at the Escalade.

The SUV revved its engine and lurched forward, tires screeching, burning rubber on the pockmarked concrete, kicking up debris as it careened forward, right at Maddox.

Maddox stood his ground for about half a second, then realizing Danko was not stopping he ducked out of the way as the SUV sped by, fishtailing, and running over Gawain's men's dead bodies.

The other truck that had transported Maddox to the hangar was still there, blocking the entrance.

Danko slammed on the brakes, but he was going too fast and

the truck skidded wide and crashed into the back of the other truck.

The sound of crunching metal reverberated and echoed throughout the hangar.

Inside the SUV Gawain, Danko, and Sonia were recovering from the impact of the airbags. They were sore feeling like they had been walloped with a beanbag full of bricks.

Gawain began looking around, regaining her senses.

Danko was shoving the now deflated airbag out of his way as Gawain screamed, "Go, go, go, what are you waiting for!"

"We just crashed into that truck. What am I supposed to do?" he screamed, panicking.

"Ram it out of the way!" Gawain shouted back.

Sonia was in the backseat. She had seen Maddox raising his hands in surrender, knowing he wasn't firing into the SUV because of her and she heard Gawain yell, "Run him over."

Sonia screamed.

Danko groaned in pain from the impact of the airbag as he threw the gear into reverse and backed up the Escalade a few feet, then tossed it back into drive and drove forward, this time slower.

Once the vehicles were bumper-to-bumper, he put his foot on the accelerator and used his truck to push the parked vehicle out of the way.

Sonia watched as Maddox tried to open her door, but it was locked.

He tried to break the glass with the butt of the machine gun, but the bulletproof glass would not budge.

"Where's your gun? I'll kill that son of a bitch myself," Gawain shouted.

"No you fucking bitch," Sonia screamed.

"I don't know where it is," Danko said as he kept both hands on the steering wheel, foot on the accelerator, pushing the SUV out of the way as they began to cough and choke from the smell of burnt rubber and fuel that was seeping inside.

Gawain was frantically looking for the gun. "Where is it?" she kept shouting.

Danko kept ramming the other vehicle as he and Gawain yelled at each other. Then everything slowed down for Sonia who fell into a phantasmagoric trance. It was as if she was having an out of body experience, but she felt calm and knew what she had to do. Sonia leaned forward toward the driver. Gawain was leaning down by the floorboard, distracted as she looked for the gun.

Danko was focused on ramming the truck out of the way.

"It's working," he said excitedly as he began to nudge it out of the way.

Sonia raised her arms, which were still handcuffed in the front. She positioned her arms so she could bring them down over Danko's head. He didn't notice as she brought her arms down fast and hard, until her forearms were pushing down on his shoulders. She then sat back letting the plastic handcuffs cut into his throat, pulling his head back toward her.

He tried to scream, but all he could do was gasp for air.

"Oh, shit," Gawain shouted. She got on her knees, and from the passenger side front seat, began to punch Sonia.

"Let go," she yelled with each punch, but Sonia had her arms around his neck tightly like an animal control noose around a wild pit bull. Sonia scooted back in her seat, making it harder for Gawain to land blows and for Danko to breathe.

As she did, her arms pulled Danko's head back further, tightening around his throat. He began to choke and fidget. Then he lost control of the vehicle, which crashed head-on into the concert wall by the door, sending chunks of the already crumbling wall against the truck.

Smoke billowed and transmission fluid spilled onto the ground.

Desperate for air and his neck bleeding from the friction of the plastic handcuffs, Danko unlocked the doors. He opened the door trying to desperately get out of the truck, but he was unable to move with Sonia's arms still clamped around his neck.

Gawain spotted the gun on the floorboard by Danko's right foot and lunged for it, but he was struggling for air, and trying to get Sonia off him, so he kept stomping on the gun, preventing Gawain from grabbing it.

Sonia's arms felt like they were being torn from her limbs so she relented, raising her arms over Danko's head setting him free.

She fell back into her seat, exhausted as Danko rubbed his throat and sucked in air.

"Get the gun, you fool," Gawain yelled at Danko as he spilled out of the SUV, gasping for air.

Danko looked up just as Maddox appeared and shot him in the face.

Gawain was stretched over into the driver's side, trying to retrieve the gun from the floor, and she screamed as Danko's blood and brain matter sprayed over her body. She felt and tasted the warm blood.

She put her hands to her face as if to make sure it wasn't her blood thinking that she had been shot too.

She wasn't shot, and all she had accomplished to do was smearing Danko's blood all over her face. She glanced at the rearview mirror, and screamed again.

Maddox reached for the rear door and opened it, Sonia at first screamed before realizing it was Maddox, then she lunged into his arms.

The Angram 2000 felt bulky between them.

"You okay?" he asked.

"I am now," she replied.

"We have to go," Maddox said.

He grabbed her by her hands, which were still handcuffed at the wrists.

He could see Gawain frantically moving about inside the SUV so he aimed the Angram submachine gun at Gawain through the driver's side open door.

"Don't," Sonia said.

Maddox looked at her and felt ashamed, but knew that it had to be done.

"I let her go and she'll come back at us looking for revenge. It's in her DNA. Trust me, I know," Maddox said.

Sonia began to say something, but Maddox turned and pulled the trigger. Click. The Agram was out of ammo.

Lucky, Maddox thought as he grabbed Sonia by the hand.

"Let's go."

SEVENTY-SIX

CHOICES

Boží Dar, Czech Republic

BACK IN THE SUV, GAWAIN HAD SCOOTED BACK ALL THE
way to the passenger side of the SUV after she saw Maddox aim
the submachine at her and then she heard the click. Out of
ammo. She was in a daze and could feel Danko's blood drying
on her skin.

She was shaking. She looked down and finally saw Danko's
gun. It was wedged underneath the accelerator pedal.

She looked outside and saw Maddox and Sonia making
their way out of the hangar.

She sat there for a moment as if going over her choices.
Choice A. She gets out of the SUV and runs off into the woods,
far away from Maddox. Or Choice B. She kills him herself.

She crawled over from the passenger seat to the driver's side
and lunged for the gun. She was going with choice B.

She picked up the gun and exited the SUV from the driver's
side, tripping on Danko's body.

She fell, skinning her knees on the cracked asphalt, broken
glass, and debris. She let out a primordial scream more from

frustration than pain. It was loud, guttural, and it made Maddox stop in his tracks.

He turned pushing Sonia behind him, reaching for the submachine gun instinctively, even though it was out of ammunition.

Gawain stood there trembling.

Her knees were bleeding, and her fine clothing, dirty and torn.

She was pointing the gun at Maddox and Sonia, saying, "You are both dead."

The submachine gun still hung loosely from its sling, out of ammo, useless.

Gawain had him dead to rights.

Then Maddox smiled at what he saw coming up behind her. Her eyes widened at his smile. A trick, perhaps.

It was Jar Lux who had come around the back of the first SUV and was standing behind Gawain with his rifle ready.

"Police, freeze," he said as she whipped around with the gun in her hand. He pulled the trigger killing her.

SEVENTY-SEVEN

UPSLOPE

Boží Dar, Czech Republic

BEFORE EVERYTHING HAD GONE DOWN INSIDE THE HANGAR, Jar Lux had been outside. He had spotted the sniper down below from where he was standing, so he tried, getting as close as he could without being noticed.

Lux had been worried. He wasn't a sniper, and he had a cheap hunting rifle.

The sniper was trained, and he had the perfect instrument of death expertly designed to do one thing: kill.

Lux put that out of his head. He was an experienced hunter and a good shot. The Sako 85 was a good rifle, but more importantly, he had the element of surprise because the sniper did not know he was watching him from the top of the slope.

If he could shoot a galloping deer or mouflon, he should be able to shoot the sniper from this distance if he had to.

Slowly, he began to make his way toward the sniper without making noise.

The sniper was using his backpack as a bipod, aimed toward the hangar.

When he was close enough to make the shot, Lux got down into a kneeling position and aimed his rifle down below.

Lux watched as Maddox was taken outside of the hangar by Gawain's men.

He watched as Maddox turned back toward the hangar, then one of the men shoved Maddox to the ground.

He watched Maddox crawl on all fours facing him while the man laughed and raised his pistol as he hovered over Maddox.

Shit. Lux thought the thug was going to execute Maddox right there and then.

He didn't have time to decide what to do, but he wasn't going to stand frozen while this man killed Maddox. So Lux ignored the sniper, and he aimed the rifle at the man further down below by the hangar who was standing over Maddox.

Lux pulled the trigger, killing the bullfrog.

All hell broke loose.

For a moment, Axel thought he might have pulled the trigger by accident, killing one of Gawain's men. Then he realized that the shot had come from behind him, upslope, so he began to turn to face in that direction, but it was too late.

He watched as a man with a rifle came rushing down the embankment fast, yelling, "POLICE!" over and over.

He couldn't turn around quick enough from the prone position he had been in and his pistol was tucked away in a hip holster.

Axel didn't know what he was going to do, but he knew one thing for sure: *I'm not going to a Czech prison.*

"Okay, take it easy," he said as the cop approached him.

Axel was expecting the Czech cavalry, but it was just one guy. One cop, armed with a pistol and a civilian hunting rifle. *What the fuck?* Axel thought. *Is this guy really a cop or one of Maddox's people?*

Lux had the rifle trained on Axel so there wasn't much he could do about that now.

"You're under arrest, on your stomach," Lux shouted. Axel did as he was told as gunfire and chaos erupted from the hangar. Both men scrambled for cover as bullets whizzed by from the direction of the hangar.

Lux looked towards the hangar then turned his attention back toward Axel when he felt his midsection on fire. He wondered why his shirt was suddenly wet.

He looked down and saw blood. He looked up and saw Axel holding a knife in his right hand. He had stood up quickly but didn't have the time to stab for the kill so he had settled with slashing Lux's chest with the razor-sharp blade which forced Lux to drop the rifle. He stepped backward and tripped landing on his butt. He scooted back in shock. He looked down at his wound then looked up and saw Axel coming toward him with the knife in his hand.

"Stop right there. Drop that knife and do not come any closer," Lux ordered, as he reached for his pistol. But instead of stopping, Axel bum-rushed the inspector who managed to grab his pistol in time to fire twice into Axel's chest.

Axel fell onto his back. The knife bounced off the ground and landed a few feet from where he fell.

Lux approached cautiously with the pistol still aimed at Axel when he heard what sounded like two cars colliding and screaming coming from the hangar.

"Shit," Lux said as he picked up the rifle and he ran down the embankment toward the hangar, leaving Axel to die in the woods.

A bleeding Lux made his way down to the hangar and he squeezed by the two smashed up SUVs.

Once inside he approached carefully towards the passenger side of one of the SUVs with his rifle ready to fire.

As he came around the back of the SUV, he saw Gawain pointing a gun at Maddox and Sonia.

"Freeze, police," he yelled as he aimed the rifle at her. She turned. He saw the gun in her hand turning in his direction. He pulled the trigger.

SEVENTY-EIGHT

WE SHOULD GO

Boží Dar, Czech Republic

AFTER LUX KILLED GAWAIN, MADDOX AND SONIA collapsed on the ground. They sat there exhausted, relieved, holding onto one another.

Lux joined them on the ground.

All three were in a daze.

"What happened?" Lux finally said.

Maddox thought about it for a moment.

"We got caught up in the middle of a board dispute."

Lux shook his head and turned toward Sonia as he pulled out a red pocketknife from his pants pocket. He pulled out a blade, and he cut off Sonia's plastic Speedcuffs.

She smiled and rubbed her raw wrists.

"Thank you, Jar. You saved our lives," Maddox said.

"Yes, thank you so much," Sonia said, not knowing who he was.

Maddox noticed the blood on Lux's clothing for the first time.

"You're shot," Maddox said.

"No. That sniper up there sliced me with a knife as I tried to arrest the prick. It's safe to say he's the one that shot Foxglove in London," Lux said.

"He was working for Gawain and Danko. That's her over there," Maddox said, pointing at her dead body. "She was a member of the board looking to take over. Her husband was Pavel Nossik."

"No shit?"

"No shit. Is the sniper dead?" Maddox asked.

"Yes. He came at me with that knife, so I shot him," Lux said.

"I want to see that asshole," Maddox said. He turned to Sonia.

"Wait here while we go and check."

"No way, I'm not staying down here by myself."

The three of them hiked up the slope.

A few minutes later, Lux, Maddox, and Sonia stood there dumbfounded.

Axel was gone. He had policed up his area, taking his rifle and his gear, except for one item that he left behind—a black ballistic chest protector with two slugs bored into it, courtesy of Lux.

"That son of a bitch," Lux said.

Maddox and Lux looked around nervously. Darkness now engulfed them and they were very exposed at the moment.

"Let's get the hell out of here," Maddox said.

"Yes. We shouldn't be standing around in open spaces with that prick out there," Lux said.

Maddox, Sonia, and Lux were walking back to Maddox's rental car when they saw the lights of a vehicle approaching them.

"Shit," Maddox said. "Get in the car," he told Sonia, but she just stood there.

"It could be townspeople or the police," Lux said, taking out his badge and holding it out in front.

The car stopped and Special Agent Beachy, Dale Shaw, and Bob Guy exited.

Maddox recognized Shaw and Guy right away.

"CIA," he whispered to Lux.

"I'm Special Agent Carey Beachy with the US Diplomatic Security. Is everything okay?" Her hand rested on the grip of a black Glock that was in a hip holster.

Lux identified himself as a police inspector with the Czech National Police. He held out his badge for her to inspect.

She covered the holster with her jacket as she glanced nervously toward Shaw. She demurred to Lux, knowing this was his jurisdiction.

"Is everyone okay?" she asked.

"There was a shoot-out back there. My car is down in Milovice. I can't get a cell signal out here to call for backup. Do you have a radio?"

"I have a handheld Motorola radio in my vehicle," Beachy said.

"Maddox. What happened here?" Dale Shaw asked as he walked past Lux toward Maddox and Sonia.

"Who are you?" Lux asked.

Shaw didn't answer so Maddox did on his behalf. "That's Dale Shaw. He's with the CIA. Him too," Maddox said, pointing at Bob Guy.

Lux turned to look at them.

"I need to talk with Mr. Maddox," Shaw said.

Lux turned to Maddox. He had his arm around Sonia. He could tell Dale Shaw was the last person Maddox wanted to talk to at that moment.

"I'm afraid that's not possible right now. Mr. Maddox and his wife were kidnapped. There are several dead bodies back there. Russian mafia. None are American. This is a matter for the National Police and I need to get them out here, right now. The Maddox's are my witnesses and I'm taking them into protective custody," Lux said.

Maddox smiled.

"May I use your radio? I require medical attention," Lux said to Beachy as he pulled the lapel of his jacket away to show his blood-soaked shirt.

"Oh shit," Beachy said.

"It looks worse than it is, but it stings something awful," Lux said, smiling.

Beachy took Lux to her vehicle where she used a two-way radio to have the embassy notify the Czech police to come out there.

Shaw took the opportunity to approach Maddox again.

"Jesus Christ, Maddox, talk to me," he said.

"We just had a shitty night, Dale. We're going home," Maddox said.

"I'm afraid that's not going to cut it," Shaw said.

"I'm the only one with authority to hold anyone here, and you're making me wonder what the CIA has to do with that shoot-out back there. How did the CIA know to come here?" Lux asked.

Maddox saw Shaw tense up. Bob Guy appeared to be hiding behind the embassy SUV.

Agent Beachy shook her head and said to Shaw, "We should go."

SEVENTY-NINE

THE POOR MAN'S ALPS

SZKLARSKA PORĘBA, POLAND

SZKLARSKA PORĘBA WAS a popular ski resort town in south-western Poland between the Karkonosze Mountains in the south and the Jizera Mountains in the west.

It was known as the poor man's Alps and was located near the Czech-Polish border, about seventy miles from Boží Dar.

For two days Axel had been holed up in one of Danko's safe houses. It had been the dedicated rendezvous location between them. The go-to place if the shit hit the fan. And back in Boží Dar, the shit had hit the fan in spades.

For a change, it was now Axel who desperately tried to get a hold of Mr. White—he was so used to calling Danko by that codename so he kept addressing him that way in his mind.

The dedicated phone set up just for communication between the two of them was disconnected.

Following protocol, Axel destroyed his phone. Then tried him on a backup drop phone but it too, was disconnected.

The last resource—as he had been explicitly told by Mr.

White to never call that number unless it was life or death—was the landline telephone in his Cyber One office in Prague.

"Hello, who is this?" A man answered the phone, not using Mr. White's passcode and it didn't sound like Mr. White's voice. He was supposed to hang up immediately, but Axel froze.

"Are you trying to reach Edvard Danko?" the man said after a few seconds of silence.

"Axel Gore, I presume? This is Lieutenant Jar Lux. We met in the woods of Boží Dar. I'll have a lifetime reminder of our meeting on my chest," Lux said.

"You shot me twice in my chest, so we're even," Axel finally said.

"It's over, Axel. Your photograph and details are going up on Interpol as we speak. You might as well let me know where you are and I'll pick you up. It will save a lot of time," Lux said.

"Is Mr. White—is Edvard Danko dead?" Axel asked.

"Yes. They're all dead. It's over."

"Interpol, huh?" Axel actually thought that was pretty cool.

"You can go to the website tonight. You'll see your details there under your real name: Brandon Jones."

Axel hung up. *Now that's not cool.* He thought Brandon Jones was gone forever.

He had to get out of Danko's safe house immediately. They had obviously accessed Mr. White's database. The one he had boasted was unhackable. Now they knew everything about him.

Axel counted the cash he had left. About twelve thousand dollars' worth of dollars, euros, and pounds. Not a fortune to run away and live his days in hiding somewhere, but enough to get him far away from Europe as fast as possible.

He could no longer use the emergency only credit card. That had to go. As did all the sim cards Danko had given him. It would be all cash and pay phones for the foreseeable future.

Ten minutes after his phone call with Lux, Axel exited the safe house located in the center of the village.

He wore blue jeans, a black T-shirt, and his olive-green army jacket. He had glued on the full beard from his kit and put in green-colored contacts. He hated putting them in, but an eye color change was appropriate if his real-life face was going to be joining Interpol's most wanted list.

He had the loaded pistol in his coat pocket and the sniper rifle was broken down and stowed in its hard case, which was in his rucksack. He knew he should have ditched it already, but not yet.

He would walk twenty minutes to Szklarska Poręba Górna railway station. From there, he would take a train to the Main Poznan railway station, where he could catch another train to Berlin.

Once in Berlin, he could purchase a one-way plane ticket to Brazil or maybe Ecuador.

He could get by with Spanish, but he didn't know a lick of Portuguese. Not that it should matter.

I don't speak Czech or Polish and it hasn't held me back. But Rio is too damned hot, he thought. He figured he had ten to fifteen hours to think about where he would go before he arrived in Berlin.

He turned onto the road leading up to the train station.

Axel smiled as he walked. In a year or two, he'd be back and Maddox would learn that he was the best in the business.

The village was sleepy and quiet during the summer so there weren't many people out and about especially on foot.

To his left, he noticed these wooden steps leading down a steep hill. He didn't know where they led, but he saw Maddox walking up the last steps as if he were out for a Sunday stroll.

Maddox smiled at Axel.

Sennight had cracked open Danko's computer like a walnut.

There would be enough data and information to make everyone happy for decades. Dale Shaw, the chairman, the Czech police, and Maddox.

That had been his caveat to Lux. He hated to put the screws to Lux after he'd saved his life, but there was no way Maddox could go back home knowing Axel was still out there.

Lux had insisted that if he didn't find him and arrest him that he would probably vanish. But Maddox wasn't so sure. The punk had a chip on his shoulder as big as the state of California.

The odds that Axel would surrender peacefully if caught were remote as the stitches in Lux's chest could attest.

When Sennight discovered that Danko had a rendezvous safe house across the Czech border into Poland, Lux knew he was out of jurisdiction.

He had given Maddox forty-eight-hours before he shared the location of the village with the Polish authorities and Interpol.

The problem was, they knew the name of the town, but not the address of the safe house.

Danko had taken that to his grave.

Maddox knew Axel wouldn't stay put for too long. And the only way to get out of the area and out of the country fast without a car was the railway station. From there, he could connect to one of the other Polish main railways and be on a train that would take him anywhere in Central Europe in mere hours. Or he could catch the train and be at Warsaw Chopin International Airport in around seven hours.

Once there, he would have many choices of places to lay low for as long as he needed.

But all those choices started in the only railway station in the village.

When Lux had called Maddox to tell him of his telephone

conversation with Axel, he'd known the sniper would head to the train station.

Maddox had already scouted the perfect spot to intercept him.

Whether he was traveling by car, on foot, or a bicycle, Maddox would see him go by from his vantage point, on a long steep staircase in a hillside where he would not be seen until he stepped up the last few steps. Which was what Maddox did when he saw Axel walking up the road toward the railway station.

"Keep those hands where I can see them," Maddox said as he slowly approached Axel.

Both men looked around to ensure no one else was there.

"I can see I still have a lot to learn in this business," Axel said.

"Too late for that."

Both men had their hands in their pocket.

Maddox gripping the Glock and Axel gripped the Beretta.

"I don't see the cavalry," Axel said.

"It's just me and you now," Maddox said.

"Like gunslingers in the old West," Axel said as he charged toward Maddox, pulling out the Beretta.

He moved fast. He pointed the gun at Maddox's face.

"Look here. And you're supposed to be the top shit," Axel grinned, "I'm going to blow your head off."

Maddox seized on Axel's mistake of getting too close and immediately reacted, taking the gun out of his hand, and pointing it back at him.

Axel looked stunned.

"They don't teach that move at Ranger school anymore?"

"Fuck you," Axel said as he lunged toward Maddox.

Maddox hit him in the throat with the butt of the gun; he fell to his knees, gasping for air.

Maddox stood over him as he continued gasping. He looked down at him and thought how he came there to kill him, but he was having second thoughts. *So what would happen if I let him go?* Between the chairman's contract on Axel's head and Jar Lux ready to sic Interpol on him he was going to end up in prison or a pine box soon enough.

As Maddox stood there, Axel suddenly leapt to his feet. He was holding his knife, sealing his fate. Maddox shot him twice in the head, just in case he was wearing a bulletproof vest as he had in Boží Dar.

EPILOGUE

It was a sticky South Florida day. A perfect day for a pool party.

"Jesus Christ, I don't know how you can live in this sauna of a state," Troy Sennight said, sweating profusely.

He was holding a handheld personal fan that he had bought at the dollar store.

"I like it, mate, feels like the Canary Islands," Tom Rose said, drinking a beer.

"We're in the shade, the beers are ice-cold, the pool is right there, there's AC inside, and you have that little gizmo in your face like a Geisha fan, what's the problem, Troy?" Maddox said, laughing.

Sonia and Tawny Tree were chatting poolside, enjoying Daiquiris made with Nicaraguan Flor de Caña rum.

"You ready for that triathlon yet?" Maddox asked Rose.

"I'm still moving around like an old man," Rose said.

"You are an old man," Sennight and Maddox said at the same time.

They laughed. After a moment of quiet, Rose said, "I spoke with the chairman."

"Oh yeah? Was he able to explain how the widow of a Russian mafia kingpin ended up on his board with the mob's favorite hacker as the network's systems guy with access to all our data?" Maddox asked facetiously in one breath.

"He said he was getting too old for this work and that's how she was able to con him. He's retiring. For good this time," Rose said.

"Good for him. I might do the same," Maddox said.

Rose leaned in, lowered his voice, and said, "He wanted to know if we would be interested in taking over the network."

"Fuck. No. You can't be serious. After all this shit? We're lucky to be alive. Sonia was almost killed. I'm done with it," Maddox said.

"But it would be different. We would be running the show. You and me in charge, with Troy handling the tech stuff. It would be great," Rose said.

"As far as I'm concerned, the network should stay dead. If it comes back up somehow, I don't want any part of it," Maddox said.

Sonia jumped into the pool.

"I'm not putting her through that shit anymore," Maddox said, getting up from his chair.

"Well, think about it mate. Couldn't do it without you."

Maddox didn't respond as he made a run for the pool and cannonball-dove right next to where Sonia was wading.

"You ass!" she shouted, splashing him with water.

"He sounds serious about being done with this," Sennight said.

"I said the same thing when I was laid up in hospital. The passing of time is a remarkable thing. He just needs more time," Rose said, drinking his beer.

"What about the agency?" Sennight asked.

"We were nice enough to share some of that data with Dale Shaw so he's happy. That's the trick with those intelligence boys. We give them little morsels and that keeps them satisfied and out of the way," Rose said.

Sennight laughed.

Maddox swam up to Sonia. "Looks like those two are up to something," she said.

Maddox shrugged, and he kissed her. They floated there together, looking up at the blue sky.

This is good. I can get used to this, he thought, and he looked at Sonia and smiled.

AUTHOR'S NOTE

I would like to ask you for a favor. If you enjoyed this book, would you please consider taking a moment and leaving your thoughts for others who might also enjoy this story?

Reviews are the best way to help me get the word out to others about my thrillers and it's an important factor that the big retailers like Amazon use when ranking books on their website.

The number of reviews helps with the ranking of the book on Amazon and other retailers which helps me with discoverability which is always a tough nut to crack for an indie author like myself.

It only takes a few seconds to leave a review, but it carries so much weight that it can make or break the visibility of the book.

Please don't feel any obligation to leave a review, just know that if you do, I will truly appreciate it.

Thank you,
Alan Petersen

ABOUT THE AUTHOR

I was born in San José, Costa Rica and grew up there and in Caracas, Venezuela. My father was an American expat who lived in Latin America for over forty years and my mother is from Costa Rica.

I moved to the USA (the state of Minnesota) to attend college where I earned a BA in Political Science and became a huge fan of espionage and political thrillers from the likes of Tom Clancy, Vince Flynn, Ken Follett, Daniel Silva, John le Carré, and others.

I married my college sweetheart, Jennifer, and we now live in California on a a quintessential San Francisco city street (17% grade) right out of Steve McQueen's Bullitt.

I like to write high-octane thrillers and I usually toss in a Latin American bent into the story in there somewhere.

I love to hear from my readers so feel free to email me at alan@alanpetersen.com. Check out my website for more information and to join my mailing list: www.AlanPetersen.com.

You can also connect with me on social media:

Proof

Made in the USA
Columbia, SC
08 April 2018